COVERT VENGEANCE

SEALS AND CIA BOOK 2

KENNEDY L. MITCHELL

*To all of us Elliot's out there.
Be your crazy ass self.*

© 2021 Kennedy L. Mitchell

All rights reserved. This book or any portion thereof may not be reproduced or used in any manner whatsoever without the express written permission of the publisher except for the use of brief quotations in a book review.

This book is a work of fiction. Any references to historical events, real people, or real places are used fictitiously. Other names, characters, places and events are products of the author's imagination, and any resemblances to actual events or places or persons, living or dead, is entirely coincidental.

Cover Design: Bookin It Designs

Editing: Hot Tree Editing

Proofreading: All Encompassing Books

❦ Created with Vellum

ABOUT THE AUTHOR

Kennedy L. Mitchell lives outside Dallas with her husband, son and two very large goldendoodles. She began writing in 2016 after a fight with her husband (You can read the fight almost verbatim in Falling for the Chance) and has no plans of stopping.

She would love to hear from you via any of the platforms below or her website www.kennedylmitchell.com You can also stay up to date on future releases through her newsletter or by joining her Facebook readers group - Kennedy's Book Boyfriend Support Group.

Thank you for reading.

ALSO BY KENNEDY L. MITCHELL

Standalone:

Finding Fate

Memories of Us

Protection Series: Interconnected Standalone

Mine to Protect

Mine to Save

Mine to Guard

Mine to Keep (Coming December 2021)

SEALs and CIA Series: Interconnected Standalone

Covert Affair

Covert Vengeance

More Than a Threat Series: A Bodyguard Romantic Suspense Connected Series

More Than a Threat

More Than a Risk

More Than a Hope

Power Play Series: A Protector Romantic Suspense Connected Series

Power Games

Power Twist

Power Switch

Power Surge

Power Term

PROLOGUE
ELLIOT

I line my lower lip in red on memory alone, my focus fixed on my partner's reflection in the motel room's full-length mirror instead of my own. With quick, fluid movements, he secures varying weapons along his tall, lean frame. Most are concealed for "in case of emergency" situations, but the few out for all to see are for a show of force rather than true necessity. Though if on the off-chance shit goes sideways during tonight's exchange, he and I are deadly enough on our own, the weapons convenient but unnecessary.

A knowing smile pulls the edge of his lips upward, no doubt sensing me monitoring his every move. There's just something about a good-looking man strapped with enough weapons to take out a small nation that does it for me. Knowing full well I'm watching, he picks up the shoulder harness, my favorite—don't ask me why, because I can't even answer that question even though I've asked myself many times—and threads his arms through the straps. The snug leather stretches across the sculpted chest I know hides beneath his fitted black dress shirt.

Kurt checks the clip of one nine-millimeter before slipping it into the holster. "If you keep looking at me like that, we'll end up back in bed and miss the meeting we've worked eighteen months for."

I give him a dramatic eye roll as a response before shooting him a wink. He isn't wrong, however; we don't have time for another distraction. I'm the reason we're pressed for time as it is. Earlier, I needed a quickie to relieve the suffocating stress this final meeting with the most dangerous arms dealer in Central and South America has amassed. An illicit shiver races down my spine at the memory of him just minutes before pinned beneath me, taking everything I gave him.

Sleeping with your partner is a big no-no in the agency, but I bet the prude asses who created that rule never ran an eighteen-month stint in the shittiest shitholes of Colombia with only their partner as a viable option to scratch the sex-deprived itch. Adding a personal layer to the mix meant complications. Like the bomb I still have yet to drop on Kurt.

I'm pregnant.

Yep. CIA Officer Elliot Smith, the rising star in the agency with over a dozen completed missions and high marks from all her superiors, is fucking pregnant.

Sure, I'm considered a badass by most people's standards, but tonight I'm just another woman afraid of what will happen next. This won't affect only my career but his too, and I'm not sure how he'll take the news. Especially since we're not in love. Well, I'm not. He's mentioned deeper feelings, but I always shift the conversation away from anything dealing with feelings when it comes up.

Convenient fuck buddies? For sure.

Love? Nope.

He's good-looking, with his dirty-blond hair and Ken Doll look-alike features, but there's no spark. Hell, there isn't even passion when we have sex. Call me crazy—most do, though never to my face if they want to keep breathing—but a man who allows me to dominate him isn't a guy I want slotted as my forever.

No fight.

No spark.

No fire.

And pregnant.

Fuck me sideways, I'm in deep shit.

Long dark brown strands of hair cascade over my bare shoulder with a soft head shake. I can't think about the whole baby thing now. Tonight my mind must be sharp, my focus solely on the operation we've been working toward for eighteen months. If we want to survive the night's events, then I need to get my shit together.

"You ready for tonight?" I ask, swiveling on my four-inch black heels. Even with the added height, I'm not at eye level with his six-foot frame. Sure, I'm vertically challenged, but I make up for it in relentless spunk and focused determination.

Though some classify it as mental instability.

I prefer spunk.

"Hell yes," Kurt groans and sits on the edge of the bed, making it creak. "I'm done with this shithole." He eyes the cheap motel room with disdain. "Everything is a go?"

I dip my chin in a curt nod. "I met with the handler early this morning." His lips purse into a thin line, clearly pissed I went out alone—again. "Don't give me that look. I can take care of myself, you know that. As far as tonight goes, the blueprints and basic software to operate the drone are on this." Stretching to the bedside table, I tug on the handle, pulling the drawer open and withdrawing a solid brick of white powder wrapped in clear cellophane.

Kurt shoots to his feet. "What the hell, Silvia?"

I fight the urge to snarl at his use of the dumbass mission name I've hated since day one. I swear I'm getting twitchy about it. Thank goodness this will all be over tonight and I can ditch this identity.

"Calm your tits," I say in obvious exasperation to his overreaction. "It's not coke." My hair glides along my shoulder with the tilt of my head. Raising the white brick to my nose, I take a sharp inhale. "At least I don't think it is." Shrugging a shoulder, I use the edge of the cheap wooden side table to rip through the thin plastic wrap.

A cloud of powder rises from the package and grows as the contents spill onto the threadbare rug. Halfway through the brick, a silver flash drive slips from the opening. I catch it before it falls to the floor.

"That," Kurt questions, narrowed eyes glaring at the thin metal balanced on my outstretched palm, "contains the blueprints and software to the most advanced military-grade drones ever created?"

I grin, plucking the little device from my palm to wipe the remaining powder from the metal cover. Once it's clean enough, I tug my canary-yellow silk cami away from my chest and slip the flash drive into my black lace bra.

"It's password protected. I've memorized it, don't worry, which is also the signal to the handler to activate the SEAL team." I tap the tip of a finger against my temple.

I fail to mention that there are two passwords needed to access the information. Not because I don't trust him but because I don't trust anyone. Old habits die hard, and after being on my own for so long, not being forthcoming with information is just that.

The first password opens the flash drive, which lets our handler know we have eyes on Rico, and leads to another login portal where the next password will need to be entered to access any of the drone information. The plan is to input password one to activate the SEALs, then use the second password as a last resort to keep Rico at the location until the SEALs arrive.

"What we have on the flash drive provides enough detail to prove what we have to sell is legit, except missing a few key details. If Rico has an issue, I'll tell him I'm not a damn idiot who brings everything to a shady-ass meeting. He thinks I'm former CIA. An officer wouldn't make the mistake of putting all their grenades in one handbasket."

Kurt groans and smiles up to the ceiling. "Only you would have a handbasket for your grenades."

"Focus. I'll input the password for the flash drive, activating the SEALs—"

"You get to have all the fun," Kurt grumbles, crossing his arms across his chest like a sulking teenager.

"I'm the lead on this mission, understood?" With my stern "get your shit together" glance, he ends the pouting with a respectful nod. "As I was saying, I'll give the signal to the SEAL team waiting to storm the compound." Inspecting my nails, I scowl at the flour caked beneath several of them. Withdrawing my knife from my pocket, I use the razor-sharp tip to scrape out the remaining powder.

"Fucking SEALs. Think they're God's gift to men and women alike. I hate those flashy bastards."

I roll my eyes and move on to the next nail. My snarky side wants to inform Kurt that it's his obvious inferiority complex that causes him to detest our military's finest, but that's not the fight I need to start right before tonight's events. I respect and honor any man or woman who fights for our country. Plus, the SEALs—hell, any special forces division—are fucking sexy as hell. They're walking killing machines, which shouldn't turn me on as much as it does. Most assume they're just a bunch of big-ass fuckers who only do what they're told. Sure, they follow orders, but most hold multiple degrees, meaning they're smart as hell along with being badass.

So damn hot.

Weighted silence settles over the motel room, both of us lost in our own thoughts. I focus mine on surviving the next twenty-four hours and how to inform Kurt of the surprise baby news.

"What about after tonight?" he asks, apprehension in his tight tone.

"What do you mean, after tonight?"

He gestures between me, then himself.

Oh. Right.

Well, this is awkward.

I could use this moment as a segue into the pregnancy news, but I go with avoidance, my tried-and-true way to deflect from too-personal conversations.

"Well, after we're home, I'll tell the higher-ups you did a phenomenal job playing the role of my personal bodyguard on this operation. It's the truth too, even though half of this country is too scared of me to try anything nefarious. I assume they'll put you on a new—"

"That's not what I mean and you know it." There's an undercurrent of anger in his voice that worries me.

Yeah, no shit. It doesn't take someone with my training to know what he's getting at. I just don't want to answer him, even though him having deeper feelings than just a fling would make the pregnancy news easier to deliver. Except I don't feel more, and the last thing I need is a rift between us before the mission is complete.

"We should go," I say instead of responding to the question that now lingers in the space between us like a cancerous fog.

Grabbing the black suit jacket off the chair back, I slip it over my shoulders and tug the cuff of each sleeve to avoid Kurt's penetrating stare like the coward I certainly am not. I don't want to hurt him by telling him the truth. The moment those two lines formed on the pregnancy test, I dreaded telling Kurt, not because I thought he would reject me but because I instantly knew I didn't want to do the parenting thing with him.

Emotions are not my strong suit. I'll run into any gunfire with a smile on my face, but try to talk about feelings and I bolt. This is why I should've been a nun. They don't have to deal with relationship shit.

Then again, they don't play with grenades, so clearly that career path was a no-go. Making bad people, and sometimes random abandoned warehouses, go boom is really cathartic. And unlike sex, there aren't strings attached when you're done.

"Right. We'll talk about us after."

The detachment in his dull tone makes the hair on the back of my neck stand on end. *Why did that sound like a threat?* I sure as hell hope he's controlled enough to keep his emotions in check tonight or he'll get us killed.

His heavy, angry stomps echo around the room while I place an extra knife inside the small black clutch. He pauses at my back. "Come on, let's get this over with."

Hot anger burns through my veins at his childlike attitude. Gritting my teeth, I snap the clutch closed and spin, ready to rip into him for allowing his emotions to show. We're CIA officers, not fucking high school sweethearts. But the threat of death and dismemberment stalls in my throat. All traces of emotion are gone, his handsome face cold and posture stiff, not an ounce of his internal anger toward my indifference visible.

Perfect.

Prologue

A final once-over in the full-length mirror shows my pristine sleek black trouser pants, the low-cut yellow cami highlighting my golden tan skin, my honey-brown eyes sharp, and long chocolate-brown hair straightened to perfection.

Picture-perfect image of the bitter, defunct CIA officer eager to sell top-secret military weaponry to the highest bidder. In this case, that's Rico Suarez, South America's most notorious and vicious arms dealer. And tonight, eighteen months of hard work will all be worth it when his reign of terror ends.

The night's thick damp air coats my throat with each inhale. On the small landing outside our room, I take a moment to scan the surrounding area for threats before descending the rickety steps. Each click of my heels against the warped wooden planks increases the vibrating tension already coiled tight in my gut. Something feels off, ominous almost, but nothing specific stands out as the reason.

A soft warm breeze moves through the parking lot, catching several locks of my hair and brushing them across my sticky cheeks. Pausing alongside the SUV, I survey the various dark corners, searching for what set off my internal warning. Hand wrapped around the passenger door's handle I turn to ask Kurt if he feels uneasy too, but his head disappears behind the roof. The following slam of a car door stops the question from ever leaving my mouth.

Swallowing down the building apprehension, I climb into the Mercedes.

Final night jitters. That's all this is.

Another crack of knuckles echoes in the small space as a fist slams against my bloody, swollen face, snapping my head to the side from the force. Rivers of blood and saliva pour over my split lower lip, dribbling down my chin and dripping to my bare shoulder. I struggle to stay conscious, trying to focus on the blurry objects moving around the room, but my right eye is completely swollen shut, the orbital bone no doubt fractured from the bastard who used brass knuckles, and the left eye isn't much better, though I can at least still see through a slim opening.

Not that I want to see how they've now switched the torture to something worse than the physical beating. Dread swims in my foggy thoughts as the blurry figure fumbles with the top of his blood-splattered jeans in front of the chair I'm restrained to, forced to take every punch and insult.

"Not so tough now, are you?" one of Rico's guards snarls from somewhere in the room. I swallow a scream of pain as the rough yank on a section of sweat-damp hair snaps my face to the ceiling. I bite my tongue until it bleeds to remain silent. "We'll have our fun—"

Before he can continue spouting the depraved plans he and his buddies have planned, a door somewhere to my left swings open. Shouts, hurried footsteps, and the clang of weapons leak into my torture chamber from the commotion going on around other areas of the house. Focusing on those sounds, I strain to catch any hint of where they're keeping Kurt, but the insistent high-pitched ringing in my battered ears and the chaos ensuing outside make it impossible.

The hectic noise fades. In the quiet, the unhurried click of boot heels drawing closer indicates the bastard who ordered my torture has finally joined the super fun "beat the drone software password out of Elliot" party.

As I fight to remain conscious, I attempt to focus on where the hell this night went sideways. One second Rico and I were discussing the basics of the drone specs I had memorized, the next we were fighting over the need for another password to access the information, and then there were seven assault rifle barrels trained at my head and Kurt's. That's all I remember before waking up in this damn torture room, the walls covered in what looks to be sound absorbing padding, meaning this room is used for one purpose often, with a killer headache secured to an uneven-legged wooden chair.

At least I have that going for me in this shit scenario. A wooden chair is easier to escape from than a metal one. This way, when the perfect moment comes, I won't need to break a wrist to slip free of the ties connecting me to the chair's legs. Hopefully that perfect moment arrives before Rico puts a bullet between my brows. Deep in my gut, I know they won't kill me until I give him what he wants.

The password.

If he gets that and escapes with the flash drive....

No, he won't. I won't allow him access to highly classified information. What our enemies could do with that information would be detrimental to our men and women fighting around the world. I'll gladly give up my life to ensure the drone's specs are never in this asshole's hands.

"Look at what they've done to your beautiful face." Rico's small hand cups my swollen cheek.

A sinister flash behind his black eyes is the only warning before he squeezes, cracking my already fractured cheekbone. This time there's no stopping the agonizing scream from erupting from my raw throat. When he drops his hand, I slump forward, panting through the overwhelming pain. A satisfied hum of approval rumbles from his chest, intensifying the hate I have for the bastard.

"Now that I have your attention. The password."

Darkness clouds my thoughts, but I push it back. I can't escape if I'm unconscious.

Keeping with my cover is my best chance of survival. That's rule number one as an officer.

Never break cover.

"Now, Rico, do you order your minions to beat the shit out of all your business partners, or is there something special about me?" My words slur from the numbness creeping across my face and swollen lips.

His responding humorless chuckle invokes a new swell of unease in my chest. "Business partner, you say." He shifts to stand in my diminished line of sight and leans closer. If it weren't for the gun aimed at my temple, I would gladly smash my forehead into his nose to wipe off his condescending grin.

That damn toothpick he always has stuck between his teeth swipes from one side of his mouth to the other as he considers me for several long seconds. "Give me what I want, and you and your partner live."

I shove the rush of relief at hearing Kurt's alive down deep.

"You think I'm a fool?" My raspy laugh scratches my dry throat. "The moment I tell you, he and I are dead."

The longer I can hold on to that second password, the more of a chance Kurt and I both have of surviving until the SEAL team arrives. It was a fail-safe I insisted the agency install as an extra level of leverage if we got in a pickle. Thank fuck I did, or we'd already be dead.

"You're dead if you don't."

"There is nothing you can do to make me give you the password."

"Is that right?" Standing tall, Rico looks to someone over my shoulder and then hitches his chin toward the closed door. "Kill him."

He's bluffing.

But even if he's not, I can't—I *won't* give it up.

The noises swell into the room when the man leaves to follow his orders. Seconds later, I understand why Rico also instructed one of his men to hold it open when the unmistakable, deafening boom of a single gunshot reverberates through the entire structure.

I stop breathing. Numbness slowly seeps through, voiding the throbbing pain.

No. Rico is bluffing. It's just a show of force to make me give up the password. Kurt is alive, and we'll make it out of this.

Guilt eats at me from the inside out at how I treated him earlier in the night, at the multiple missed opportunities to tell him about the baby.

I swallow down the panic threatening to get me fucking killed.

"Now, give me the second password, and I'll make it quick for you." Reaching out, he runs a finger along the inside of my thigh. "After you give me what you've flaunted and denied me these several months."

I have to keep him talking, to give the SEAL team a chance to storm the compound and capture his evil ass and save mine. But when that will happen, I'm not sure. With the hit to my head knocking me out, I have no idea how long I was unconscious before waking up in this room.

"I'll get what I want in the end, I assure you of that. It's up to you if we put that extensive pain tolerance training to the test before you die."

Dread threatens to seize the air in my lungs, but I reel it back and focus on the all-consuming pain radiating from every part of my body. Adjusting on the hard seat, I ease against the chair to discreetly assess the strength and stability of the back. Darting my eyes from Rico, I take in every detail I can with my limited vision.

Four armed guards, one with his AR pointed at my head, and the smug asshole in front of me. But since the moment Rico entered the room, his men have relaxed, like their boss's evil presence alone boosts their certainty of containing me.

Their gross miscalculation will be my gain.

Hopefully.

Now the agony of waiting until the best moment for the escape attempt.

"How about this?" I offer. Patches of darkness swim across my vision, but I force them away with several slow blinks. "You let me go, and then I'll take the flash drive that you stole from me and sell it to someone more hospitable than this shit."

Rico chewed on his toothpick for a moment. "And why would I do that?" he asks.

For just a moment, I unleash all my pent-up rage, allowing it to bubble to the surface. Rico's eyes widen a fraction. He stands a little taller, no doubt catching a hint of the crazy I hide inside me.

"Because," I say like a curse, "if you don't let me go right now, I promise you I'll slaughter every fucker in the room and then come after you and everyone you love."

Reaching behind his back, Rico withdraws a silver pistol and levels the long barrel at my head. "Not if you're dead like your partner."

I steel my features to keep the guilt and anguish from showing.

"I *will* kill you for this," I state, meaning every damn word. Even if I'm not 100 percent sure how I'll follow through, considering I'm secured to the fucking chair and surrounded by guards.

With a knowing smirk, Rico cocks the hammer of the revolver. "The password to the software. Now."

"Go to hell, you rat bastard. I hope you get fucked in the—"

A boom vibrates throughout the room, followed quickly by blinding pain.

"Fuck," I scream as blood erupts from the gunshot wound to my thigh. Sucking down gulps of air, I do my best to glare at Rico. "You're so fucking dead," I hiss through my dry sobs.

"The password."

"You shot me," I say with a maniacal laugh. "Holy fuck, you really think I double-crossed you."

Rico steps close and leans into my space. The hot tip of the barrel burns the skin beneath my chin as he uses it to tip my face up to meet his.

"That's where you're wrong, Officer Smith." If they could, my eyes would widen with shock. *How in the hell does he know my real name? Shit, that means only one thing—a motherfucking leak.* "I know who you are, who you *still* work for. And I also know we have little time."

For the first time since this shit show started, I doubt I'll make it out of this alive. Clearly someone sold me and Kurt out, but who?

"Get her up and ready for transport," he barks in Spanish at the four guards. "We're taking her with us."

Without another word to me, Rico storms out, tucking that damn gun into the back of his slacks before he slams the door shut behind him.

The sense of the guards shifting about hits me just before a bruising grip wraps around one ankle. A sharp sting registers where the plastic digs into my bare flesh before vanishing.

Hope sparks.

Transport means I'll be moved unrestrained.

Seems the best moment for escape has arrived.

While the guard works on the other restraint, I carefully slip the stiletto off one freed foot. When he shifts to release my hands, I fake passing out, slumping all the way forward while using the moment to double-check that the other guards are immersed in their hushed argument.

They're idiots thinking the beating and a single bullet wound will stop someone like me.

The instant the final restraint slips from my wrist, I coil my remaining energy and snap into action. In one fluid motion, I leap from the chair, whipping it around to smash against the head of the guard who freed me.

Splinters spray everywhere when it connects with his shocked face. He sails across the small room, collapsing in the corner. *One down, three to go.* Twisting around, I race toward the guard who's raising his gun and dive, slamming my shoulder into his soft gut. He stumbles backward, the wall catching him before we collapse to the floor. With a quick twirl, I move to his back, yank the AR from his grip, and sweep the barrel toward the other two and the one I stunned, who's staggering to his feet.

Pop.

Pop.

Pop.

Three bodies slump to floor, crimson puddles growing beneath them. The final guard leans forward, writhing in my arms to escape my hold. The air forcefully escapes my lungs when he slams backward. Keeping hold of the rifle, I yank it all the way back and twist the strap until it's tightly tangled around his throat.

Dropping my weight to the floor, I hold tight to the strap, cutting off his air supply. The man shifts from side to side, turning desperately, trying to dislodge my hold, but I grit my teeth, straining to keep my grip secure. He stumbles forward, falling to his knees, fingers clawing at my forearms and leaving bloody tracks in their wake.

My muscles quiver, but I hold tight until his fight lessens before stopping completely as his hands fall to the floor. I count to five before easing back and unwinding the shoulder strap from the dead man's neck. Gun freed, I shove my knee between his shoulder blades, sending him falling face-first to the floor, joining his buddies in the body pile. To ensure he's *dead* dead, I fire a single round into the back of his head.

Breaths ragged, I stumble forward, landing on my knees. Warm, sticky liquid oozes around my fingers when I press them against the weeping bullet wound.

Two breaths. I give myself two deep breaths to shove the debilitating pain and rising panic into the very back of my mind, where it won't hinder my escape and get me killed. Only when Kurt, who I have to believe is still alive to maintain my sanity, and I are out of this mess can I allow the pain to distract me.

If I pass out now among the pile of dead bodies I'm obviously responsible for, I'm dead. So that means no passing out coupled with getting the fuck out of here.

My lungs burn, each breath like shards of glass slicing down my throat. Pressing the butt of the AR to the floor, I clench my teeth and slowly rise from the blood-coated floor.

Using the gun as a makeshift cane, I limp toward the door, dragging my wounded leg uselessly behind me. Ear pressed to the metal, I attempt to listen but can't hear a damn thing. Guess whatever soundproofing or sound absorbing shit works both ways. Hopefully the area beyond the door is empty, Rico's men getting ready for whatever departure he mentioned.

The room sways, my eyes rolling to the back of my head. My shoulder collides with the door, and I roll to my back to stay upright. Closing both eyes, I inhale several rapid breaths and shove back unconsciousness by sheer will alone. Thankfully, I've been trained by the best on how to deal with pain and continue on to complete the mission.

A blessing and a curse to be owned by the CIA.

Tonight, it feels like more of a curse.

Time to turn this operation back in our favor.

First I need to locate Kurt, then get the hell out of this compound before the SEALs show up and start raining bullets down on Rico and his men. Unless the rat who leaked our true identity didn't push the "go" signal through, or worse, sent men to ambush the SEALs before they even reached the compound grounds.

I swipe at the liquid dripping over my brows with my forearm. Biting my split lower lip, I use the sharp sting to refocus my wandering, slightly panicked thoughts. Now is not the time for questions. Now is the time to fight, find my *alive* partner*please let him be alive*and get us the hell home.

With three quick confidence-building pants, I twist the metal knob and ease the door open an inch.

Peering through the small fissure, I survey the living room where our meeting was initially held. Empty. Daring to open the door an inch more, I hover a finger over the trigger, ready for anything.

Shuffling over the threshold, I use the wall as leverage to keep me upright and position the butt of the gun to my shoulder. Another sweep around the expansive area, and something in the room across from where I stand makes me do a double take.

No.

My heart stalls, and time stops. All the fight and anger drains from my veins, leaving soul-crushing emptiness in its wake.

A pathetic whimper crawls up my throat as I take in the slumped body, still secured to a chair with the head angled back unnaturally. Even with the distance and my partial vision, the gaping hole and blood that trickles from the wound are clear. The body wears a familiar black dress shirt, shoulder holster, and black slacks—Kurt's standard uniform during this operation as my personal bodyguard.

I stare at the gruesome scene, my guilt growing, slowly strangling me from the inside out.

I killed my partner.

I mentally slap myself.

No. Rico killed Kurt. He didn't pull the trigger, but he issued the direct order. Rico killed Kurt. The rat who leaked our operation details killed Kurt.

That reassuring statement repeats over and over in my mind, suppressing the debilitating guilt and replacing it with hate and rage. That's what I have to hold on to. That rage instead of grief. Anger will be the fuel to get me home so I can figure out exactly what happened tonight and execute my vengeance.

Stepping deeper into the living area, I sweep the gun toward a sound on instinct alone, firing one shot. Rico's man collapses, revealing another right behind him, gun raised and ready.

Our guns fire in unison. Pain slices along my neck like a branding iron pressing to my skin. Collapsing, I drop the gun, which clatters beside me on the tile floor. With what little strength I can muster, I press a clammy palm to the deep cut and hold tight to slow the leaking blood.

Beneath my limp body, the floor trembles. Seconds later, chaos erupts everywhere. The explosion of many automatic guns firing at once vibrates through the room. Thankfully, with the dullness of my hearing as I slowly slip into shock, I barely hear the war going on all around me.

Everything feels light as I float upward toward the ceiling. Jostled, my limp body sways as I'm secured against something solid. Darkness engulfs my vision. Even with my eyes open, I can't make out the face of the person racing down a set of stairs with me in his arms. On the edge of unconsciousness, I feel my arms and legs flop around with each quick step of my savior.

Or captor.

The sticky, warm air that settles along my bare, clammy skin is my only sign that we breached the house and have moved outside. Two, maybe three steps after leaving the house in our wake, the air vibrates. The hold keeping me to a solid chest loosens, and I float through the air, falling fast, the moist earth doing nothing to cushion my impact as I'm thrown like a rag doll. Body twisted on the ground, unable to move, I watch bright flames cutting through the darkness. Somewhere close, a man screams name after name. Heat warms my cold cheeks, soothing me with a false sense of security.

Unable to keep fighting the pull, I give in to the extreme pain and massive blood loss and slip into the beckoning darkness.

1

TONY

I curse the morning light that streaks through the living room's cheap metal blinds, shooting through my closed eyelids. Not ready for another boring-ass day stuck behind a cramped desk, I roll over to my stomach and toss the pillow over my head, dousing me in darkness. Particles of dust float up from the secondhand couch's cushion, and a loose spring stabs into my lower ribs, reminding me I passed out in the living room instead of in the comfortable bed only a few feet down the hall.

Mouth dry and throat parched, I attempt to swallow down the sour taste coating my mouth only for my tongue to stick to the roof. A steady throb pounds against my skull, making me groan and squeeze my lids tighter. Waking up each morning hungover and then being hungover until I get off work and make it to the bar to start the nightly ritual over again is the new norm. It's not that great—fucking sucks monkey dick, actually—but at least it helps the memories fade and numb the pain.

I shift to a more comfortable position, my back muscles flexing, sending tiny pinpricks flaring along the scars and skin grafts. Because of the severity of several burns, the doctors believe these random tingling sensations are permanent. I should be thankful they could repair what they did; at least now I have a chance to return to active duty in the future.

A SEAL stuck behind a desk, forced to sort through mission reports instead of being out on said mission, is no SEAL at all. CO Williams hasn't stated exactly what he needs from me to prove I'm ready to join what's left of my team, but hopefully it's soon. I can't take much more waiting around to take my revenge on the fucker who killed half my men.

Who almost killed me.

I must have dozed off, because a thundering assault against the front door jerks me awake. The pillow tumbles to the floor, allowing the streams of light to blind me as I squint across the room. Heart hammering from the spike in adrenaline, I command it to slow as I lie waiting. Another bang rattles the cheap wooden door. Blinking to clear the haze, I stare at the door. *Who the fuck is here so damn early?* No one comes by anymore, not even my best friend and fellow SEAL, Gabe Wilcox. Everyone says I'm fucking miserable to be around, no longer the life of the party like I was before. The pain and memories have dragged me too deep into rage and desperation since being released from the hospital.

When the knocking persists, I press against the cushions and swing both legs around. Not in any hurry, unlike the person still attacking my apartment door, I stretch both arms high overhead, wincing slightly at the tug and burning sensation from the movement.

My rock-hard cock bobs up from my lap like it's fucking laughing at me, reminding me how long it's been since I've gotten laid. Waking up with morning wood at my age is a sad, sad state.

"Fuck." I groan and rub the sleep from my eyes with the heels of both palms. The throbbing in my head intensifies as the person set on breaking down my door doesn't relent. "I'm fucking coming," I shout, only to have my voice break.

Chapter 1

I don't even deserve to be labeled a SEAL at this point.

Snagging a pair of dirty gym shorts off the floor, I tug them up as I make my way toward the door. Thankfully, the massive hard-on got the memo that I'm in no state to rectify the horny issue and calmed the fuck down. Though the person with the balls to knock on my door this early in the morning might deserve to be greeted with me tenting out the front of my shorts.

Not bothering with checking the peephole, I snap the deadbolt free and yank the door open. G's still-knocking fist nearly clocks me between the eyes.

"The fuck?" I snap as I stumble back to keep from having my nose broken.

"I've been knocking for fifteen damn minutes, Flakes. What the hell? I thought you were dead in there."

"I feel like I am," I grumble. "Though my morning wood says otherwise."

"Um" comes a familiar feminine voice from behind G. Lucia moves around my best friend's bulky frame and offers a small wave. "Please don't talk about your dick in front of me. Been there, done that. Didn't—"

"Why are you two here?" This morning is already shitty enough. I don't need the reminder that the one woman I thought I could love back in college blew me off and is now married to my best friend.

Instead of answering, Lucia steps around her asshole husband, her round pregnant belly brushing against his side as she walks into the apartment uninvited.

"Come on in, I guess," I grumble while running a hand over my short hair. Leaning against the still-open door, I eye Lucia as she inspects the apartment. It's a shithole. It was the day I moved in after the divorce, but it's slightly worse for wear nowadays. I was a trained killer, not a housekeeper.

Her small nose scrunches in clear disgust. "Your place is filthy," Lucia remarks from where she stands in the middle of the dismal living room, turning in a slow circle, eyeing the empty bottles and take-out containers scattered along the coffee table and kitchen counter.

"Sorry, wasn't expecting company."

"Clearly," G mumbles as he passes, slamming a shoulder to the center of my chest.

"The fuck, Wilcox?" I snap, and shove him between the shoulder blades.

G turns with a feral gleam in his eye as he advances a step, his hands curled into tight fists.

"Stop acting like damn kids." Lucia's exasperated tone doesn't match the smile she's attempting to hide as she watches us be our normal jackass selves.

"He started it," I say, pointing to G.

"Just keeping you on your toes," he responds with a haughty look.

The moment his words register, the joy that sparked to life from the friendly sparring snuffs out.

"Why?" I grumble. "It's not like my reflexes matter behind a damn desk." Turning away from their shared worried look, I start for the kitchen area. "Either of you want a beer?"

"That's a hard no for Luce, and, fuck dude, it's not even seven yet." I shrug, deflecting the concern in his voice. "Flakes...."

"Suit yourself." Moving around Lucia for the kitchen, I give her belly an awkward pat. "Hi, baby."

Her responding carefree laugh and snort make the corners of my lips twitch in an almost smile. Something I haven't done in a long, long time.

"You idiotic water mammal. That's not how you greet a pregnant woman. "

I do it again just to make her laugh again and piss G off.

"Stop touching my wife," he warns. Arms crossed, focused gaze zeroed in on my hand still resting on her belly, he's clearly annoyed, but there's something else.

Moving my hand, I study his stiff posture. He was tense the moment he walked into the apartment. Hell, he was itching for a fight. Was that for my sake or his because he's worked up about something?

"What's up your G-string?" I ask over my shoulder as I tug open the yellow eighties fridge and pull out two bottles of water. Shoulder pressed to a cabinet, I toss one bottle to Lucia, who catches it midair.

"Don't mind him," she says with an eye roll. "He's officially entered the overly obsessed protecting stage."

I raise both brows at my brooding friend as I take a long gulp, nearly groaning with relief as the cool liquid soothes my tacky mouth and dry throat. "Surely he remembers you're a CIA officer and can protect yourself?"

That could be classified as the understatement of the year. Officer Lucia Rizzo, now Wilcox, can kick anyone's ass, man or woman, and almost cut off a guy's nuts—I know that one from personal experience—without breaking a sweat. Hell, some SEALs in G's platoon are terrified of her.

Thinking about his platoon immediately brings mine—what's left of mine—back to the forefront of my mind, a wave of grief tagging along with it.

Where my thoughts drifted must show on my face, because the next thing I know, a half-full water bottle collides with the center of my chest. I narrow my eyes at the smirking brunette.

"I'm discovering through this pregnancy that all the normal dad-to-be scenarios are next-level intense with this guy," she says, hooking a thumb toward the clearly unamused G.

"I'm a SEAL. Next-level intense is in our blood, sweetheart." Falling to the couch, he coughs when dust and who knows what else billows into the air. "Fucking hell. You need a maid."

"And I need you two to tell me why you're here." Draining the bottle, I toss it into the overflowing recycle bin. I wince at the growing pile on the floor. *Okay, maybe they have a point on this place being disgusting.*

"We're here because, for one, we're worried about you." I follow Lucia as she steps closer. She turns a pleading look from me to the water bottle at my feet. I huff a laugh and do what she can't—bend down and get it for her. I gently place it into her waiting hand. "We haven't seen you, the asshole Flakes we all know and love, in forever." Her softer tone bleeds with concern.

I grunt an acknowledgment. "We can always go grab a drink, just you and me." I shoot her my tried-and-true cocky smirk that I don't even remotely feel.

"Don't you try that shit with me." A long red nail digs into the center of my chest. "He's your best friend. Best. Friend." That finger swings toward G. "And he fucking needs your sorry ass right now. I'm pregnant, Tony."

"Obviously."

G growls. "Shut your damn mouth, fucker. Don't talk to my wife like that."

Lucia groans and tips her face to the ceiling. Gabe and I glare at each other while she mumbles something about infuriating water mammals.

"Listen. I'm going to leave, and you two are going to talk your shit out." When I open my mouth, she shuts it with a "I will kill you slowly" glare. "And once you two are besties once more, we'll talk about why I made my overprotective ass of a husband bring me here at the ass crack of dawn. And let me tell you this, Anthony"—oh hell, she's serious if I'm getting the full first name—"it wasn't to witness this pigsty." Chastised in the way only Lucia can make a trained killer feel smaller than an ant, I lower my gaze to the carpet, mumbling my apologies. "Until then, I'll go pick up my package while you two work through your motherfucking feelings."

The picture frames that literally came with the apartment rattle against the yellowed drywall when the door slams in her wake.

"Hormones?" I ask Gabe, who's busy staring at the door his feisty-ass wife just stormed through. "You want to go after her, don't you?"

"I don't fucking get it," he says, sounding lost. My attention perks. Gabe is the best damn SEAL I know. If he feels lost, something must be really wrong. "I know she can take care of herself but, I can't relax when she's not around."

"That's normal though, right? For most dudes to want to protect their pregnant wife? Like Lucia said, we're intense protectors in normal situations. Toss in the pregnancy and that urge is just riding you harder now. You're just being you."

"She says I'm an overbearing asshole."

"Well, I say that every day, so that shouldn't be fresh news."

Finally looking away from the door, he smirks. "True. Just haven't had you around lately to hear my daily affirmations, I guess."

So we're going there. We haven't had this conversation in a while, so I shouldn't be surprised.

Keeping my ruined back angled to the wall, I move to sit at the two-person round table just off the kitchen in what is considered a dining room. Weight pressed back, I balance on the two rear legs and rock back and forth while debating a response.

"You might have to find someone new to bolster your confidence at the base, G. Not sure when I'll be back to help."

I keep my attention fixed on the chipping tabletop, feeling more than seeing him move across the room. Across from me, a wide hand grasps the back of the other chair at the table and tugs, the legs rasping along the worn beige carpet.

Forearms pressed to the table, he clasps his hands. "You know the CO is only waiting for your final psych evaluation to come back before approving you for active duty. Which is on you. Not him, not me. You, Flakes."

"I don't know shit." Okay, maybe I know what he's talking about, but denial feels like the best route in this moment. Denial is my go-to these days for most things.

"You need to move on, Tony."

My rapping fingers pause, curling into a tight fist. "Move on," I state with cold detachment. "If it were that fucking easy, don't you think I would have by now? But I can't move on, like you said, from the constant damn pain that wakes me up in the middle of the night unless I'm too drunk to feel, or the vivid flashbacks and nightmares of being blown up, of my men not responding when I called their names." Heavy labored breaths send my chest heaving up and down. Heat blisters beneath my skin from my growing rage. "You think I should forget it all, just wake up and act like nothing happened, like my life wasn't fucking ruined that night. How can I forget that I'm a fucking scarred mess when every stretch or move reminds me of how parts of tactical gear were melted into my body? And how will I ever, *ever*," I say, hissing the word, "stop thinking, stop knowing I should've died with my men?"

G doesn't utter a word or shrink away when I lean closer and fist the front of his T-shirt.

"Get the hell out of my place if your advice is simply to move on. There is no moving on, not for me. There's only locating that bastard who wrecked my world, and making him pay for what he took from me, from other families. And I'm not an idiot thinking that will take away the pain or bring back my men, but I'm damn positive it will feel fucking amazing watching him die by my hand."

Weighted silence settles between us, only my rapid gasps filling the quiet.

"Good."

All the fight fueling the adrenaline rushes from my veins. Releasing him, I fall back into the chair, unsure of how to respond.

"Good?"

G's chin dips in acknowledgment. "Yes, good. I understand it won't be easy. Every day you'll think about the men you lost and feel suffocating guilt like a damn weight on your chest because those men died following your orders." There's no holding back the emotions his words invoke like a physical punch. "But you didn't kill them, Flakes. You were following orders, and the mission went to shit, completely out of your control. Someone out there triggered the explosives that blew up the main house on that bastard's compound. Some damn mole is responsible for informing that Suarez bastard that your platoon was in route. Their deaths are not on you. Our hands are permanently colored red from all the blood on them, but your team's is not in the mix."

The steady thud of my heart hammers against my chest as I stare, jaw slack, across the table at my friend, wondering when in the hell he became so insightful.

Chapter 1

"Drinking won't fix anything," he adds.

"I know," I admit with a resigned sigh. "But it sure as hell makes things easier to deal with on a day—"

"The fuck did you just say to me?" Gabe bolts out of the chair, sending it toppling to the ground behind him. With one hard shove, he launches the table between us into the living room.

Still in shock at his sudden mood change, I nearly fall on my ass when he steps closer, a menacing glint in his eyes. Retreating, I suck in a tight breath when my back hits the wall, trapped.

He pauses, so close our noses almost touch. "We are Navy fucking SEALs. We do not do things the easy way. We make shit harder just because we can live through it and smile on the other side. We meet issues head-on, not drowning in a bottle. Make things *easier*? That word is not in our vocabulary, SEAL."

I can't breathe. The intensity radiating off him, the strength in his words, makes me long for that matching passion. Makes me remember what it's like to now wallow and mourn and sit stagnant as the world moves on.

Makes me want to live the life I know I'm capable of. Not because I've moved on but because I can't dwell here in this sad state any longer or else I risk being stuck here for the rest of what would be a miserable life.

Stern eyes search mine, almost like he's reading the thoughts running through my head.

"Are you going to get your shit together and be the damn godfather my kid will need you to be?"

My response is automatic, with a renewed strength in my voice I haven't felt in months.

"Yes."

"Are you going to get your shit together, meet with the counselor, and get cleared for active duty?"

"Hell yes."

"Are you going to act like the SEAL you are, the team lead your remaining team needs you to be?"

"Yes."

Stepping back, Gabe rests his palms on my bare shoulders and smiles.

"Good. I know it's a long road, but this is a start. Which means now," he says, clapping his hands and rubbing them together conspiringly, "we can move on to the good stuff."

It's like live wires are zapping energy into my veins. Almost jittery with excitement, I search for something to do. Lip curling in disgust, I rip a garbage bag from the barely used roll and begin shoving litter into the depths. Lucia was right, this place is a pigsty.

"If by good stuff, you're wanting to share all the positives of pregnancy sex, I'm out. That's not my idea of the good stuff." I sniff a dirty sock and gag. Shoving that into the bag, I move to the stack of empty Chinese food containers and used utensils covering the entire surface of the coffee table.

"That's not what I meant, but now that you mention it, it's fucking amazing. Her tits are enormous, and don't get me started on the kinky—"

Without turning, I chuck an empty white cardboard carton in his direction. "For the love of everything that's holy, please stop."

Gabe's still smiling like he's the funniest fucker in the world when he sits on the sofa's rounded armrest. "Fine. Are you ready to hear this?"

"I'm legit nervous about what's going to come out of your mouth after that TMI disclosure."

"We have a lead."

Everything stills. Even my heart freezes for a second before stuttering into hyperdrive. My hand hovers over a plastic water bottle, my unseeing gaze locked on it as I repeat his four words over in my mind.

"A lead," I state, trying not to get too excited before I confirm I heard him right.

"That's what I said. A lead on Rico Suarez."

The full bag of trash slips from my fingers, some contents I just stuffed inside tumbling back out to the floor. Straightening to my full height, I cross both arms over my chest and widen my stance. "Tell me everything you know."

"It's not much, but Luce says there's recent activity coming out of Colombia. Seems the world's most wanted arms dealer is looking to sell top-secret blueprints and software to an advanced military-grade drone."

"What?" I say in utter shock. "It's been eight months since that flash drive and the bastard himself vanished. Why is he trying to offload it now? What's his endgame?"

Something isn't adding up. Rico is smart enough to not attempt to sell that information through CIA-tracked channels.

Gabe lifts a single shoulder and leans forward to press both elbows on the tops of his thighs. "Luce has a few theories about the timing and his endgame."

"The theories aside, what does that mean for a mission? Intel from before is dated. The asshole's no doubt changed locations, altered trade routes and resources. He's a sneaky fucker, which is why we could never pin him down long enough to form a solid plan of attack before the CIA inserted their operative, and we all know how that turned out."

"If you'd give me a chance, I'll get to the best part." I flip him the bird while swooping an arm down to grab the bag of trash. "You know the woman you pulled from the house before it exploded?"

I grit my teeth to keep me from lashing out a string of curses. Of course I know who he's referring to. It's hard to forget the nameless woman who accompanies you in your nightly nightmares.

"What about her?" I'm not sure what will happen to my mental status if he tells me she works for Rico and my men died without me all because of her. I might lose it.

In that moment, surrounded by gunfire, I couldn't just step over the beaten woman's body, leaving her to bleed out on the floor. Something demanded I haul her against my chest and get her to the chopper. Even to this day, no matter how many times I've tried, I can't pinpoint exactly what kept me from moving on.

"She'll lead us to Rico Suarez."

For the second time in a matter of minutes, the world stills, and my mind goes blank.

I blink at my friend, lost on what to say next. "What do you mean, lead us to that bastard?" Dragging the bag of trash, I take a challenging step toward G, but he holds up a hand, stopping my advance, and points to the door.

"Luce has all the information. We're meeting with CO Williams, Lucia, and the CIA officer at 1000 hours." Slipping off the armrest to the couch cushion, he relaxes back and interlaces his fingers behind his head like he has all the time in the world. "Take a shower and get dressed. It's time to enact your revenge on that bastard."

Hell yes.

Hopefully this CIA officer will be less headstrong than G's wife.

If she's anything like Lucia, finding Rico and killing the bastard will be the least of my worries.

2

ELLIOT

"And how did that woman's comment to your post make you feel?"

I barely stifle the urge to throw the metal chair presently making my ass numb into our group counselor's placid face. The therapist and the others sitting in the small circle with me are morons. No, scratch that—they're ungrateful, weak-minded morons. Each person in this facility has no idea their so-called anger management issues are nothing compared to the colossal shit storm going on in the rest of the world while they complain about menial things that made them pissy.

Unlike me.

I'm aware of the good, the bad, and the ugly going on outside these walls, all around the globe. It's the bad, ugly, and the utterly depraved issues I've seen, and some I've done, that keep me wide awake at night.

"She had her friends like her bitchy comment," the kid, who looks no older than fourteen, says with a pout. Collapsing against his chair, he crosses his arms, reminding me of a toddler throwing a tantrum.

At the thought, I glide my hand over my lower stomach, fingers gathering the scratchy blue scrub material until it's held tight in my fist. My baby would never throw a tantrum, or live its life blissfully unaware of what its mommy does. Even though I only knew about the possibility of a baby for less than twenty-four hours, the grief of loss still hits me hard when I least expect it.

The group therapist's all-seeing gaze shifts from the rambling kid to my fisted hand, and she arches a questioning brow. Being the mature adult I am not, I stick my tongue out between pursed lips and relax the hand on my abdomen, dropping it back to my side.

"Do you have something to add today, Leslie?"

I grind my back teeth at the name I hate more than the last one the agency gave me.

"All good in the hood," I say in a singsong voice with a broad fake smile.

His eyes narrow at my attempt to deflect from the mess of emotions constantly warring inside me. This guy is an actual therapist, one of the best the West Coast CIA location has on staff, and he's stuck here wasting time with these spoiled nitwits all because of me.

I'm not like everyone else here, secluded away at the fancy-schmancy SoCal anger management facility. Other patients are here because they punched a photographer in the face or took a nine iron to their boyfriend's one-of-a-kind sports car and are now serving out their judge-mandated sentence.

Me? Well, I'm a different, more volatile and violent set of anger management issues.

I come with grenades, guns, and a lot of instability.

Before the failed operation in Colombia, I was a little irrational, maybe stabbing someone when they wouldn't talk or blowing up a building because I couldn't find a door. But now I'm riding the crazy train full speed ahead, fueled solely by the desperate need for vengeance, and I'm fully on board with doing whatever is required to ensure it happens.

However, the agency assholes don't see my need for Rico's blood as urgent as I do. By sticking me here, guarded and monitored at all times, they're keeping me from locating Rico and ending him—piece by piece. He took my partner, my career, and maybe my one chance at having a family of my own. The moment I can get out of here, without getting caught again—yes, I said again—I'll find Rico and take everything from him like he did me.

Lost in detailing Rico's live autopsy, I almost don't register a new sound outside the group therapy room, growing louder. Drowning out the pop star's high-pitched voice as she describes attacking her fiancé with a bat when she caught him with the pool boy, I focus all my attention on the rhythmic click.

Heels, the owner's stride long and labored. My dark hair swishes in its high ponytail as I tilt my head toward the door with a pointed look at the therapist. His slight head shake sends my piqued interest into overdrive.

Very interesting. An unknown guest is approaching, no doubt here for me. Hopefully it's not for another round of integration. The agency and navy assumed I was the leak that ruined the operation and left one officer and several SEALs dead. Not even fully recovered, they ripped me out of the hospital, locked me at a black site, and grilled me for days, trying to break me.

But I wasn't their leak, my survival of that messed-up mission a fluke, not a plan devised by myself to allow Rico to go free and me barely escape like some of the directors believed. Apparently surviving a failed mission pointed to you as a traitor instead of praised for your badass combat and survival skills.

At the nearly inaudible twist of metal hinges, I ready my now fully healed body for anything. Muscles tense, hands and fingers loose at my side, I train my full focus on the single door leading to the hallway.

My fight-or-flight drains when a tall, familiar, and very pregnant female steps through the open door and into the room.

Even if I hadn't met Officer Wilcox before and known she's CIA, there's no mistaking that she's an immediate threat. It's the way she carries herself, even while pregnant, and takes in the entire room in one quick sweep, calculating everything. I recognize all this the second she enters the room because I do it myself. We were both trained by the best.

All CIA officers have this cold, analyzing look about them. A look that says, "If you see me, you're already dead." I wanted a pattern with that saying made for maybe a cross-stitching team-building exercise, but I never got a reply from the email I sent the secretary of state.

Officer Wilcox surveys the room with a bland smile until her gaze locks on me. "Leslie," she says in an overly cheery voice. "I've been looking everywhere for you."

As one, the others around the circle turn to face her. Officer Wilcox and I both have long dark hair, hers fuller and mine board straight, but that's where our similarities stop. So that's a no on the quick cover story that she's my sister.

"Aunt Lue," I say with enthusiasm just as fake as she showed.

Her sharp gaze cuts to the therapist, who doesn't appear alarmed or concerned about the officer in the room. "I'm checking my niece out for a few days. I've already cleared it with the other doctors."

By doctors, she probably means my superiors who have me locked away here until who knows when. Fuck knows they don't have an answer for that question every time I ask.

With awkward goodbye waves from the others and a few pleas to take them with me, I release a breath the moment the door shuts behind us. I glance one way down the hall, then the other, finding both directions empty.

"Honestly, I don't even care if you're here to kill me. I'm just damn grateful that you cut group therapy short."

Officer Wilcox snorts a laugh and starts down the hall, not bothering to make sure I'm following. "That bad?"

"Yep." Keeping up with her long strides is easy considering she's in heels and I'm barefoot, even though her legs are almost twice the length of mine. "So what are your orders this time, Officer Wilcox? More questions? Oh, maybe this time some electric shock therapy."

She was one of the many ordered to interrogate me after Colombia, to uncover the truth. Who knows if my director believed I leaked the details of the operation, but they put me through a full interrogation just the same. CIA Officer Wilcox believed me from the first meeting. I'm fairly positive she's the reason they sent me to this fancy facility instead of leaving me decaying somewhere in an unmarked grave.

"Pretty sure last time I told you to call me Lucia," she says with a side-eye glance. "And what the hell? You know we haven't done electric shock for interrogation in ages. It's so eighties."

"Right." I draw out the word, emphasizing my doubt, considering she avoided answering my question. "And if we're going the personal route, then please use my real name. I don't know who creates my cover identity names, but I seriously want to throat-punch them. I mean, come on. Leslie Lilac Little? Who does that to someone and doesn't expect violent repercussions?"

Lucia smiles but keeps her focus down the hall. "You should've heard the name they gave me when I ran an op at Coronado. Just as terrible." Her features soften as if reliving fond memories. "I'm sure you want to know why I'm here, and I'll clear up your two questions. No, I'm not here to kill you, and no to the electric shock." We take a right at the front desk, going toward the female living quarters. "I'll shoot you straight, Elliot, because I know you're not one to bullshit." I dip my chin in agreement. "I'm trusting you. Everyone says I'm insane for choosing you for this operation."

I consider her statement for a second. "They're right. I could run."

She slows our pace as we weave through a small group of patients. "True, but you won't."

"What makes you sure? You know nothing about me."

She pauses and spins toward me. Her unwavering stare burns, like she can see through to my soul. "That's a lie. I know you better than you know yourself these days, Officer Smith. And I know *you know* that to be the truth."

I do know, but that doesn't mean I have to like it. After being released from the hospital, Lucia was the one who went through every inch of my life. Question after question to find the truth, or verifying it, in my case, that I wasn't the mole.

"Now, we have to hurry," she says and starts walking toward my cell—I mean room. "We're on a time crunch, and you can't meet with the CO wearing that." Her long red nails make a zigzag line, showing my current scrub attire is not acceptable.

"Shoes would be great if you can convince the assholes here to give me mine back."

"From what I read on the way here, that's your fault. Using shoelaces as a weapon and an escape accessory will force those overseeing your confinement to take all potential weapons away. But you're right, you need shoes for this meeting. I already asked for them to bring up a pair of boots from your storage container."

At my door, she pushes it open and gestures for me to enter first.

Keeping one eye on her, I step inside, never turning my back to the obvious threat. Inside the small ten-by-ten room, I narrow my focus on the black tank and jeans resting on the all-white bedding.

"I'll give you some privacy to change, but we need to leave in fifteen minutes."

Gratitude washes over me as I pick up the soft black cotton shirt, rubbing the material between my thumb and finger. "Thank you," I say as I run my other hand over the ripped black jeans. "The CO or whoever won't care that I'm wearing something this casual?"

When she doesn't respond, I find her smiling like she's in on some kind of secret I'm not. "Oh, he won't mind. The other two who will attend the meeting with us are going to hate it."

"Then why have me wear it?" What kind of mind games is she playing? Immediately my training kicks in, searching for signs of a trap.

"Because you seem like an all-black-clothing type girl with an edge." She shrugs, like understanding that little piece of me isn't as big a deal to her as it is to me. "And I need you to trust me, to be comfortable and compliant during the meeting while you listen to my proposal."

"I'm not going to like it, am I?" Already stripping off the scrub top, I release a soft sigh when the thin, soft cotton tank slips over my skin.

"Depends."

"On what?"

"On what you're willing to put up with to get what you want."

Chapter 2

I pause, gaze meeting hers. "And what do I want?"

"Vengeance on Rico Suarez."

Well, hell. Now she has my full attention. "Is this some kind of trap?" I say, tightening my grip on the jeans. "I've asked for months to be released from this fancy-ass prison so I can hunt that bastard. What's changed?"

The smile on Lucia's face drops, making my stomach do the same.

Suddenly too tired to stand, I perch on the side of the bed. "What's he done now?" My gut twists with nerves. If he's injured more innocent civilians or killed more soldiers with the guns he sold our enemies—

"Just focus on getting dressed. I'll explain the details on the way to the meeting. But if you play your cards right and I'm able to sell this crazy operation to the CO, you'll not only get your vengeance on Rico but your job back too." She glances at the phone in her hand. "Seven minutes."

With that bomb, she steps back, allowing the door to snicker closed.

Rico and my career back on track?

Hell to the yes.

"I don't understand his ultimate endgame," I mutter to myself, staring out the dark-tinted window as we cross the sky-high bridge to Coronado Island. "Let's say he figured out a way to replicate the password I put in for the drone's blueprints. There's no way he also miraculously figured out the fourteen-character complex password for the software too."

"Agreed." Lucia shifts in her seat behind the wheel, unable to get comfortable despite the luxury ride. "But it's our first lead in eight months. We have to jump on it."

"Maybe *that's* the plan," I murmur, thinking over the various possibilities. "To draw us back to Colombia without a solid plan in place."

"Or," she draws out, "not so much *us* but just you."

My ponytail swishes as I tilt my head one way, then the other. "Possibly. He showed creepy interest in me those few times we met. He could be after me since I got away just to prove that he can catch me and finish the job his men botched. Or to lure me back because he knows I'm the only one he can reach with the password to the drone software."

"Your tone makes you sound okay with either scenario."

Twisting in the smooth leather seat, I rest a black motorcycle boot on the dash and shift to get comfortable.

"Shouldn't I be? If I go back to Colombia, I won't make it out alive. I've accepted that from the moment I woke up after surgery and knew I'd do anything to take that bastard down. As long as he's gone, I'm okay if I am too."

"And if he captures you?"

I shrug. "Well, then, I'll put up with whatever he can throw at me until I can figure out a way to kill him myself."

Lucia hums a noncommittal response.

Head rested back, I study the various condos and houses shifting past the window until they morph into high-end shops and hotels.

"So this plan you're pitching to this CO Williams guy is me going down to Colombia, figuring out where Rico is hiding out these days, and taking him out?"

"Not exactly, but the middle part sounds about right." I watch her out of the corner of my eye as a smile tugs at her full lips. My gaze dips to her enormous belly that's almost brushing the steering wheel.

"How far along are you?"

She purses her lips and shoots me a glance before flicking the blinker on to turn into the gated military base. "Eight months."

I blink, working to keep my features neutral. Same as I would've been.

Once we're allowed entrance, the guard waves us through, and Lucia whips the SUV into an accessible parking space. I huff a laugh and move to unbuckle the seat belt, but Lucia stops me with a tight grip around my wrist.

Chapter 2

"I understand it. The grief pressed into you from every side, even when there wasn't any actual proof of something being there to grieve. Don't let anyone, even that dumbass shrink or doctors at that facility, tell you it was nothing and to move on. Don't let them make you believe you don't have the right to grieve what you lost. But also don't let that grief prompt you to make mistakes or rash decisions that could get you killed. Mourn the baby you lost. Mourn what was taken from you. You're allowed that."

Heart racing, I can't rip away from the intensity behind her hazel eyes. She means every damn word.

When I woke up, the doctors informed me I had lost the baby like it was nothing. They said it so casually while they listed off my other injuries and wounds. It was never brought up again. It's like my baby was a dirty little secret and the agency was happy when they could sweep it under the rug and move on.

"Okay," I rasp. Licking my dry lips, I swallow and nod. "Okay. Thank you."

"You're welcome. I see a lot of me in you, Elliot. So much passion, determination, and—"

"Mental instability?"

That wide smile of Lucia's spreads across her face. "Well, I think that comes with anyone who joins the CIA. We're all too damn smart for our own good."

"I like the way you think. 'Too damn smart for our own good.' Has a nice ring to it. We should cross-stitch it on matching pillows or something."

"You'll get through this and get your career back on track. But, Elliot, I need to know I can trust you. That if I convince those responsible for approving the operation that you'll stay in line. No disappearing and forming your own plan or taking out the team members who are going—"

I hold up both hands and scoot until I plaster my back against the door. "Whoa there, new friend. Team members? I'm better alone where I can—"

"With your history and fixation on Rico, that won't happen.

Maybe if you wouldn't have escaped the heavily guarded facility and tried to get across the border *twice*, I might have been able to convince everyone you could do it alone. But not a chance now. Plus, if Rico is trying to draw you out, no matter his reasons, having a team who has your back is needed."

I open my mouth to tell her to take me back to the facility, then snap it shut. "Fine," I hiss. Yanking the handle, I shove the door open with the toe of my black boot. "Let's get this over with."

Our car doors slam shut at the same time. With her long legs, she makes it around the front of the SUV before me. "If I weren't pregnant, I'd kick your ass for your shit attitude. Do you or do you not want your life back?"

I seal my lids and count to twenty, inhaling and exhaling in deep, slow breaths. "You're right. You're giving me an out that doesn't end with me disappearing like our agency likes to do to officers they no longer have a need for." I gesture toward the set of metal doors I assume is the entrance to the building. "Lead the way to my future freedom."

3

ELLIOT

"Enter," a deep, commanding voice calls from behind the wide, dark wooden door.

The moment it swings open, a billow of arctic air caresses across my warm cheeks. Goose bumps sprout along my bare arms, my only reaction to the change in temperature as we move deeper into the CO's expansive office.

After a quick scan, I note only one exit—the door we just came through—a comfortable sitting area with large leather chairs on one side, a massive wooden desk with a man dressed in fatigues studying a paper in his hand, and two men also dressed in fatigues standing at ease along a bookcase spanning the other long wall.

It doesn't take even half a second to identify the two men with their lean bulk and intense focus.

SEALs.

Both men's eyes track my every movement. The stacked one with blue eyes swings his concentrated gaze to Lucia and tracks down her pregnant frame in a slow, calculated perusal. My defenses snap to attention, not at all approving of his focus on her. With a quick sidestep, I place myself in front of Lucia, blocking what I can of her larger frame from his line of sight.

His thick blond brows rise along his forehead, and his lips press into a tight line as if to keep himself from speaking.

The SEAL beside him, who's not as bulky as his creepy friend but still tall and no doubt ripped beneath those stiff clothes, stands up straighter as if preparing for a fight.

I'm no idiot. I'm well aware I don't stand a chance between two SEALs, but I'll fight to the death to protect my new friend and the baby in her belly.

Feeling her shift behind me, I don't startle or break my stare-off with the SEALs when Lucia gently grasps my elbow and tugs.

"Officer Smith." I cock my head to the side as a sign I'm listening, not daring to glance away from the two threats. "It's okay."

"I don't like him," I say, not clarifying which male I'm referring to. Because honestly, they're both making me a little twitchy at the moment.

Her soft chuckle eases some of the tension from my taut muscles.

"Well, the one who looks like he's about to explode out of his fatigues is my husband." When her words register, the rigidity in his stance and mine relaxes. "And the other, well, I don't really like him either, but he grows on you—eventually. And they're kind of a package deal."

"Lovers?" I take in the two with a new outlook, borderline fascination. I mean... whatever floats her boat if she doesn't mind sharing her husband with another guy. I could totally see the benefits and appeal.

The two exchange a panicked look and shift to put additional space between them.

"That's a no, just best friends. Have been since the academy," Lucia says around three fingers pressed to her lips, clearly trying to hide her grin. "Both are senior officers over different platoons." She points to the blond one first. "My husband, Sr. Officer Gabe Wilcox, and Sr. Officer Tony Hackenbreg."

I point to my chest. "Officer Elliot Smith." Swiveling on my boot heels, I move to one of the two chairs in front of the large desk and fall into it. "Nice office."

Peering over the edge of the manila folder, the man behind the desk furrows his brow. His gaze slides to Lucia, who now stands just to my left. "She's not nearly as disciplined as you were in our first meeting, Officer Wilcox."

Lucia glances down at me and inclines her head toward the bald man.

"Thankfully the Army's bullshit never stuck," I say while shifting to get comfortable in the stiff leather. "You get what you see with me. I might not stand, sit, and jump at your every command, but I'm a damn good officer."

Slowly the CO lowers the folder and reaches over, sliding another, much thicker one closer. A stamp with big red block letters reads CONFIDENTIAL across the front.

"A damn good officer, you say?" He flips open the file, revealing a stack of papers with more black lines through them than clear letters. "Your file states that before Colombia, your operation record was stellar. All twelve of your targets were...." He peers up over the rim of his reading glasses.

"Handled," I fill in for him.

He nods and glances back at the paper. "However, your mental health has consistently been a concern, it seems. Defiant, lack of respect to supervisors, zero self-preservation, apparent dissociative behavior, self-harm—"

I hold up a hand, stopping him. "Um, what was that last one?" Maybe he has the wrong file, though the other issues he listed are correct.

His eyes skim down the page, flipping to the next one. "Says here you've shot yourself."

I bark a humorless laugh, drawing the CO's attention back to me instead of the dumb, inaccurate file. "Well, yeah, sure, that happened. But they're taking it out of context. I didn't do it to hurt myself. I shot myself in the shoulder to shoot the guy strangling me. I thought it was pretty brilliant."

His responding nod is slow and uncertain. "And it also lists a fractured wrist?"

"To escape zip ties." I leave off the "duh" at the end. Pretty sure that would send both SEALs currently vibrating with restrained anger at how I'm talking to their CO into a frenzy.

"And the incident when you cut yourself?"

"Yeah, that one I'll give them. But again, it wasn't to self-harm but rather to cut the damn tracker out of my forearm."

Everyone in the room seems to pause at that revelation. Sighing through my nose, I hold up my forearm to display the nasty jagged scar. "It was a bitch to dig out. But apparently the agency isn't behind the 'my body, my choice' movement and inserted a new tracker between my shoulder blades where I can't get to it." I glance over my shoulder at the two men and waggle my brows. "Yet."

Relaxing back in the chair, I almost laugh out loud at the CO's slow blinks like I'm some kind of circus freak. Maybe I am.

I'll give the agency credit. The dissociative behavior assessment is accurate, but then again, that's what makes me a good officer. And fucking fun as hell to hang out with, if you ask me.

But don't ask others.

He clears his throat and flips to the next page. "Your file also states you were caught twice trying to cross the border after escaping the facility where the CIA has you recovering."

My back goes ramrod straight. "Recovering?" I laugh. "Not even close. They're just biding their time until they figure out what to do with me. They haven't decided if I'm damaged goods or not, and I get their pickle. I'm not sure yet either."

He hums his agreement and continues reading, this time to himself. Halfway down the page, his black brows shoot up his forehead seconds before he stares across the desk with amusement in his kind eyes.

"Am I reading this correctly? After the first escape attempt, they found you with an assault shotgun, two grenades, and a six-pack of Red Bull?"

I nod. "Yep. Blueberry. My favorite. They don't allow it in that damn facility. I was totally jonesing for one the moment I hopped the fence." Leaning toward the desk, I point to the file. "Does it list

Chapter 3

anything good in there? Like my hobbies or nonlethal skill set? I can make a mean margarita and have recently taken up cross-stitching." I shrug at his questioning look. "What? It's cathartic. Keeps my hands nimble and involves a sharp object. Win-win."

The corner of his mouth tilts upward. It thrills me to no end knowing I'm pushing his patience and also entertaining him at the same time.

"Officer Wilcox," he says, his features visibly softening when he looks to the woman still standing beside me. "You have the floor. Present the details of the operation you're suggesting. Based on what I've seen and read so far, you can only imagine how skeptical I am that this will be the right path to Rico Suarez."

With a resigned sigh, she nods and leans a thigh against the back of my chair.

"Eight months ago, the joint mission between the CIA and SEALs to apprehend Rico Suarez was a failure resulting in a flash drive with military-grade drone blueprints and software going missing, as well as one CIA officer and five SEALs dead." My heart squeezes painfully at the reminder. "Since that night, the arms dealer has been quiet. Fewer shipments going overseas, he changed up trade routes, didn't return to his normal hideouts. That is until five days ago, when the blueprints went up for sale. My analysts are working on gathering new data on Rico, but he's ghosting us, like he did all those years before Officer Smith and her partner immersed themselves in Colombia and gained his trust. We need to find him, get the flash drive, and bring him into custody. "

I raise my hand like a third-grader needing some clarification on that last part.

"Yes, Elliot," Lucia says cautiously.

"When you say the word custody, does that mean dead?" When she narrows her eyes, I hold up both hands in surrender. "Just asking for a friend."

"No, custody means alive. We know our enemies buy his weapons, which results in the deaths of our soldiers, but I have a lead on a rumor that one of our allies is also stockpiling weapons behind our backs, and we need to know why. Therefore, we need him alive. We need him to talk."

"Well." I blow out a puff of air. "That's a letdown. Can I call dibs on killing him when you're done interrogating him?"

"Let's focus on the mission first, shall we, Officer Smith?" CO Williams says, ending our conversation.

After a confirming nod, I twist to face Lucia and motion for her to continue.

"I'm proposing we send Officer Smith plus a small team to locate and capture Suarez before the sale is completed on the flash drive."

"Time frame?" CO Williams questions.

"Fully organized and ready to send the team in less than a week."

"Permission to speak, sir."

Chin to my shoulder, I give my full attention to the SEAL who's stepped forward. His dark eyes glare down at me, his hands fisted at his side.

"Granted."

"Based on the information in Officer Smith's file, she is a liability to the mission, not an asset. We need to find another avenue to Suarez."

"Excuse me?" In a smooth move, I stand to face him. "A liability? I'm pretty damn sure that's you, considering this operation is on land, where your synchronized swimming routines won't do us any good."

A genuine smile pulls at my lips, feeling completely foreign, when he takes a challenging step closer.

"Enough, Hackenbreg." I shoot the annoying yet crazy-hot SEAL a wink and ease back into the chair, putting my back to him like I don't consider him the threat he clearly is. "That goes for you too, Officer Smith." He turns a weary gaze to Lucia. "I'm inclined to agree with Hackenbreg. Why her?"

Lucia starts, but I hold up a hand. Looking the CO straight in the eye, I lean forward and clasp my hands.

"Because I got to Rico once before, and I can do it again. I know his suppliers, and they know me. This time around, I don't have to play nice to gain their favor to grow closer to Rico. This time I get to do what I do best—get shit done. If I make it known to Rico that I'm local and looking for him, he *will* find me. No other officer has what I offer. It's me, or Rico goes on selling weapons to bastards who kill our friends, our men and women in uniform, and innocent bystanders caught in the middle. If I'm on this mission, we'll find Rico, but without me, you can guarantee he'll keep ghosting you, and that flash drive and all the information inside will vanish with him.

"I know what my file says. I know what others say about me as an officer and as a person, and I don't care. I do what needs to be done to complete the mission with minimal casualties. Colombia is on me. I was the lead officer, and it went fucking sideways. This is my chance to vindicate myself and not only get me back on the agency's good side but serve a heavy dose of vengeance at the same time. I will not fuck this up if given the opportunity. Sir."

CO Williams holds my stare for several long seconds before relaxing back into his chair and closing the file. Rubbing at his dark brows with a thumb and finger, he stays silent. No one in the room dares to interrupt him as he weighs the information provided.

"If I agree to this mission, there will be conditions."

"Of course, sir," Lucia says with a curt nod.

I take in the way her back is ramrod straight, her feet spread and hands clasped behind her back. Even though it's been a while since she served in the Army, it seems her training stuck.

A snort gets caught in my throat. Nothing in my short stint in the Army stuck. They tried to break me then, as others have before and since, but here I am. Proving them all wrong.

"Based on the time both Hackenbreg and Smith have been sidelined, I'd need full assessments on their readiness for active duty. Stamina, firearms, and others before I approve either for the mission."

"Sounds like fun," I say, earning me a side-eye glare from Lucia. "What?"

The mention of the SEAL being sidelined too doesn't miss my attention, but instead of asking now, I tuck it away for later. I need a full rundown of the guy before I'm saddled with babysitting him in Colombia.

"Two weeks to complete the testing and gather any additional intel so the three won't be walking in blind. This isn't a suicide mission." The CO's glare shifts from me to just over my shoulder, angled in the direction of the two SEALs.

"Three, sir?" Hackenbreg steps up to stand beside my chair. "The more who go in—"

"Yes, three. Smith to get us to Suarez, you to ensure her safety and apprehend the bastard, and another to babysit you two."

"Hey," Hackenbreg and I grumble at the same time.

"I don't need a babysitter," I state.

"Your file says otherwise." Well, he has me there. But I really don't like being made out to be the kid who needs one of the backpack leashes because they're a runner. "I'll review the details and let you know my decision. Dismissed."

As one, the three behind me twist around and march toward the door. Not wanting to be left behind, I leap from the chair and hurry to catch up.

Before the door shuts, the CO calls my name, stopping me. The door's wooden edges dig into my hand as I hold it open with me half in the hallway and half in the office.

"Yeah?"

"You're heading down a dangerous path. Don't lose sight of what matters most."

Um, what the what? "My country always comes first, sir. You never have to question that with me."

"I'm not talking about where your clear loyalty lies. It's you, Elliot. Don't lose your focus on who you are. I've seen the signs after failed missions, the grief that settles behind one's eyes. There's no coming back if you lose the sense of self that tethers you to your reason for living."

My mouth gapes as my jaw hangs open. *What did he just say to me?*

"That's some deep shit, sir," I reply. "Ever think of tossing the military career aside and writing inspirational cross-stitching patterns?"

Chapter 3

Even from across the room, the subtle twitch of his lips and chest vibrating from the restrained chuckle are clear.

"It's my backup plan. I'll have a decision on the mission by the end of the day. Dismissed."

When the door snickers shut, I lean against it and blow out a slow breath. "I think I just got Yoda'd."

The sense of eyes on me has my defenses rushing to the surface. Slowly I scan the long hall only to locate the source of the sensation standing just five feet away, posted along a stack of metal filing cabinets.

We each take the other in, assessing the way I would any mark to identify weakness and immediate threats. His dark cropped hair is a standard military cut that looks cheesy on most but not on him. Somehow it draws attention to his golden skin and dark almond-shaped eyes that currently scan me from crown to toe. A straight nose that fits perfectly with the harsh lines of a square jaw, accentuated by perfectly kissable lips.

Add in the strength that radiates off him and the menace in his eyes, like he's plotting my death, and I struggle to not close the distance between us, wrap my legs around his waist, and find out if his lips are as soft as they look.

When his dark eyes finally meet my own, I grin.

"I think we got off on the wrong foot." Shoving off the door, I move toward him with my hand held out. "Officer Elliot Smith."

"I'm not buying it." When he doesn't take my hand and crosses his arms over his chest instead, I mimic his combative stance.

"Not buying what exactly?"

"That you won't bolt the second the chopper lands in Colombia."

I grit my teeth. "Guess I'll have fun proving you wrong, then, sailor."

"You do that." Spinning on the heels of his black boots, he puts his back to me.

In three quick jogging steps, I catch up and do my best to match his long powerful strides with my shorter ones.

"Why you?" I ask.

He cuts me a look out of the corner of his eye. "Why me what?"

"You heard why they want me on the mission, but no one mentioned why you were chosen to go with me. If you think I'm a liability, why not bow out and let someone else take your place?"

At the top of the stairs, he pauses and turns. With each step he draws closer, I retreat until my back presses against the cool wall. Dark eyes stare down from where he towers over me. My heart reacts, thundering against my chest, and my breaths grow shallow, though not from fear but something hotter, now sizzling in my veins.

Holy seaman, Batman. The intensity of this guy combined with his good looks might make me combust right here in the stairwell.

"No one is taking my place on the mission. Rico Suarez is mine."

That clears the lust fogging my focus. I tilt my head, considering his words and the passion in them. "What did he do to you?"

Something like shock flashes across his features. With one more considering stare, he twists and hurries down the stairs.

Instead of immediately following, I take a quick second to mentally slap horny Elliot—which doesn't help since horny Elliot likes it rough—to bring bitchy, get-shit-done Officer Smith back to the surface.

After several deep, controlled breaths, I jog down the stairs and through the community space at the bottom. With a clang, the metal door pops open, the late-morning sun already chasing the coolness from the air. At the base of the steps, Hackenbreg, Wilcox, and Lucia stand huddled together, locked in some kind of deep conversation.

"Just don't, please," I overhear Hackenbreg saying as I approach. He glances my direction and runs a hand over his short hair before replacing his cap.

"I don't understand why, but okay." Lucia hitches her chin, beckoning me closer. "Good job in there."

Faking a smile, I tuck both hands into the back pockets of my jeans and join the trio.

"Glad you could dress up for the occasion," Hackenbreg says like he's bored.

Chapter 3

I hook a thumb toward my current warden. "She did it. Said you guys would hate it."

Both men turn their attention to Lucia. My instincts urge me to step in front of her, to protect her from the two obvious threats to her and her baby.

"There's always a reason behind your games, Luce. So what gives?" Her husband smiles down at her like she's the most precious being he's ever beheld. Jealousy takes root in my gut, twisting and then growing with every second he studies her.

She shrugs and gives his shoulder a push. "It was more for her than you guys." She turns to face me, a wide smile on her face. "You've been hidden away for months. You needed a bit of normalcy to remind you of who you are. Plus, it was all you had, and your tiny ass would not fit into anything of mine."

I raise my brows and give my five-foot-five frame a slow once-over, then shrug. "Sorry we can't all come from the Amazon, Wonder Woman. Some of us come in a more compact size." Shifting my focus to Hackenbreg, I fold both arms across my chest. "Listen, Hackenbreg. I get you don't trust me, but I promise if this operation is a go, I won't let you die on my watch. I'll have your back if you have mine. We both want him taken out, though my plan might be a little less humane than yours."

"Really? Try me."

Tapping a finger against my lips, I stare up at the cloudless sky as I shift through the various gruesome details I've plotted regarding how to dismember that bastard Rico.

"Well, considering my love for explosives, lately I prefer the dream of shoving a grenade up his ass and pulling the pin out with a hot poker." Both men cringe, but I swear something like approval shines in Hackenbreg's eyes. "But it changes on the daily, each worse than the last. Check in with me tomorrow and I'll update you on my 'how I want to torture and kill Rico' daydream."

"Holy shit, you're fucking crazy," he murmurs with a slight shake of his head. Slowly, like he's weighing the options, he uncrosses his arms and lifts his hand between us. "As long as you're on our side, be as batshit as you want to be. Sr. Officer Tony Hackenbreg." With a small victorious smile, I slap my hand into his and give it a firm shake. "But if Lucia here has her way—which she typically does around here—and this mission moves ahead, then I guess you should call me Tony."

Satisfaction blooms in my gut.

First-name basis with a good-looking, intense Navy SEAL who—bonus—will help me get to Rico Suarez?

Yes, ma'am.

"You guys want to go get a drink while we wait for the verdict?" Lucia suggests.

"Yes, please," I chime in as the two men also agree.

And just like that, for the first time in ages, I don't feel utterly alone.

4

TONY

For the past few hours, all I could do was watch and listen, learning little through the light conversation that flowed between the other three. Positioned by the front windows, the shifting sun's glaring rays indicate how long it's been since we arrived at the bar next door to G and Lucia's condo.

"Here's your refill, darlin'." The sweating glass hovers in my line of sight, briefly blocking my view across the table to Officer Smith. When it lingers longer than necessary, I flick an annoyed gaze to the server. Not noticing my agitation, she bats long fake eyelashes in my direction and bites at her lower lip. "See anything else you like?"

Ah hell. Nine months ago, I would've taken her up on the flirting for a quick fuck in the stockroom during her break. Hell, maybe she's acting this way because I *did* that nine months ago. But after the messed-up mission and now Officer Smith, the server's coy antics do nothing but rub me the wrong way.

"Thanks," I grunt and set the glass down beside G's beer. Without a second glance, I refocus across the intimate high-top table on the imbalanced, beautiful anomaly.

Lucia says something, making everyone laugh. Elliot smacks the table, making all our drinks quiver, her boisterous cackle drawing attention from other tables. It's her broad smile that has me entranced. There's an edge to it, just like the rest of her. It's almost like there's two sides to Officer Elliot Smith: the one she allows everyone to see, the hard-ass, tiny bit crazy CIA officer who's climbing the ranks in the agency, and the other side of the coin that she keeps hidden.

I might not have the same lie-detecting talents as Lucia, but something tells me Elliot Smith is not all that she seems. Add in her smart mouth, curves for days, and fight I'm willing to bet transitions into the bedroom, and I'm drawn to her, eager to learn more about the woman and officer.

Earlier, Lucia questioned why I didn't want Elliot to find out I was the one who carried her out of the house in Colombia or that it was my team who lost so many in the explosion.

I'm not quite sure why, but I just don't want her knowing. Not yet.

Maybe I don't want her pity when she finds out about the injuries I sustained or for her to feel obligated to thank me for doing my job.

I consider that for a second and fight a smile. The Elliot I've seen so far would probably give me a fist bump and send me a thank-you basket filled with grenade-shaped fruit—or real grenades if she could find them.

Taking a long gulp of water, Elliot diverts her attention from whatever G is explaining to Lucia using a napkin and cardboard coaster and hitches her chin at the water glass.

"Not a drinker?" Something greedy churns in my chest as her amber eyes follow the movement of my throat with each long swallow.

Wiping a few stray drops with the back of my hand, I set the glass back down. "Normally, yeah, but maybe a little too much these days. I figured I should put the all-nighters behind me if we're about to be assessed for active duty."

"And I'm sure your liver is rejoicing," Lucia says out of the corner of her mouth.

I gesture to the glass of white wine sitting on the table in front of

Chapter 4

her. "Should you be having that while pregnant? You're growing my godkid in there. I need that"—I circle my palm, indicating her belly's entire circumference—"in tip-top shape."

Lucia grips the edge of the table, her knuckles going white. At the promise of death behind her eyes, I inch toward G for protection.

"It's fine in small amounts, asshole," she hisses. "I'm not going on a chardonnay bender."

"Sorry," I mutter, holding up both palms. In search for a savior from Lucia's wrath, I turn to Elliot, who's grinning ear to ear, clearly entertained. "So, Elliot, you from around the SoCal area?"

Her silky brown ponytail swishes side to side, drawing my focus. Bet it would look amazing wrapped around my fist.

"Nope, Northern California. Napa area." That earlier wide smile dims and goes stiff. "My life was fairly boring before the current gig with the agency."

I study her blank face and empty amber eyes. Something tells me that's not the whole truth. Hell, all of it might be a lie.

"Right," I drawl. Even Lucia has her full witchy focus on Elliot now. "Where are you staying now? I think CO Williams mentioned something about a facility. What's that all about?"

I say a silent prayer to anyone who will listen that it's not a mental health facility or hospital psych ward. Based on what I've seen and heard in the last several hours, there's a good chance her room has padding on the walls for her safety and others.

Lucia coughs into her hand, dragging my attention to her. "The agency has her in a local exclusive anger management facility," she clarifies.

I can't help the laugh that bubbles up, but Elliot's sharp glare cuts it off quick.

"Yeah, yeah, laugh it up. The place is fucking terrible besides the five-star food they serve." The table rattles when she slams her elbow onto the top and holds up a single finger. "Reason one, no alcohol or Red Bull. That's a new form of torture even the CIA won't attempt. Way too inhumane, if you ask my opinion. Reason two..." She flicks up her middle finger and gives it a wiggle in my direction. "Daily group therapy where I'm forced to listen to these self-centered idiots drone on and on about how they got their feelings hurt over a dumb comment on social media." She flicks up a third finger. "And three, no guns or grenades allowed on the property. I feel fucking naked."

G asks her something, but I can't focus on the conversation. The moment the word "naked" left her lips, my cock stirred to life, and mental images of her began flipping through. I stifle a groan and shift on the stool to ease the discomfort. I want to blame it on the fact that it's been almost a year since I've touched a woman, but I know that's only half the cause. The other half is that she's fucking beautiful, and some fucked-up part of me is turned the hell on by her crazy ass. My dominant side, the one that helps me lead a team of alpha males into battle, thrums to see if she's just as crazy in bed and to see how long it will take for her to submit.

Being full in all the right places that make a woman beautiful is just the start of what had me instantly captivated the moment she walked into the CO's office. Without an ounce of makeup on, Elliot is the most stunning woman in the room. I've caught several blatant stares, so I know it's not just me who sees it. Gold-flecked amber eyes pop against her tan skin, accentuated by long black lashes. Soft, full cheeks that make you want to cup your hands around them and drag her face to your own. And then there's her long, thin neck that's just begging me to wrap a hand around it while I—

A hard punch to the bicep snaps me out of the short porno reel. Lip curled in a snarl, I hit G back just as hard.

"What the fuck was that for?" I growl. Reaching between my legs, I adjust my rock-hard dick to keep it from tapping the bottom of the table.

G shoots me a knowing smirk and then turns his attention back across the table to his wife. "Say that again, sweetheart. Something about Elliot moving in with our boy Flakes here."

What the fuck did I miss while daydreaming about bending Elliot over?

"What the hell did you just say?" I question G while watching the other two.

"We knew you weren't listening," Lucia chastises. I grumble

Chapter 4

under my breath, making her grin. "As I was saying, CO Williams messaged me stating the operation is a go, but with one additional condition. He doesn't want Elliot to go back to the facility on the off chance that our mole or Rico himself knows where to find her now that she's been off the property. Which means I need to find a secure place for her to live until the physical assessments are done and you leave for Colombia."

The thought of Elliot seeing the dump I live in makes me cringe. "Then call a damn real estate agent or find her an apartment." Realizing how callous that sounds, I shoot Elliot an apologetic shrug. "Sorry, nothing against you." Though my aversion to a temporary roommate has everything to do with her.

"None taken. Though it could've been fun." She waggles both dark brows suggestively. "We could always explore the lovers' angle between you and the Greek god here. I'd totally watch to see who ends up on top."

"What?" I sputter, not knowing what else to say to that random, disgusting comment.

"Ew," Lucia says, fake gagging.

"Not fucking happening, Smith."

G and I slide an inch in the opposite direction along our stools. I can't even look at him after that comment. Hell, it might be a week before we can even spar with that unpleasant image seeded into my brain.

"So that's a no, then." Elliot lifts a bare shoulder and picks up her beer. "Pity." She takes a quick drink, but I catch a mischievous smirk before it's hidden behind the lip of the brown bottle. "All jokes about some hot guy-on-guy action aside, I'm 100 percent on board with not going back to that hellhole. No need to find me a place though. I can find somewhere on my own as long as the agency hasn't frozen my bank accounts."

Lucia pats Elliot on the shoulder with a sad half smile. "Sorry, Elliot, but there's no way in hell my superiors will approve of you living on your own after... well, everything." Elliot tilts her head side to side as if weighing the truth in Lucia's statement. "And you can't stay with us," she says, pointing between herself and G. "Which leaves us with Tony. Or"—I groan at her mischievous tone—"I'm sure one of the guys in Gabe's platoon wouldn't mind a sexy, fun bunkmate for a few days."

I narrow my brows at the grinning she-devil. Lucia knows exactly what she's doing, suggesting Elliot stay with another guy. Hell, knowing her witchy senses, Lucia is very aware of the fact that I've been hard for Elliot since the moment she walked into the office.

"Stop with the mind games," I grumble, spinning my nearly empty glass, making it wobble on the fake wood tabletop.

"Whatever do you mean, Anthony?" Lucia bats her lashes my way before sneaking a knowing look at her husband. "Plus, it could be good for you two."

"What do you mean, good for us?" Elliot's nimble fingers mindlessly peel the label off the beer bottle, her calculating gaze bouncing around the bar area. Something she does every other minute. It's an odd sensation knowing there's someone else capable and aware to shoulder the burden of assessing your surroundings.

"To get comfortable around each other, use the time to become a highly functioning unit. You two have never worked together before, and we don't have much time to prepare you for the mission in the long run."

"Sounds legit," Elliot says after a minute. Her amber eyes find mine, brows raised in a silent question. "I'm game if you are. I promise to not blow your place up or watch porn too loud."

A swig of water flows down the wrong pipe when I bark a laugh in shock at her comment. Eyes wide, tears building in my lower lids, I erupt into a coughing fit to not drown. How ironic would that be for a SEAL to dry-drown?

Almost as if Elliot can read my mind, sensing the irony, she looks away with a knowing half smile.

Oh hell. This woman is unlike any woman I've ever been around. And that's saying a lot.

What the hell has Lucia gotten me into?

Chapter 4

"Sorry about the AC being broken," I grumble for the third time while fiddling with the knobs, hoping this time it will magically work. "Getting it fixed has been on the to-do list for a while, but waiting around at the mechanic's for an afternoon hasn't been high on the agenda."

And just like the other times I apologized for my shit truck, she waves me off and goes back to staring out the passenger window. "I told you it's fine. I'm not some damn delicate flower that will wilt in the heat. You're doing me a favor by helping me get my stuff. I appreciate the ride, AC or not."

Elbow on the door, I rub a hand over my mouth, contemplating her response. At every turn, she surprises me with either her laid-back attitude, shocking comments, or excitement over anything with firepower. It's a pleasant diversion. The burning along my back is there, though dulled with my mind focused elsewhere. Same with the grief I've carried around like an elephant on my chest since I woke up from surgery. It's not gone, but less than it was.

Trees and houses stacked on top of each other blur outside the windshield as we haul down the highway toward the anger management facility where Elliot's stayed the last few months. Humming to herself, she taps a beat with two fingers on the cracked leather seat, her head back against the headrest, eyes closed.

Content. She looks perfectly content in my old truck with sweat rolling down her temples and a barely there smile tugging on the corners of her lips. I catch myself looking at her more than the road.

"Guess I'm not used to being around women like you," I admit.

"And what's that?"

"Easygoing, comfortable, grateful."

Her chest rises and falls with a harsh laugh. "Then you haven't been hanging around the right women."

"You might be right."

"I know I am." Sitting up straight, she twists and rests a jean-clad thigh on the bench seat. The bare skin beneath the rips and tears pushes against the strips of strings along her knee. "You married?"

My knuckles go white as I tighten my grip on the wheel. "Not anymore. Divorced over a year ago."

"Hmm." I can feel her assessing gaze taking me in, but I keep my focus out the windshield. Though it's killing me wondering if she sees me being divorced as a fault or not. "The split her fault or yours?"

"I'd love to put the blame on both of us, but it was me. The best thing I ever did for her was sign those divorce papers and let her go live a life without me in it. I'm a womanizing asshole if you ask most people. Hell, even G would say that about me."

Her head cocks to the side. "I guess that's good for the future Mrs. Hackenbreg."

I cut my eyes her way. "I'm scared to ask why."

"Practice makes perfect, right?"

The unexpected bark of a laugh has me leaning forward, the motion tugging the tight skin along my back. Holding in a wince, I settle back against the seat and fight to relax my spasming muscles. "The shit you say is...."

"Absurd? Funny? Out of nowhere?"

"Distracting," I state out of fucking nowhere. Before I can come up with a better answer than that, I catch her smiling and nodding.

Soft cheeks bunch until her amber eyes are barely visible. "I'll take that all day, every day. With what all we do and see on a daily basis, distraction is a slice of bliss from it all, don't you think?"

"Agreed. And you're welcome. For the ride, that is. The ex got most of, well, everything, which is why I'm driving this hunk of junk." Having to sell my new truck to afford rent in San Diego was a slap to the ball sack, but at least it's all done and behind me. Now we can both move on. Free to live our lives the way we want, when we want, and with whom we want.

"It gets you where you need to go. Seems to me you have it better than most. Plus, there's nothing wrong with enjoying the fresh air. I've missed it." As if to prove a point, she cranks the metal arm around

Chapter 4

and around, lowering the glass until she can hang her head out. Like a mad snake, her dark ponytail whips behind her as she grins like a madwoman, cheeks vibrating from the force of the wind.

A wave of heat washes over me as nervous energy takes hold. Reaching across the bench seat, I grab her shoulder and pull her back into the truck. We veer a little into the other lane, the headlights of an oncoming truck flashing. Yanking the wheel back, I straighten us out and grip the wheel tight with both hands.

"What do you mean, miss it?"

Arm on the door, she rests her cheek on her forearm. "I'm not allowed a lot of freedoms," she admits. "Because of what I know, plus the multiple escape attempts, but also the threat of Rico finding me. The agency hasn't found the mole who sold me and my partner out that night, so they're extra cautious to keep my location secret." Licking her lips, she shifts to study me. "When Lucia said he's selling the flash drive, I honestly wasn't surprised, more shocked that it didn't happen sooner to draw me out. Him coming out of hiding now feels like it has more to do with me than what's on that flash drive."

I tap my thumb on the hard plastic wheel, letting that revelation sink in. "Because you have the password?"

She shakes her head, then nods and shrugs a single small shoulder. The movement draws my attention to her slight frame. If you saw her on the street, you wouldn't have the faintest clue the power housed in such a bite-size body.

"I don't feel like it's about the password anymore. He's trying to draw me out for a more personal reason. Don't ask me why I think that, I just do. The software means nothing anymore. I think he wants me, only me, because I'm the only officer who got close. I lied to his face time and time again, and he didn't know until some fucking insider told him what I am. Top that little shot to the ego with the fact that I didn't die like he planned, and now he wants to finish it once and for all."

"Why? Why risk all this, the heat of the SEALs and CIA, just to kill you? What did you do to him? Slice off his dick or something?"

I wouldn't put it past her, and losing my favorite body part would drive me to getting revenge no matter the cost.

Elliot's boisterous laugh reverberates in the cab even above the roaring wind. "I would so do that, and almost have." I cringe away from her, which earns me another laugh and a hard shove to the shoulder. "That's a story for another day. As for Rico, he's an egotistical narcissist with a god complex. I got close without his detection, and the bastard's precious overinflated ego can't take the fact that I almost had him and also lived. I know the mole who sold us out also knows I survived and fed that information to Rico." Her small hand reaches up, tracing a single finger along a thick pink scar. "I almost didn't survive that night. If it weren't for someone dragging me out of that house...." She shakes her head. "Anyway, earlier, Rico had held me in a room, let his thugs beat the shit out of me, ensuring I wasn't a threat—or so they thought—and put a bullet in my thigh with every intention of torturing me to death for the audacity of almost taking him down. The fact that I escaped, killed his men, and lived eats at him every damn day." Her smile turns sharp. "And that makes me beyond happy. Downright giddy when I think about him somewhere in Colombia fuming that I'm alive despite his best efforts."

I can't help my smile as it grows, making my cheeks burn from lack of use. "You're crazy as shit, you know that, right?"

"Someone's crazy is another's normal. But you and I, what we do and who we are, is not normal. So you calling me crazy is a little ridiculous. You throw yourself into situations ninety-nine percent of the world would piss themselves even thinking about. You push yourself to the limit every day to make sure you're the best in every situation. Bloodlust for our enemies thrums through your veins, fed by the arrogance of knowing you can kill a human with a single move. Me, crazy? Look in the mirror, Seaman."

The truck swerves off the road when I whip my face her way, jaw slack. "What the hell did you call me?"

"Seaman."

"I'm a senior fucking officer, not a—"

"Don't take offense. I just like saying the word. But now that I know it bothers you so much...." Her thin, dark brows bounce along her forehead. "Take your next right, Seaman."

Grumbling under my breath about pain-in-my-ass officers, I turn the wheel with the heel of my hand. "Anything else I should know about you besides being annoying as shit?"

"Well, let's see here. You already know I like explosives. It's kind of my thing. Give me any type of chemical and I can whip you up a bomb. Depending on the ingredient, it can range from a small boom to take out a wall for an escape route to a big one that will implode a midsize building."

"Holy hell," I murmur. My stomach cramps at the mention of a building imploding. The noises, smells, and pain from that night come flooding back. Heart hammering, I suck in a deep breath and hold it, attempting to chase away the oncoming flashback.

"Hot, right?" When I don't respond, she shakes her head and throws an arm out the window. Weaving her hand through the pressing wind, she moves like there's actual music coming out of the busted radio. "Get it? Explosives. Hot. Because fire?"

"Right." What I will not say is it's also hot as in sexy as hell. Who knew her level of badassery would be a fucking turn-on?

"I can drive anything," she continues. The sound of her voice calms me, like a balm to my panicking thoughts. "From tanks to helicopters, but planes are trickier. I can land one but not fly it well."

"So what you really mean is you can crash it."

"Basically."

"Good to know."

"I'm also trained on every weapon our military has invented, including rocket launchers, which are fun as hell to play with. All forms of martial arts and hand-to-hand combat. I wanted to pick up some MMA fights as a side gig, you know, to get some of this restless energy out, but my superiors thought it would blow my cover. I think it was more of a liability thing. So instead I picked up cross-stitching. Not nearly as violent but, oddly enough, just as cathartic."

I can't stop laughing. Really laughing, because the shit that comes out of her mouth is unbelievable. "Holy fuck, Elliot. How old are you?" When she doesn't immediately respond, I chance a glance her way only to find her smile gone and a cold, emotionless mask in its place. I shift along the seat. "You don't have to answer if—"

"Not that," she says, sitting straighter in the seat to lean forward, elbows resting on the dash as she peers out the windshield. Her eyes narrow to slits. "Do you see that?" Reaching out, she points toward a diminishing billow of dust caught in the high-beam headlights. "Slow down. It looks like someone turned off the road and drove through the dirt, but security wouldn't be this far from the main building."

I ease my foot off the gas until we're creeping up the slight incline toward the dust cloud. Before the truck comes to a stop, the passenger door swings open, and Elliot leaps out.

With a curse, I slam on the brake and throw the gearshift into Park. Metal hinges groan in protest when I shove the door open, the entire truck rocking when I slam it shut to round the hood. On the shoulder, Elliot squats low, fingers moving as she studies the dirt. My knees pop when I squat beside her.

"This isn't on the security ATVs' typical route." Eyeing the tracks, she places a thumb in the tread impressions. "I don't know what kind of all-terrain tire makes this kind of track."

Bending closer, I use my phone's flashlight to highlight the various ridges. "Based on the width between the tracks, I'm going with a dirt bike. Make that dirt bikes. Two for sure." Twisting on the balls of my feet, I face Elliot. "You said security drives ATVs."

She nods. A spark lights in her eyes, and a slow smile pulls up at the corners of her lips.

"Oh, what if Rico found me?" Popping up to stand, she grabs my elbow and drags me up with her. "Less than twenty-four hours after my location was public knowledge. This has to be Rico and his fuckers coming to get me." A sharp clap rings through the night when she slaps her hands together. "Oh, this will be fun. We need to get to the facility and sneak me back inside. That way we can meet them head-on when they come for me."

"What?" I question cautiously. "We don't know for certain that it's

Rico's men. What if it's just a terrible driver?" The energy thrumming off her tells me whatever plan she's concocting in that violent mind of hers will happen whether or not I'm on board. "Fine," I say with a resigned sigh. "Get in the truck, and tell me your plan along the way."

She lets out an excited squeak and throws her arms around my neck. Instinctively I wrap an arm around her trim waist, keeping her sealed against me.

"This is going to be so much fun." Releasing me, she jogs back to the truck. At the passenger door, she turns and flicks her wrist in an impatient wave. "Come on, or we'll miss our window to lay a trap."

Feeding off her excitement, despite knowing this is a terrible and possibly illegal idea, anticipation that only the thrill of a fight can trigger zips through my veins. I hold up a finger, rewarding me with an annoyed huff, and shoot off a 911 text to Lucia to cover our asses if things go sideways.

Maybe Elliot was right earlier and I'm just as crazy as I claim she is, because this undiluted thrill at the thought of a standoff with an arms dealer and his army isn't normal. Good thing I've never been what others consider normal.

And it seems I've met my equal with Officer Elliot Smith.

5

ELLIOT

Stomach twisting with nervous energy, I start for the main building, ready to have some fun if it really is Rico and his men here to find me. A hand engulfs my shoulder and hauls me backward before I can take a step.

"Better plan," Tony says into my ear. A delicious tingle races down my spine at the feel of his lips against my skin. He hunches low, bringing me down with him, taking cover between a row of cars in the sparse parking lot. "Let's make sure it's Rico's men before we storm through the front doors and prepare for a fight." He surveys the area and runs a hand over his face. "Okay, let's start with a perimeter check. You know the security routes and schedule from the previous recon, correct?"

"Yeah, but—"

"I'm willing to guess if Suarez is behind this, they'll look for weaknesses in security to not tip anyone off before entering the main building. If you wanted to break into the facility while alerting no one, where would you strike?"

I give myself a second to flip through everything I know about the security for this place. "The southeast corner. There's a gap in the guard routes."

Before I can say anything more, Tony swivels on the balls of his feet and jogs across the parking lot. Once we're somewhat concealed in the shadows, I tap his shoulder. He pauses and looks down at me expectantly. "So... we're going southeast, I take it?"

He turns my face, now at eye level with his chest instead of his muscular back. "Are you serious?"

"Okay, so that's my one teeny tiny flaw." I pinch two fingers together, leaving a small gap between them. "I'm more of a 'turn right by the McDonald's and a left at the dead body' directions type girl."

Slipping behind a tree, Tony checks every direction before turning his full focus back to me. Despite what we're doing, I swear he's fighting a smile.

"You're telling me you're directionally challenged." I nod, the tip of my ponytail popping my upper back. "Which way is north?" he asks. Looking to my left, then right, I give up and just point up at the dark sky. "You're not kidding, are you?"

I huff and cross both arms over my chest. "I never kid about my one flaw."

His straight white teeth catch the bright beam illuminating the high wrought iron fence. "The one? You sure about that, Half Pint?"

Something warm blooms in my chest at the nickname I really should hate but somehow don't because it came from his lips. "Yep, one flaw. Now come on. You be my compass, and I'll be your weapon."

"I'm a weapon too," he grumbles.

Patting his shoulder, I give him a little shove in the direction I assume is southeast. "This isn't a dick measuring contest."

"Too bad. I enjoy winning those."

"Is it really a contest when the other person doesn't even have the right equipment for the measuring?"

Tony grumbles under his breath about crazy-ass female officers. I can't help but smile. Between the thrill of the hunt and Tony, I feel lighter than I have in a long while. It's nice sharing the weight of the operation with someone who's as competent as you. A pang of grief and guilt squeezes my heart as I think about Kurt. He was a decent officer. But the difference between a decent officer and a fucking SEAL is like comparing apples and hand grenades. Sure, apples could be deadly if used with a combination of other things, but a hand grenade is primed and ready, built for destruction.

Our steps are light and nearly silent as we race along the fence line, weaving between trees to avoid cameras and the monitoring security personnel. Sweat gathers along my forehead and rolls down my temples, dripping off my jaw. Lifting the hem of my tank, I swipe the moisture before it can fall into my eyes. I catch Tony watching me out of the corner of his eye.

"This is fun, right?" I say under my breath.

We pause beside a wide tree trunk and squat low.

Instead of responding, though the excitement in his sparkling dark eyes tells me he agrees, Tony points over my shoulder. Leaning to the side to see what's going on, I immediately shuffle around to get a better look. I catch three figures, all dressed in black, huddled together along the fence.

"What are they doing?" I whisper, not looking away from them.

"Planning their entry, waiting for others, waiting for a signal from inside." Adjusting his weight, his knee bumps into my thigh, nearly knocking me over. He wraps a hand around my bicep in a strong yet gentle hold to keep me upright. Just like earlier, when he held me after my impromptu hug, a sense of familiarity knocks me off-kilter.

Odd. I've never met this guy before today. Why would my body respond to him like I have?

Shoving that question down to process later—or never, knowing my propensity for denial and avoidance—I hitch my chin in their direction. "We need to get closer. I can't tell shit from here without a scope."

With a single confirming nod, he keeps low and moves through the shadows, closing the distance between us and the unknown figures. My thighs and hamstrings burn from the strain of racing across the short distance in a half crouch.

As we draw closer, deep male voices filter through the night.

Above the summer insects, humming in a familiar pitch and cadence has me tugging Tony to a stop and angling my ear in their direction.

"Why does that voice sound familiar?" I whisper more to myself, but Tony's eyes slide to meet mine. "Not Rico. Sorry, Seaman." His lips press into a tight line in an obvious display of his displeasure. Him and me both. I was so looking forward to a fun, unfair fight. "But still familiar."

As I rack my brain to recall where I've met or heard one of the unknown characters, a fight starts between the three. Forgetting about the security lights, too caught up in their argument, all three shift into the bright beam. The moment the larger of the trio's features are visible, I curse.

"You have to be fucking kidding me." Annoyed that I got myself and Tony worked up over nothing, I fall back, landing on my ass. Resting a forearm on each knee, I shake my head while staring into the dirt. "I really thought, maybe...." Blowing out a breath, I tip my face up to the sky. "I wanted it to be Rico or his men so badly, I guess I jumped to conclusions."

"You're not making sense," Tony says while keeping an eye trained just over my shoulder to the three men. "Do you or do you not recognize those people?"

"One of them, yeah." Pointing in their direction, I indicate to the larger of the three. "That big fucker. He used to be a patient here. We had a run-in, I guess you could call it, one day when we couldn't agree to disagree."

"Explain." Tony twists, taking a knee beside me.

"I wasn't a fan of the conditions of why he was a patient. Most of the people here are harmless, just destroying stuff in their rage or saying dumb shit on social media. But that guy, his story, it's different. He took his anger out on those close to him." My lip pulls up in a snarl as I picture his cocky, smug face. "He paid off a judge to not go to jail for beating his girlfriend and instead was sent here for therapy. I found out she spent a week in the hospital because of the 'incident.'"

Chapter 5

"And let me guess. When you say you two had a run-in, you mean to say you provoked him to strike first, then beat the shit out of him."

I flash Tony a sly grin. "Less than twenty-four hours together and you already get me. Yes, I showed him how displeased I was with his presence here. He was released, cured per his therapist and attorney, two weeks ago."

A loud curse has us both turning our attention back to the men.

"What do you want to bet someone like him wouldn't let a woman teaching him a lesson slide without retribution and would plot a half-assed plan to get back at her while she sleeps?" Tony's large hands curl into white-knuckled fists. "Men like him don't deserve to be fucking breathing. We're meant to protect, not hurt the vulnerable."

A half snort slips out and I slap a hand over my nose, remembering we're within earshot of the men currently trying to figure out how to scale the twelve-foot wrought iron fence. "Most of the men in my line of work don't agree with you. They don't care if you come with an innie or an outie—"

"Are you referring to a dick as an outie and a pussy as an innie?"

"Well, yeah. Anyway, I think you've lived a sheltered life if you think there aren't more like that bastard than there are of men who think like you."

"Or maybe you've been hanging around the wrong men."

I tilt my head, conceding that comment as a win for him. "Seems like we've both been hanging around the wrong sex." Pushing back up to the balls of my feet, I point to the group. We both huff a laugh when one of the three makes it halfway up the fence only to fall backward, landing on his ass with a painful grunt. "So, what do we do about these idiots?"

Tony remains silent for a few moments. "Well, we're already here, and they're attempting to sneak into a private facility. Technically, they're about to trespass."

"And I think I heard one say they have a gun," I whisper enthusiastically.

Tony tilts his head in their direction and nods. "Agreed, I just heard it too. We should stop them before someone gets hurt."

As one, we stand. "We could get into a shitload of trouble for this," I whisper as we step from the shadows. The men are too engrossed in their conversation to notice us moving closer. It helps that I'm in all black and Tony is still wearing his dark fatigues.

"Nah, I texted Lucia before we got back into the truck. Told her we thought Rico's men had found you and we were headed to investigate. She said silence the threat. How were we to know it wasn't some of Rico's hired thugs and instead some bitch-ass dude who deserves a lesson in how to treat women?"

"Why were you sidelined?" The question slips past my lips before I can stop it.

The air ripples around Tony with the tension that's replaced the earlier ease.

Before he can answer—hell, maybe he wouldn't have anyway—one man finally takes notice of our lazy approach and curses before taking off at a dead sprint in the opposite direction. Another twists to look over his shoulder, eyes going wide when he takes us in. Immediately he follows the path of his friend, leaving the biggest one of the bunch standing all alone.

"You," he snarls.

My steps slow as he charges toward me. The grass slips beneath my boots as I widen my stance, ready to take the brunt of the impact.

In an unexpected turn of events, Tony steps in front of me, pulls his clenched fist back, and then thrusts it forward. Having timed it perfectly, the snap of bones and smack of flesh radiate through the night. The asshole sails backward a few feet, never finding his footing again, and falls to the ground.

Tony shakes out his fist, wiggling his fingers. "That felt good." I shove his arm. Pointing to the clearly unconscious man, I raise both hands in question. "What?" He laughs. "You already got a piece of him. It's my turn."

Grinning, I shake my head in pure amusement.

"I think we're going to be great friends, Sr. Officer Tony Hackenbreg."

Chapter 5

The same fist that knocked a man on his ass hovers between us. Careful of his tender knuckles, I tap my own to his.

"Same, Officer Badass. Now, let's go find this asshole's friends."

"This is the best burger I've ever eaten," I say, ending on a moan that draws the attention of a few of the guys down the bar.

"Most of us come here after missions," he says before taking a big bite of his own burger. "That's why it's mostly guys in here."

I swivel on the well-worn stool to take in the entire bar area. Wiping my mouth with a rough paper napkin, I turn back to Tony. "So most are SEALs like you?"

He nods, his features now weary. "It's kind of known as our bar. A lot of groupies hang around waiting for attention." He inclines his head toward the two women sitting at a table toward the back by the pool tables.

Jealousy flares within me when both of the beautiful women smile at Tony's brief attention.

Going back to my burger, we eat in silence watching a baseball game on the fuzzy TV behind the bar. Loud male laughter, the crack of pool balls smacking together, and the low vibrations of the bar's booming jukebox fill the small intimate area.

"I wish we had something like this," I admit before shoving a ketchup-slathered fry into my mouth. "But everything is so secretive, there's no camaraderie among the officers. Especially for me."

"Why do you say that?" Raising a hand, Tony flags down the bartender and points to my empty beer bottle. "She'll have another, and I'll take another water."

"Thanks. And I say especially for me because I'm slightly driven, if you haven't noticed." He shoots a side-eye glance my way and then winks. "That's intimidating to others. I'd like to say the male officers are worse in the way they treat competition, but it's the women."

"I don't understand that. Why be an asshole when someone gets what they deserve because of hard work?" I arch a brow, surprised by his insight. "What? Clearly you're not a slacker. You don't achieve all the shit you've listed by sucking some upper-level guy's cock. It's hard work to hone your body into a weapon and learn all the shit you know."

My elbow clunks to the smooth wooden bar top, and I rest my cheek on my palm, facing him. "You might be the only person who hasn't assumed I fucked my way through the agency."

His features turn pensive, a line forming between his pulled brows. "Had you ever met a SEAL before me and G?" I shake my head. "We see things differently. That someone could sleep their way up the ranks isn't a possibility with us. We get to our level by working harder than everyone else. There is zero room for making it as a SEAL by anything other than blood, sweat, and hours of training." His lips press together like he's debating his next words. "Lucia and I have a long history. When she first arrived on base, I wasn't happy. Hell, I was downright pissed at seeing her. I accused her of what others have of you, that she slept her way into the CIA." I narrow my eyes with the promise of death. He chuckles and holds up a hand to keep me from tackling him off his bar stool. "I said it out of anger. I knew she would never do that."

With one more glare, I turn back to my food. "I like her."

Tony nods. "She's good people. Talented as hell, and as much as she drives my ass crazy, she's the perfect match for G." A warm grin softens his features. "He'll be a great dad."

The mention of their baby is like a punch to the gut. I suck in a breath, the wind hissing through my teeth. Thankfully Tony doesn't notice, or he probably did and said nothing.

"She believed me," I say quickly to derail my grief-riddled thoughts. "After Colombia went to shit, I was interrogated by several officers, but Lucia was always in my corner. I owe her for saving my life. All it would've taken was a hint of belief from her that I could've been the mole and I wouldn't have lived to see the next sunrise."

"Damn, your agency is brutal. Why do you work for them?"

"It's what I know, and at this point, it's too late to think of doing anything else. The moment I signed to be an active officer, I knew I was in it for life. For someone like me, there's no leaving the CIA breathing. I know too much, have done things our government can't afford to have exposed. So the moment I stop being an asset, I'll disappear like many before me."

The beer bottle slips from my grasp. I gawk at Tony as he takes a long pull, finishing the bottle. "What the hell?" I exclaim, grabbing it back from him.

"Sorry, that heavy of a conversation deserved a drink." Not sure why, but suddenly I'm laughing. *Really* laughing. "And here I thought I had it bad being sidelined behind a desk. You're having to worry about being offed by your employer."

Wiping at the corners of both eyes, I motion toward the bartender for another beer. "You never answered me about why you're sidelined."

With a sexy groan that sends a vibration from his chest directly to the apex of my thighs, he rubs a hand over his short hair.

"Injured during a mission."

"Still recovering?" *Please say no.* That would mean Lucia planned to send him in before he's physically ready, which I'm not okay with.

"Not physically. I've been holding out on taking my psych eval that will allow me back on active duty."

"Why? Don't you want to be back out there?"

Tony stares into his water glass as if the ice holds all the answers.

"I do, but it's complicated. Don't be thinking I'm damaged goods. It's not that. I just have other shit to work through too."

Absentmindedly, I stroke the thin puckered scar along my neck. "Don't we all? If you say you're good, then that's good enough for me." A rogue drop of beer slips down my chin after a quick drink. I wipe it with the back of my hand, drying it off on my jeans. "Since the mission is a go, we'll have to go through those performance tests, I guess. Any clue what he'll want to see?"

"None. Maybe Lucia can give us a hint tomorrow." Looking at his watch, he curses and reaches for his wallet. "It's almost midnight. Sorry, didn't mean to keep you out this late."

"It... it was fun." Leaning over, I rest my temple on his firm shoulder. His long fingers pause their flipping through several bills. Allowing my lids to flutter closed, I sigh. "Thank you for the much-needed distraction, Seaman."

"Any time, Half Pint."

He doesn't make a move to leave, allowing me a second to savor every sensation, committing the joy of the simplistic, warm moment to my few happy memories before we finally head out.

As we drive home, I can't help but hope there will be more nights like tonight in my future.

And there's a growing desire for them all to be with him.

6

ELLIOT

The sensation of being watched jerks me awake. Keeping my breaths deep and even, eyes softly closed, I focus my other senses around the room. An unfamiliar scent, woodsy with a hint of vanilla—unlike Tony's spicy citrus—wafts up my nose.

Not Tony, then.

A soft brush of moving air along the exposed skin of the arm resting outside the covers shifts the tiny hairs and snaps me into action. My every move to dissolve the obvious threat is instinctual at this point in my career. The hand buried under the pillow palms the hidden Glock's grip. Eye snapping open, I bolt upright with the loaded gun raised in front of me.

I blink, squeezing my lids shut, hoping that will help me better understand the SEAL standing in the middle of the room with his hands held up in surrender.

"What the hell are you doing in here?" Swinging both legs around, I slowly stand, not daring to shift my aim. Sure, he's Lucia's husband, so obviously she trusts him, but they've trained me to not lower my guard for anyone.

"You two overslept," he says slowly. "Lower the fucking gun, Elliot. I'm not a threat."

I scoff. "Yes, you are, because clearly you're lying. I don't oversleep, because I hardly sleep at all." Yet my mouth is tacky, like I've been knocked out for hours or sedated. That plus my lethargic muscles and fog coating my sluggish thoughts point to him telling the truth. But that couldn't be, could it? I hitch my chin at his watch. "What time is it?"

The smug ass drops his hands and shoves them into his loose gym shorts. "Eight thirty, sleeping beauty."

My jaw drops. Gaping at the man, I lower both arms, the gun swinging to my side. "That's impossible."

Gabe rocks back on his heels and hums a noncommittal response as he pulls a phone out and tosses it to the bed. The screen lights up, showing the time: 8:32 a.m.

Holy seaman, Robin.

"That's impossible," I whisper. The mattress sinks beneath my ass when I fall back.

"That's what he said too." Only now do I register the deep male voice grumbling curses, followed by a door slamming. "Apparently he's taking the first shower. We expect you two at the base at 0900, and it takes approximately fifteen minutes to get there from this apartment. I suggest you both hurry the hell up to not be late on your first day back in the game."

Cursing under my breath, I rub the heels of both hands into my eye sockets. Realizing I'm still holding the gun, I release the clip and remove the bullet from the chamber, tossing it all to the bed beside me.

"What the hell did you two get into last night?"

"Kicked some assholes' asses," I mutter while wiping the corners of my lips, checking for dried drool.

"After that," he says, but his tone sounds distracted. When I glance over, I find him using the toe of his tennis shoe to widen the opening of my duffel.

"Grabbed a burger. I had a few beers, came back here, and apparently passed out cold. Get the hell out of my stuff." Pitching forward, I

Chapter 6

grip a corner of the green canvas and yank it closed. "My shit, my business."

He lifts a single brow and looks at the bed. "I'm surprised he's out there and you're in here."

From my spot on the bed, I take in the sparse bedroom. All four walls clear of pictures of any kind, personal or purchased. Solid, comfortable-as-hell bed. On the wall opposite the footboard hangs a huge-ass TV with all kinds of cords dangling beneath connected to a gaming system. Total bachelor's room. Is the lack of personality in the room due to him moving here after the divorce, or does he not care about aesthetics in general?

"Why are you surprised?" I ask absentmindedly. "We played Rock Paper Scissors for it. I won fair and square."

Gabe's serious features shift with the slight tilt of his lips. "Of course you did." Taking in the room, he cringes. "He gave his ex-wife most of what he had to help her start over. That's why this place looks like shit. He tell you about that?" Running a hand through my loose hair, I nod. "It happened over a year ago, and he's still here. If you ask me, he's punishing himself for—"

"Thank fuck no one's asking you, G."

At the sound of his voice, I swing my attention to the doorway. My eyes widen and my stomach does this weird flipping, tingling thing at the sight of Tony nude from the waist up, a tiny white cotton towel barely secured around trim hips. Water droplets slip down the center of his golden chest, bending around the curves of his pecs before tumbling over every bump of his abs.

The two men trade comments, but I don't comprehend their words. I'm too focused on memorizing everything from Tony's defined calves and thick, muscular thighs up to the distinct bulge beneath the towel that has me chewing on the corner of my lips. I bet he's as big there as he is everywhere else.

"Elliot." Gabe's humor-filled voice rattles through the small space. I tear my focus from Tony's distracting hard body, one of the toughest acts I've done in a long fucking time. I shoot the smirking asshole the bird. Of course he saw me checking out his friend. "If you want a shower, you have three minutes."

My hair slides along my shoulders with my head shake. Snatching both wide handles of my duffel in one hand, I stand. "I'm good. I'll just change. What's today's test anyway?"

"Endurance."

Tony and I share a look, his gaze dropping to take in my bare legs that extend beneath the hem of the large T-shirt I slept in. It doesn't hide much, the bottom barely covering my pink boy shorts. A smirk pulls at my lips, knowing he just checked me out. Maybe not as blatantly as I did him, but still, a new flicker of heat now dances behind his brown eyes.

"Perfect," I say to Gabe but don't break eye contact with Tony. "Now I know what to wear." Stepping aside to let me pass, Tony keeps his back to the wall. I pause in front of him. "Do you have any coffee?"

"That's a good idea," Gabe says from his spot in the middle of the room.

Tony doesn't move an inch, his bare chest barely moving up and down with his calm breaths. I tilt my head, trying to figure out why he isn't hurrying to get dressed when we're obviously running short on time. Running late because we both slept in.

"We have a unique outlook on endurance," Gabe continues.

"So basically they plan to run us until we can't take another step without collapsing," I say. Both men nod in agreement. "Then yeah, I'll still need that coffee. Even if I puke it up in the end, I need that jolt of caffeine to get this day o' fun underway."

"Is that outfit really necessary?" Tony grumbles, commenting yet again on my workout attire as we jog across the packed parking lot toward a nondescript building.

"Is being hard of hearing a seaman thing or just a you thing? It's going to be fucking hot as Satan's ball sac today, and I don't know what your CO will throw at us. Running? Probably. Swimming?

Chapter 6

Knowing you guys, most likely. Sparring for hours? Sounds like a good time, but who knows? We don't know specifics, and this ensemble ensures I'm prepared for any scenario he throws at me."

Plus, I'm obsessed with the way my ass looks in these snug black athletic shorts. I haven't been able to wear my own clothes in months. Having shit that fits is a comfort I didn't realize I desperately missed. And bonus, Tony keeps falling behind a few steps, indicating he appreciates the tight fit too.

"This is our gym. You realize that, right? Every available fucker in there will be watching." I shrug, not at all bothered. I've worked in a male-dominated career. I know men will watch no matter what I wear. "Is that what you're aiming for?"

The tip of my ponytail flicks from shoulder to shoulder. "That's not my intention, but if it's the byproduct, then it is what it is. I wore this for me, because I like it and feel good in it. Why should I give two fucks about what they think or do?"

He grips the dull metal handle before I do and holds it. Hand to the top of my brows, I tilt my face up, squinting to figure out what he's waiting for.

"You really mean that, don't you?"

"Of course. What a dumb thing to lie about."

The morning sun blazes all around him, making him look like some kind of fire god. "You're not wearing those and that"—he motions to the tight razorback top with a built-in sports bra that hugs my chest in all the right places—"to make anyone jealous?" Again I shake my head. "Not to draw attention?" My lips dip in a frown. "Not to drive me insane?"

Ah, so that's what he's getting at. He's already distracted by me. Tongue pressed to the inside of my cheek, I shoot him a closed-mouth smile. "Well, Seaman, you caught me there. Because what's the fun of being insane if you can't bring others down with you?"

Tony's chuckle makes me smile wider. "Well, all right, then, Half Pint. Let's do this."

A billowing all-male stench of sweat, body odor, and blood assaults me the moment we step inside the open-plan building. I immediately scan the area, searching for exits, threats, and weak points. To the left, several treadmills line the far wall, all facing the center of the room. In the back are the free weights, and four separate sparring mat squares sit in the middle.

Adrenaline-injecting music vibrates through the space from several overhead speakers, making the air almost shimmer with each thrum of bass. Lucia, Gabe, and another man dressed in fatigues stand along the left near the treadmills. Without a word, I turn on the balls of my tennis shoes, the rubber squeaking on slip-resistant flooring, and start toward the small group.

"Oh good, you're finally here," Lucia drawls, focusing on the phone in her hands, thumbs flying across the screen. "Stevens here is evaluating your performance throughout the day. He'll submit his unbiased results to CO Williams at the end." I hold back a groan. I never got that coffee, and "throughout the day" does not sound fun. "First, a one-mile warmup on the treadmills"—her red nail points to the machines—"before heading to the beach for a timed twelve-mile run."

Clearing my throat to get her attention, I slowly raise my hand. Lucia flicks her gaze over the edge of the phone screen and quirks a brow.

"What do I get when I win?"

"This isn't a competition—"

"What makes you think you'll win, Half Pint?" Tony cuts Lucia off, turning to me.

Anger and desire swirl at that condescending nickname in his deep, seductive-as-hell voice, confusing the hell out of me. Part of me wants to tackle him to the floor and beat his ass for the dumbass nickname. The other part, well, that wants to tackle him and keep him pinned there for a whole different reason.

Bet he'd fight to be on top.

"What are we betting?" I say instead of answering his stupid question. He knows exactly why: because I won't accept anything else while still breathing.

Humor flicks across his features, faint lines spreading out from the corners of his eyes with amusement. "Sleeping arrangements. For a week. Winner gets the bed and loser pays for dinner."

"Hell yes. Deal." We bump knuckles in agreement and turn in unison to Lucia, who looks baffled and annoyed. "Winnings settled, let's work on some kind of point system to keep score. For each of the various tasks they put us through today, winner gets a million points."

A muttered "What the fuck?" comes from the man I don't know while Tony's cocky-ass smile turns nearly feral. "Perfect."

"A million points?" Lucia mumbles around the fingers she's using to physically pinch her smile together.

"Go big or go home. That's the saying, right?" I say over my shoulder as I move toward the treadmill. I pause, foot hovering over the belt. "The one I cross-stitched last month said 'Go big or die.' I like that version better." With a dismissive shrug, I hop onto the treadmill.

Tony stomps onto the one beside me. "First one to a mile win's the first million points?"

At my nod, he presses a button on the controls; the belt slowly rolls around until it hums beneath him. I curse under my breath at the very important seconds I just gave up not being ready, then turn to the unfamiliar controls. Erratic beeps sound as I try to match his quick speed. Anticipation and excitement mix, amping up my adrenaline, a heady mixture that has forever been an accelerant to my competitive side.

"Guys, this is a motherfucking warm-up."

I wave a hand, dismissing Lucia's concern, and continue hitting the button until my tennis shoes pound in a rapid cadence against the whirling belt.

"You're going down," Tony calls beside me.

"What will your friends say when you get your ass handed to you by a girl?"

"We won't be surprised," someone shouts, and a rumble of male laughter fills the brief gap between songs.

"You're not a girl," Tony mocks, followed by three quick beeps inching up his speed.

"Pretty sure the lady bits between my thighs say I am."

He groans and misses half a step, throwing off his smooth rhythm. "You're not a typical girl," he corrects, breaths coming quicker now. "You're like Harley Quinn with special forces training."

"Wow," I reply. "Thank you. She's so damn hot."

"That's what you're taking away from that?"

"What? I'm just saying I would."

"Stop," he hisses. Out of the corner of my eye, I catch him adjusting himself. "You're doing this shit on purpose."

"Doing what?" I say, faking innocence as I jab my thumb against the up arrow, increasing my speed to the max.

"You two take this fucking seriously," Gabe yells. "Now, step it up, Flakes. Don't let her win, damnit."

A louder rumble of laughter fills the space. The music turned down at some point.

I flick Gabe both middle fingers. "Bros before hoes, seriously," I say between three counts of quick short inhales. "Lucia, you're in my corner, right? Women before wieners."

Another loud cackle of laughter makes me smile. Several of the guys who were already working out when we walked in now stand close, watching.

"A hundred on the crazy one," someone calls out.

"I'll take that motherfucking bet," Tony shouts back, pushing his treadmill to the max. "You're going down."

I glance at the console. Only a quarter mile left. The itching burn along my thighs and the stabbing pain in my side point to this being a terrible decision to kick off the competition before we stretched.

Eh, too late now.

As much fun as I'm having, it's also a bizarre aphrodisiac, and while I'm very aware of the fact that I'll lose this round—I'm crazy, not stupid—but I sure as hell won't make it easy for him. The harder I push him now, the less he'll have later in the day. That's when I'll have a chance to beat a physically fit, highly trained male. Today I'll give him a run for his money in every way until either I win or my body gives out.

Being super competitive has always been one of my best traits and helped me in this secretly violent, lonely life I live.

Tony's machine is the first to beep, signaling he reached the mile mark. With a victorious roar, he slams his fist to the emergency stop button and leaps off to victory run around the building, arms held high, roaring with pride. A mere thirty seconds after his, my machine beeps, and the belt slows to a much more humane pace.

Smiling, I stop the belt completely and lumber off, legs feeling like Jell-O beneath my slight weight. The only way to make this feel better and even have a chance at winning anything today is to stretch. Legs stick straight, I walk my hands down my thighs, past my knees, along my shins to wrap around my ankles. The deep stretch pulls in all the right places, a soft pleasure-filled moan slipping out when I sink a little deeper. Counting to thirty twice, I walk my way back up my body. My movements pause when I find every set of eyes on some part of me.

"What?" I question.

Gabe clears his throat and turns around, muttering something under his breath. Lucia smiles and follows him. The others just stand, blank-faced and barely blinking, except Tony. Still breathing hard, he barrels through the small group with a wide grin, aiming straight for me.

"One million points to the SEALs." That whips the others out of their speechless, kind of creepy trance. With a few whoops and back slaps, they dissipate, returning to their regularly scheduled workouts. A firm fist hovering, he waits for me to bump it with my own before flaring his fingers out like a firework. "Nicely done though. I thought we'd be here for another hour with how slow you were running."

A snort crawls up my throat, but I cover it with a forced cough before anyone hears it.

"Whatever. I took it easy on you and you know it," I say, lying through my teeth.

His responding half smirk tells me knows every word is false.

"Right, Half Pint." Turning to the man Lucia introduced as

Stevens, Tony points at him. "What's next? I'm ready to make my next million points."

Cocky, insufferable asshole.

And fucking hell, it would be a whole lot easier to hate him for those qualities if he wasn't also endearing, funny, and sexier than a bedazzled gold hand grenade.

These next few weeks could be the longest of my life.

7

TONY

The water-saturated sand gives beneath my pounding steps, leaving size thirteen shoe impressions until the next wave sweeps away the evidence of me ever being there. A thin layer of sweat coats every inch of my skin. It even rains from the tips of my short hair with each forceful step. Full focus down the crowded beach, I work to empty my thoughts, to find the zone needed for this run. Except the tiny woman, who somehow keeps up with her shorter strides, keeps distracting me.

Not that I mind this kind of diversion, no matter the effect on my performance.

An up-close view of her perfect tits bouncing is enough to captivate any man, though sometimes I ease back a few strides to watch that ass.

Groaning low, I turn my thoughts to something else before my twitching dick stands at full attention. Though I haven't thought about her in a while, the mental image of Mom's snarling face turns my hardening cock to an overcooked noodle. A flash of anger from simply picturing that hateful perfect face speeds up my long, quick strides.

Together, Elliot and I weave around the happy beachgoers enjoying the scorching weather. Twice now I've caught Elliot watching a young family with a look of longing before that aloof mask snaps back into place. This complicated woman isn't fooling me. She's not the heartless, slightly unstable, career-driven officer she works hard to make everyone believe.

Three quick beeps from my watch signal we've reached the halfway mark and need to turn, heading back toward the base. With a grunt to draw her attention, I slow, twisting a finger in the air, indicating to turn back. I don't even have to wonder if she follows before I twist and start running again. She's at my shoulder, keeping pace seconds later.

Sweat rolls down the side of her face, her high ponytail whipping in the wind like a trailing flag. Catching me watching, she winks.

"I love running," she says between deep, steady breaths. Mile six and the woman's breaths are barely labored, unlike mine. The last several months of sitting on my ass, pouring alcohol and fast food into my body clearly took its toll on my endurance if the rattle in my lungs means anything. "It's incredibly freeing, you know? Just you and the wind, nothing mattering except putting one foot in front of the other."

I grunt a noncommittal response, though I agree with her assessment. Swimming and running, two places where I normally excel by pushing life's concerns and the day's worries away, everything blank inside my head. In the focused zone, there's no pain, no lung-scorching dry, hot labored breaths, no concept of time, just you and the peaceful silence of nothing. It's a characteristic I developed as a kid out of necessity because of nightly screaming insults. Not wanting to hear your mom berate and demean your father made being able to tune everything out a needed skill.

"Hey," Elliot says, snapping me out of the worst of my childhood memories I'd somehow lost myself in. "Slow your damn roll, Seaman." I'm about to ask what she means when the twinge in my thigh muscle and burn along my hamstrings draws my awareness of how fast I'm sprinting down the beach.

Chapter 7

"Sorry," I say, gulping down as much oxygen as I can. "About. That."

"Wanna talk about who you were running for up there?" She taps her temple. "I'm a good listener."

"What... talking about?" A stab of pain bursts through my side that reminds me of being fucking shot and causes my steps to slow. I grit my teeth, pushing past the side stitch. Holy hell, how did I forget how much being out of shape fucking sucks? I'm a sad, sad state. A Navy SEAL with a fucking side stitch from a brief run. When was the last time I had one of these?

Hell, maybe I'm not mission ready after all if I'm unable to complete a simple twelve-mile run without collapsing.

She swerves close and pumps her shoulder against my bicep. "Fine. Avoidance is my go-to too, so no hard feelings. Just know we're all running from something. It's not just you."

"How... you... talking?" *Oh damnit to hell.* My weak, out-of-shape ass is an embarrassing excuse for a dude. Hell, they might take my damn SEAL card if anyone sees how much I'm struggling just to suck down enough air to live.

"What was that?" I shoot her a glare, earning me a full smile. "Fine, be rude. To answer your questions, there's nothing to do at that damn facility but plot Rico's violent death and work out. I told you I enjoy running."

I grunt, unable to respond with actual words.

Lips parted in a wide happy smile, she looks to be having the most fun she's had in years, just running free out here on the beach. I almost lose my cadence at the sight of her breathtaking beauty. There's an innocence about her at this moment. All the sharp edges that the CIA no doubt put there smoothed, making her look young and free. Not the first time since she dropped into my life yesterday morning, I'm stunned by her raw beauty. Not beautiful in the traditional sense, but everything combined about Elliot makes her striking. And when she smiles like all she wants in life are simplistic pleasures, I turn into a lost fool.

Which makes her dangerous to the imaginary walls I've

constructed, protecting not only my heart but my freedom. Again, images of Mom's irate yet perfect features flash like a horror film through my mind.

I choke down the growing feelings for Elliot and push them deep to forget. I've worked my entire life keeping all women—including my ex-wife—at arm's length to prevent myself from being swallowed whole by a woman. I won't be one of those fools blinded by love and beauty, forced to give all of themselves to keep their partner happy.

I dwell on my shitty childhood, focusing on what my abusive mother taught me, making the next few miles fly by with each breath slicing through the dry, raw flesh of my lungs.

"Tony," she calls, pulling my attention to my right with her strange tone. "No hard feelings, okay?"

Before I can question what she's talking about, all I see is her fine ass hauling in a dead sprint.

Grinding my back teeth, I push myself harder, commanding my legs to move faster, and zero in on her flopping ponytail as my aim. But each time I draw close, she finds another burst of energy, sprinting just out of my reach. Sucking in ragged breaths, I shove past my body's current limit. The scarred, healing skin along my back pinches and pulls like never before, making it feel like it's on fire once again.

Then it's over. Two steps. Two motherfucking steps is all she wins by.

Rough grains of sand scrape against my palms and knees when I collapse forward. Squeezing my lids shut to keep the sweat out, I suck down greedy gulps of air.

The sensation of others standing close, their shadows casting a small reprieve from the blistering sun, has me pulling my gaze upward. Standing in a circle, arms crossed, several sets of eyes stare down at me. A bright glare breaks through the group when Elliot shoulders her way between two SEALs. Tits bouncing with every deep breath, she holds a hand out to help me up.

"What the fuck was that, Hackenbreg?" one fucker says the moment I'm upright, getting into my face. "You let her beat you?"

Jaw clenched, breaths whistling through my teeth, I muster a reserve of energy to shove the SEAL away from me. He retreats a step, a spark of fight flaring in his narrowed eyes. We square off, fists now raised, ready to fight when Elliot steps between us, hands on her hips.

"Well, if he would've taken this seriously and not flirted with every beautiful half-naked woman begging for his attention, maybe he would've won." Everyone, including me, blinks down at Elliot, surrounded by seven trained killers and dusting the sand off her hands like she didn't give two shits. "Ugh, how do y'all deal with this shit? Sand is annoying as fuck, which is why sex on the beach is only a good idea in cocktail form." Peering up through her lashes wet from the sweat dripping down her brow, she meets my confused gaze. "It was a step too far in the 'show Elliot how superior SEALs are over CIA officers when you ducked into that one blonde's beach tent. I don't know whether to be impressed or pissed."

The one asshole who was just ready to beat my face in for losing barks out a laugh. "Of course he did." His hard slap to my back squelches when it connects with my soaked T-shirt. A sharp hiss whistles through my teeth in my attempt to control the pain from his contact. "That's our Hackenbreg for you. Never passes up easy pussy." Dropping his hand, he steps closer to the unamused Elliot with a cocky-ass smirk. My hands curl back into tight fists. "Not me though. I like a challenge."

"Good for you, sailor," she says, her smile sharp instead of soft like when we were running. "Come on. Let's walk this off." She pushes through the group of men and glances back at me with an expectant look. "Lucia has another form of torture for us. I have a feeling you're a shoo-in to win this one considering your affinity for the water."

I shove through the group, confusion and anger fueling my quick steps at her dismissing her clear win and thinking she needed to defend me. *Me.* Only when the group is several feet behind us do I grip her shoulder and tug her to a stop.

"What the hell was that, Half Pint?" A single dark brow rises, and she shrugs, turning to keep walking toward the pools. "I could've handled the backlash of those dumbasses on my own. You won fair and square because my fat ass is so fucking out of shape." Groaning in annoyance at myself, I run a hand over my hair, flinging sweat droplets all around me.

"If you want to run together in the mornings, depending on our assessment schedule, I'm down. Running on the beach is hella fun." Her gaze softens and turns unfocused as she stares out over the ocean. "I bet the sunrise is gorgeous here."

"It is, but the sunset is better. The way it dips below the ocean, leaving the water and clouds painted in color and bringing a crisp breeze as it fades, is everything you never knew you needed in life."

Elliot bites at her lower lip as she steals a side-eye peek my way. "That's quite poetic for a seaman."

Chuckling, I give her a playful shove and point toward the pool deck. "Come on, I see Stevens up there by the pools."

My tired muscles protest as I march through the shifting loose sand. I'm already running on empty, but thankfully swimming is invigorating, not draining for me. But from the worried expression on Elliot's face, it seems she feels the opposite.

I watch her eye the water. "You know how to swim, right?"

"Yeah, of course. It's all good." But her body language screams the complete opposite.

"What?" I question as we sit on a side bench to pull off our shoes. "You seem off."

"I almost died in the water," she says as she tugs off her socks and stuffs them inside her shoes. "I haven't been a fan of pools or any body of water since."

"Shit," I curse under my breath. She's making it out like it wasn't a big deal, but in the short time I've known this woman, I haven't seen her like this. If I didn't think she'd kick my ass for even thinking this, I'd say it's fear stiffening her movements. "You don't have to—"

I flinch when she slowly turns on the bench to stare me down with a look of promised death in her amber eyes. There's nothing

Chapter 7

familiar in her stone-cold features. This is CIA Officer Smith. And a depraved side of me finds it hot even if she might fuck me and eat my head praying-mantis style.

Apparently I really need to stop staying up watching Animal Planet.

"I'm fine. Let's get this over with."

I've only known this woman for twenty-four hours, but I know there's no use arguing. Her small bare feet don't make a sound on the concrete deck as she moves to the edge of the pool. With a few minutes until we start, she uses the time to stretch. Twisting to put her back toward me and Stevens, she spreads her legs and bends forward at the waist. That bitable ass I'm growing desperate to grab handfuls of while slamming into her thrusts into the air.

My steps falter when she leans from one foot to the other, that ass wiggling like a damn invitation to the world to appreciate. Scanning the pool deck, I catch Stevens blatantly staring, licking his lips at her ass on display. In two strides, I'm in front of him, blocking his view.

"Problem?" I command.

"N-No, sir," the young officer stutters.

"Then turn the fuck around and treat her with the fucking respect she deserves."

As soon as he obeys, I swivel around and march over to where she's still stretching. My palm tingles with the itch to smack that ass to show her the attention she's attracting. Folding my fingers inward, I clench them into a tight fist.

"Elliot," I somehow say through gritted teeth.

"What's up?" She looks up from where her nose almost brushes the concrete. Long dark lashes fan up and down. "Oh shit, is it time to start? I didn't hear the whistle."

"You're...." When I can't find the words, I motion toward her upturned ass, pointing out where her ass cheeks are literally hanging out.

"Oh." She stands and tugs the hem of those damn teasing short-ass shorts down an inch. "I need to stretch after that run to not cramp up in the water." The honesty in her voice makes me believe her oblivious innocence. How she could be so damn deadly and unaware at the same time, I don't know. "It's just you and Stevens here, right?" She shifts to look around me. "Is there an issue?"

"Yes. You deserve better than to have us drooling over your ass without you knowing."

In a smooth motion, she rolls up and pokes me in the chest with a single finger. "Did you say us?"

I groan and run a hand down my face at the word slip.

"Just watch it in that outfit. You're better than some fucker getting a B-roll film for his spank bank." That only makes her smile widen. "Come on," I say with a resigned sigh. "Let's get this over with. Hopefully this is the last assessment for the day. I'm fucking whipped."

Stepping up to the edge of the pool, we hang our toes over the edge. My feet look like water skis compared to her tiny ones.

"What size shoe do you even wear?" I ask absentmindedly while inspecting her mouse-size feet.

"I mean, I'm not trying to brag, but I can sneak into the kids' section to score some mega deals."

Head back, face tilted up to the warm sun, I bellow a genuine laugh. I tilt slightly off balance when she gives me a playful shove.

"First to one mile wins," Stevens says from somewhere behind us.

"One million to one million," Elliot says, frowning at the water like it's a viable threat. "This is it, Seaman. Whoever wins this is the victor of the day."

"You gonna be okay?" I ask, concern for her well-being slowly overtaking the drive to win.

"Shut the fuck up."

All righty then. Guess that's a yes.

The moment the whistle's shrill slices through the air, I push off the edge, diving into the soothing clear water. My tense muscles immediately relax as I propel down the lane. My running gear absorbs the water, adding additional drag, but I adjust accordingly. By the second turn, I've fallen into a smooth rhythm, that blissful blank peace settling over my thoughts. Nothing can bother me here.

Chapter 7

Not my memories, not my failures, not even the sinking Elliot, whose dark hair floats up above her head as she descends to the pool's bottom.

Bubbles billow out of my mouth when the scene playing out in front of me registers. Not wasting time to surface for air, I angle for the bottom, feet kicking, to dive toward the limp figure. Panic threatens to cloud my mind, but I shove it aside as I wrap an arm around her tiny waist, kicking off the bottom and rocketing toward the surface. I gasp for air when we breach the surface. Using my free arm, I propel us toward the side where Stevens waits, his hands outstretched.

The moment Elliot's limp body is in his arms, he hauls her out of the water, laying her carefully along the rough concrete. With a hard shove, I leverage myself out of the water and kneel near her head, sweeping away the dark hair covering her face. Lids shut, blueish lips parted, she doesn't move when I shout her name.

"Go get a medic," I shout to Stevens, who immediately disappears. "What the hell did you do to yourself, Half Pint?"

Layering one hand over the other, I push down on her sternum, starting chest compressions. Nose pinched, I lean down to seal my lips to hers. Her chest inflates with my two forced breaths. I sit back on my heels, monitoring for any sign of life. When nothing happens, I go back to chest compressions. The second time I force my air down her lungs, her small body jolts, twitching along the concrete. Rotating her on her side, I smack between her shoulder blades as water forcefully expels out of her open mouth, gurgling coughs forcing what remains from her lungs.

The pound of approaching footsteps signals the medics.

Slowly, those dark lashes fan up and down. Her amber eyes find mine. "Did I win?" she croaks.

Anger like I've never known from fading panic floods my veins. "Did you win? Elliot, you fucking drowned. *Drowned*, and you're asking if you won? What the hell happened?"

"Oh." A trembling hand swipes over her brow. "Do I win on a technicality or something?"

Unable to stop myself, I lash out a hand, wrapping my thumb and two fingers around her chin in a tight hold. Something fires behind her glassy eyes, clearing away the lingering confusion. "Don't you ever fucking do that again. You hear me?" I clear my throat to stop the tremble. "I'll give you the damn win. Never fucking again."

"Or what?" she croaks, but there's a tilt to her voice that suggests a heated challenge.

"Don't push me, Elliot. I'll wear your ass out if you disobey me on this."

"I think that's more of an incentive," she rasps.

At that moment, a swarm of people descends, pushing me away from Elliot and ending our intense stare-down. With a hard shove, I stand while they check her vitals and ask a series of basic questions. Knowing she's in good hands, I force myself to turn and walk away. I can't stay and watch. Seeing her lying weak and hurting is almost too much for my control. A large part of me wants to scoop her into my arms and haul her back to my place to watch over her, while the other wants to bend her over and smack her pretty ass until it's fire red for being so damn irresponsible with her own life.

But I won't. She can't happen. No one like her can infiltrate my life.

Just like that idiot said on the beach, I never pass up easy pussy. No one except G knows why I keep it that way. If I want to keep control over my life, I need to stay on the easy lay, no emotional connection path. Because women like Elliot are dangerous.

And I swore to myself a long time ago that I'd never lose myself to a woman.

No matter how perfect they are.

———

A low screech pierces the steam-filled bathroom as I wipe away the condensation coating the mirror hanging above the sink. Facing my reflection, I twist to study the scars littering the length of my back. With a single finger, I gently prod at one near my left shoul-

Chapter 7

der, checking for feeling. Nothing. My hand falls to my side. Zero nerves left, but it's not the numb sections that are slowly driving me insane with the insistent sensations. It's the wounds where they extracted pieces of brick and other debris from deep in my muscle.

Disgusting.

Before Colombia, my skin was covered in scars, but not like this. Now my back looks like a damn patchwork quilt made of skin.

Turning back to face the sink, I grip the sides and hang my head. Broken, scarred, and broke. Maybe I won't have to worry about Elliot overtaking my life. She wouldn't be interested in a loser like me anyway. It's for the best, even though the thought of her not wanting me as much as I long for her hurts like a dull knife to the abdomen.

The clatter of the bathroom door vibrating on its hinges at the same time the front door slams shut has me standing tall, watching the white door's reflection as if I can see beyond.

"You have to be fucking kidding me," Lucia's angry voice booms through the apartment. "I leave for a doctor appointment and you die? What the fuck happened out there, Officer Smith?"

Padding across the tile, I lean a shoulder against the closed door and angle my ear in their direction to catch Elliot's response.

"Nothing happened."

I glare down at my bare toes, anger at the indifference in her tone rising once again. That's the exact response she gave me every time I asked during the tense-as-hell truck ride home. Of course, the crazy, stubborn woman wouldn't go to the hospital to get checked out like the medics suggested. Instead, she demanded I bring her back here.

"Elliot, I swear—"

"What do you want from me?" Elliot snaps, the first flare of anger —hell, any emotion—I've heard since I resurrected her dead ass. "Nothing happened. I was swimming, pushing myself to keep pace with my seaman." A groan rumbles in my chest, and I roll my eyes at her dumb nickname, though I don't miss her calling me hers, which shouldn't make me as fucking happy as it does. "I felt my body shutting down. I guess I pushed myself too hard during the beach run and chose not to listen to the warning signs. I kept pushing like I always do, assuming I'd scavenge a reserve of energy, but clearly I was wrong and passed out. And passing out in the water is not ideal. Zero out of ten, don't recommend it."

My forehead connects with the door. I'm going to wear her ass out for this nonchalant bullshit she's got going on regarding her life.

"Why in the hell did you push yourself that hard?"

"Because I fucking can." The tension in Elliot's voice makes me wonder if she's more unnerved about the incident than she's letting on. Maybe she's skilled at deflecting emotions to hide what's really going on inside that mind of hers.

"You're telling me you were willing to die to win something that was never meant to be a competition in the first place but rather a test on your individual mission readiness?"

"Don't you dare judge me for my tactics that have kept me alive. I push myself past my limits repeatedly, so if it happens in the field I'm prepared and don't die alone with no one ever coming to find my body. If we die out there as an officer, it's like we never existed in the first place. So fuck me if I do what I can during training to ensure I always come home."

When the silence that meets Elliot's declaration stretches, I lean closer to the door to catch any hint of a sound.

Shit, what if Elliot hurt Lucia or Lucia snapped and injured Elliot?

Or, my other head interjects, *they're in there making out.*

The door shakes beneath my shoulder, and a pounding echoes through the bathroom.

"Shit," I curse and step away from the door, cautiously eyeing the handle. "What?" I bark to the person on the other side.

"Stop your snooping and get your ass out here. Fair's fair. I'm ordering dinner."

Only when her footsteps fade and both women's voices pick back up do I open the door. Poking my head through the small gap into the hall, I listen to ensure Lucia and Elliot are in the living room. I release a relieved sigh as I head down the hall for the bedroom and lock the door behind me.

Am I embarrassed of my ruined back? Hell yes. But with Elliot, it's deeper than vanity, more like self-preservation. If she sees my back, the scars fresh and obvious, she'll want to know what happened. I'm not ready to explain that night, to be forced to voice the most terrifying and painful moment of my life.

The night I saved her life and almost lost my own.

8

ELLIOT

"You're better than this, Elliot," Lucia says in a tone that leaves me feeling chastised.

"I'm really, *really* not," I grumble. "Pizza?" I shout over my shoulder down the hall. An enthusiastic "Hell yes" from the bedroom lifts my spirits. Pulling out my phone, I search for places close by that offer delivery.

"So, what's on tomorrow's agenda?" I ask Lucia as I scroll through the options, hoping to distract her from her anger at my earlier mishap. No one more than me wants to move past what happened today in the pool. The fact that I let my past overtake my thoughts, sending me into a panic attack in the middle of the pool, is possibly the most embarrassing moment of my life.

Lucia watches me from her perch on the couch's armrest. "CO Williams wants a weapons assessment tomorrow, but I'm wondering if that's a good idea after today."

"Why? I'm golden. I was only unconscious—"

"You mean dead."

"Yeah, whatever. I was only out for, what… a few seconds? I've had worse." When she doesn't respond, I peek up from the phone screen. "What? We all have a near-death or resuscitation situation during training at least once. Didn't you?" I tilt my head, my wet hair slipping from one shoulder to the other.

"No, can't say I've endured a situation quite like that. Apparently you and I didn't receive the same form of training."

"Oh. Have you always been on the intelligence side of things?" Her blank face gives nothing away as she dips her chin in acknowledgment. "Well, that was never my path. When they pulled me from basic training, they only offered the active officer role as a possibility. It was that or a discharge on the grounds of bad conduct, which would've resulted in me going to jail." Lucia's eyes widen. I wave off her alarm. "Long story, best told over a few bottles of tequila."

"I just assumed we all had the same courses and challenges during training."

"Maybe it's like that for everyone else and I was a unique case." I force a smile, hoping that eases her stress, which is clear from her rigid posture and furrowed brow. She doesn't need to know the details on how thoroughly the agency prepares its active officers for torture, nor do I want to retell the horrific stories I wish I could forget. "You staying for dinner?" I ask to lighten the heavy mood that settled between us. Nothing like death and torture to bring a room down. "It's pizza night here once I find a place that looks decent. Any suggestions?"

Lucia pushes off the armrest to stand, a low groan slipping past her lips. "No, I need to head home, where my overprotective water mammal is waiting for me." She glances at her watch and smiles, chewing on her lip. "He's probably already worn a path through the condo since I'm running a few minutes late and haven't called."

"Doesn't bother you?" I ask while scrolling through the options for pizza. "It sounds controlling as hell."

Lucia rakes a few fingers through her dark hair, fluffing the top. "No, it's not controlling, more protective, leaning toward possessive. And yeah, if any other guy would've treated me like Gabe does daily, I would've walked away, but with Gabe, it's different. Having him worry about me, be concerned for my well-being, is sweet and makes me feel... I don't know. Like a girl, I guess."

"But you *are* a girl," I say slowly and reach out to pat the top of her head. I was the one who died today, and here she is offering crazy talk.

She swats my hand away, laughing. "Come on, you know what I mean. Don't you ever want to be that woman who's taken care of, protected instead of always being in charge? Having someone just so focused on you that they worry about everything, giving you a break from constantly being on alert? There's something to be said about a man who is fully aware that I can kill him or any threat in thirty different ways, yet still sees me as vulnerable—cherished like a one-of-a-kind jewel. No, that doesn't make sense for guys like Gabe. More like a one-of-a-kind customized weapon. It's nice to turn everything off and just be taken care of for once."

I scrunch my nose like the idea actually stinks. "Give up control? I don't think so."

"When you find the right person, it just kind of happens. Don't diss it until you've let yourself go knowing there's someone there to catch you when you fall."

With a smile and goodbye wave, she exits the apartment, leaving me staring at the door, wondering if she's right or crazier than I am.

"I prefer that place." Reaching around my shoulder, Tony taps the phone screen, pulling up a pizza place website. But I'm frozen, unable to move with his breath brushing past my ear and the feel of his body heat encircling me. The way he towers over me, I should hate feeling this small, but I feel sheltered.

Protected.

Um, hell no. I am not turning into a sentimental senile woman like Lucia has. No, thank you. Only feeling guilt, anger, and pain works great for me. Just. Fucking. Great.

Forcing my feet to move, I take several steps toward the kitchen, putting much-needed distance between us, and clear my throat. I can do this—whatever this is. I'm a badass officer with no soul and zero emotions. I will not crush on the sexy-as-hell SEAL who smells divine and has muscles I want to lick and nibble, teasing him to the breaking point.

My stomach flips at the mental image of him naked. Careful to keep the movement subtle, I press my thighs together to quell the low throb building at the apex.

Okay, maybe I'm past crush and have barreled straight into infatuation. Shit, when did that happen?

I sneak a peek across the living room, where he's now relaxed back against the couch, an arm tucked behind his head, dark eyes watching me.

Okay, how does he even make lounging sexy?

Oh hell, I'm in major trouble.

And that's bad coming from the girl who drowned earlier.

Belly full and utterly exhausted from the day, I should be dead asleep, but I'm not. With an annoyed huff, I flop to my opposite side, nose grazing the couch cushion. A billow of dust tickles my nose. Ugh. Flopping to my back, I glower at the water-stained ceiling that's taunted me for the last few hours. Reaching to the floor, I grab my phone to check the time.

Three in the morning.

At this rate, I might as well stay awake until the 5:00 a.m. alarm.

A creak from the hall has me sitting up, feet planted on the floor in one fluid motion. In the yellowed glow from the front light, a shadow shifts as a body ambles down the short hallway.

"Get in the damn bed, Elliot" comes a low, gruff voice. Tony scrubs a hand over his face and yawns wide. "I can't sleep with you twitching and grunting out here."

"Your couch sucks," I grumble. "But a bet's a bet. You won the bed."

"We can share," he offers. "It's big enough, and I promise I won't bite."

What does it say about me that I'm slightly disappointed at that promise?

Messed-up. That's what it says.

Chapter 8

I'm as crazy as everyone claims, I guess.

I'm about to protest when he releases a frustrated groan and steps in front of me. In one swift movement, I'm hauled off the couch and tossed over his shoulder. My ratty sleep shirt rides up my back, leaving my florescent blue boy shorts exposed to the cool night air. My cheeks flush when his hand engulfs the back of one thigh, keeping my legs secured as he turns into the bedroom.

He pauses at the edge of the bed and unceremoniously drops me. The mattress gives beneath my slight weight, popping me back up a few inches before cradling me back in its comfort.

"You're a bossy ass, you know that?" I say as I adjust my shirt.

"I'm a SEAL. Comes with the territory." The bed shifts as he falls onto the opposite side. Punching the pillow a few times, he turns to his side to face the opposite direction. "Good night, Elliot."

"Night." I blink into the darkness, trying to slow my rapid pulse. The ease of last night's sleep seems out of reach tonight. But as the seconds tick on and his soft breaths fill the room, my muscles relax, my mind slowing the rapid thoughts, and before I know it, I finally find the sleep I've been chasing all night.

I wake up in an oven. Or that's what it feels like, at least. Sweat coats my skin, causing my thin T-shirt to cling uncomfortably to my back and arms. Blinking past the grogginess of a deep sleep, I give my eyes a second to adjust to the dark room.

That's when I notice all the things wrong. Movement along my chest, a rhythmic push and intense heat soaking through my shirt, inching up my body temperature. Careful to not wake Tony, I shuffle backward, my skin sticking to his. Across the bed, covers pulled back, cool air sweeps along my bare skin. Running both hands through my hair, I curse the universe for sticking me with this SEAL. Why couldn't he have been ugly, or a dick, or worse, an ugly dick? Instead, it's Tony. A male who, in my sleep, I scooted toward and forced my body against in a one-sided cuddle.

But here's the thing. I do not cuddle. Hell, I barely hug, and snuggling is just one prolonged, awkward hug. At least that's what I've always considered it to be. But the more distance I wiggle between me and the sleeping man, the deeper the ache to curl my small body back around his.

Almost as if he senses the loss in his sleep, Tony's hand flops to the mattress and reaches across the sheets, his fingers searching.

His T-shirt-covered chest rises and falls in rapid succession. A low groan escapes his parted lips. Those corded muscles twitch, flexing and relaxing while his face pinches in what I would guess is pain. A mournful whimper has the hairs along my arms and back of my neck rising. Without second-guessing myself, I reach across the empty divide and grab the offered hand, interlacing our fingers.

The effect of the contact is instantaneous. With a heavy breath, Tony settles, relaxing into the mattress and pillow.

I stare in wonder at our joined hands. How did such a simple touch calm the massive warrior beside me? *My* touch at that. I'm used to my touch causing fear or pain, not comfort. But yet here I am, giving him something that a part of me has longed for myself. How many nights have I lain awake, replaying all the times I should've died, or the days spent susceptible to my uncle's abuse? All those times, how nice would it have been to have someone hold me, to calm my mind and fears with a simple touch?

Before I can dive any deeper down that black hole of confusing thoughts, the blare of my alarm snaps Tony awake, going from dead asleep to sitting up in bed, bleary eyes scanning the dark bedroom. I slide my hand from his before he notices and stretch to reach my phone on the floor.

Tony scrubs the sleep from his eyes, mumbling something about the time while I turn off the alarm and check my email, hoping for something from my handler. But the inbox is empty just like it was the last time I checked. The agency has been unusually quiet since I left the facility, which isn't a good sign. Worry about what they're planning builds, pressing on my chest like a heavy weight. There's no need to stress over it until I know what to expect, but there's no way

Chapter 8

they'll let me go out on this mission without testing my loyalties. What that testing might encompass scares the shit out of me, almost enough to say screw it to the early morning run and just burrow back under the covers for a few hours—or the rest of my life.

The SEALs' CO required an assessment on physical abilities before clearing Tony and me for the mission, but the CIA will need to see I'm still the coldhearted spy they created. I've been out of the game, sidelined for too long at that dumb facility, and they'll need to know my head is in the right space in case of capture. As crazy as I make myself appear to the rest of the world, I am mentally ready for anything Rico can throw at me, but after the agency's level of demanding, borderline inhumane assessments, who knows what will be left of me?

"Seriously?" Tony says beside me, leaning back against the headboard and shutting his eyes. His voice is deep and scratchy from sleep—sexy as hell, if you ask me. "You died yesterday. Can't you take a day off to mourn those few moments?"

"Nope," I say, popping the *p*. "Rise and shine, Seaman. We have a sunrise to catch."

"You should've been a SEAL," I hear him mutter under his breath and preen at the compliment.

Twisting to face his side of the bed to make some snarky comment, I seal my lips and cock my head, studying him as he sits on the opposite edge of the bed. The white undershirt he slept in is soaked from the nightmare or because of the heat he's constantly emitting, I'm not sure. But either way, why wear it at all?

"You always wear so many clothes to bed?" I question, my voice high and tight as I stretch both arms, fingers interlaced high above my head.

Tony stiffens, every muscle along his back flexing as he bolts off the bed.

"I'll be ready in five, and I'm leaving with or without you, Half Pint, so I suggest you be ready too."

I watch, not understanding the shift from sleepy, sexy Tony to guarded asshole. He slams drawers as he rifles through the dresser, pulling out running gear, then storms across the hall before smashing the bathroom door shut.

Touchy.

But *why* is what I desperately need to know.

"Stop being a sore loser," I say, laughing, and shove my shoulder against Tony's bicep.

A dull burn blooms through my cheeks from smiling all damn day. It was hella fun kicking his ass in the weapons assessment, but playing with him through it all was the highlight of maybe my life. Despite the seriousness of the day, we joked and teased each other relentlessly, laughed until my stomach hurt, and still passed every test thrown at us with flying colors.

Who knew working out alongside someone could be so damn entertaining and utterly distracting in a way I didn't know I was desperate for?

"Another shot for the fucking winner of the day," Tony calls down the bar and jerks a thumb my way.

Hooking my boot heels on the lower rung of the bar stool, I push myself up and offer the applauding bar patrons my best princess wave. A firm grip around my wrist yanks me down, holding on until he's sure I won't topple off the side. Considering I'm on my third shot of Patrón, he has reason to be concerned that my ass might tumble off the smooth wooden stool top. Tony shoots me a grin, shaking his head in what I hope is amusement, and takes a sip from the beer bottle pressed to his lower lip.

"For real though, great job today," he says, wiping a rogue drop of liquid from his mouth with the back of his hand. "It was damn impressive to see you handle all those weapons."

"Impressive or hot?"

I immediately seal my lips shut. *Damnit, Elliot, where the hell did that come from?*

"Both," he says. Those dark eyes sweep over my face, urging me to

Chapter 8

shift closer—or maybe that's the tequila. His heated gaze dips to my lips, flaring when I sweep the tip of my tongue along the middle.

Something shifted between us today, at least for me anyway. Maybe from waking up curled against his back and never wanting to let go or observing him fire all those weapons with deadly aim, whatever it is, I can't stop myself from wanting all of him. Bad. Going from hating each other to friends was nice, but now I want more. I could blame it on the fact that I haven't been with anyone since Colombia, but I would only be lying to myself. It's all him and who I am when he's around.

Movement in my periphery has me tensing, ready for a fight, but instead of a threat, a woman with full blonde hair and bright red lips weaves past me and settles on the other side of Tony. My loose grip tightens around the chilled shot glass as jealousy burns through my veins, eradicating the heat and desire.

Instead of tormenting myself by listening to their conversation, I down the shot and slam the glass to the bar. The angry sound draws a confused glance from Tony before he turns his attention back to the woman clearly attempting to find herself a good time for the night.

The round edge of the bar presses into my ribs as I pitch forward, looking around Tony's wide shoulders to study the woman whose laugh mimics a tickled hyena. Fluffy blonde hair frames her sweet features with big blue eyes, long dark lashes, flawless makeup, and, ugh, of course, she has great boobs too. Why can't the pretty ones have concave boobs to at least give the rest of us a fighting chance at scoring some male attention?

One thing is certain, I really don't like her touching what I'm considering as mine. My training urges me to rip her off him and demand a fight to the death—okay, maybe that's an Elliot thing and not an agency training thing.

My jealous, and somewhat wobbly, gaze falls to her perky full breasts pouring out of the snug top, then to my own decent B-cups and back again. Shit, what if Tony is more of a tits guy than an ass man? If that's the case, I don't stand a chance at taking this further than friends. I'm no fool. I'm well aware all the squats and running do great things for my petite legs and ass. But boobs, unless I'm willing to pay for big ones, aren't in the cards.

As the seconds tick by with the two engaged in conversation—well, Tony talks while the woman laughs and touches him every chance she gets—I sink deeper into my self-critical thoughts. In normal circumstances, I'm confident in my abilities, but this, flirting and competing for attention, I'm a shit show. I'm out of my element with no simple way to find my equilibrium again.

And I fucking hate it. These feelings of inferiority and jealousy are dangerous for someone in my line of work, because feelings leave you vulnerable. And if I'm vulnerable because of how I feel about Tony, then that means he's a weakness. *My* weakness.

Grabbing the beer bottle off the bar top, I tilt it back, finishing the remaining liquid and slamming the bottle back to the bar. I can't have weaknesses. That shit gets you and everyone you love killed.

Nausea turns the tequila and beer over in my stomach at the idea of the CIA discovering my budding feelings for the SEAL beside me. I shove a fist into my abdomen to keep from vomiting. No. They won't find out about him, about who he is to me now even if he doesn't want me in return. It's one-sided, but they'll use my feelings for him against me to break me. All those assholes who've hated my success would love to find this new pressure point of mine and use it to their full advantage.

A shiver of fear races down my spine. The anticipation of when I'll hear from my employer has ratcheted up throughout the day. Even with the liquor, Tony's easy smiles, and our distracting banter, the anxiety of what's coming has held my thoughts in a tight grip.

The clack of pool balls and someone bumping against my shoulder snaps me back to the here and now. If I want to keep Tony, and what's left of my innocence, safe, I need to get him and what fairy-tale ending he makes me yearn for out of my system. The best way to do that is to lose myself in someone else. Thank goodness the bar is packed full of eligible men who would gladly help me smother the flame Tony sparked in my desolate heart.

Screwing someone else isn't appealing in the slightest, but it's

Chapter 8

what I *have* to do for both of us. A good shock to the system will remind me I'm forever on my own, with no one in the wings to depend on, and the emptiness that follows a mediocre night keeps me safe.

Despite my reluctance and growing disgust at myself, I order another beer and slide off the stool. Ignoring Tony calling me back, I weave through the crowd, making my way toward the single pool table. The four men gathered around the table follow my every step as I approach, their game momentarily forgotten. Interest sparks with two of them while their friends offer a welcoming head lift and turn back to the game.

"You wanna play, sweetheart?" asks the one licking his lips as his eyes rake up and down my body. Guess the black-on-black jeans, tank, and boots look gets this guy—clearly not a SEAL—hot. At my shy nod, he rounds the table. I tilt my face up to his and force a sweet smile.

I dig into my back pocket for cash and slap two twenties on the side of the pool table. "Very interested in playing with you. Just let me know how many." Oh fuck, I'm laying it on thick. This guy now thinks I'm looking for a mini harem for the night. Which… I shake my head to stop the thought.

His brows shoot up, his forehead dipping beneath his shaggy dirty-blond hair that's in desperate need of a haircut. "You can play with me any time you want. I'm game for anything for someone as smoking hot as you."

I shove my hands in my front pockets to keep from strangling the idiot and doing womankind a major favor. Instead, I bump his arm with my shoulder—his soft arm despite the obvious attempt at flexing. His cocky smile says he doesn't know I'm comparing his noodle arms to Tony's thick, corded muscles that I've mapped and memorized for the past couple days. The guy says something that I don't even bother to listen to, instead responding with what I hope is a flirty laugh. Who knows, maybe it comes out more manic than flirty, but I can only use what I've got, and I have crazy in spades.

An hour ticks by, slower than any torture session I've been victim to, me smiling, laughing, and faking happy. After the first thirty minutes, I'm pretty sure my fake smile slipped into more of a grimace, but the guy trying way too hard doesn't notice since his focus has been on my ass the entire time. No matter how hard I try to forget about Tony, to make my lady bits get excited about the sexist idiot, I can't. I'm a little grossed out at the thought of what he's hiding beneath those starched khaki shorts and polo.

At the start of the current game, I announced it would be my last, blatantly ignoring Tweedledum's agreement that he was playing *this* game. Hips pressed against the wooden edge, I stretch across the green felt, cue in hand. With my full focus on ending this shit show and sinking the eight ball into the right center pocket, I miss the shuffle of movement at my back. I'm so focused that when a hand slips into my back pocket and squeezes a handful of my ass, all I do is blink in astonishment.

Honestly, I didn't think he had the balls to touch a woman without her consent, and besides, my annoyance at his antics the last hour has been clear as fucking glacial water.

Inhaling to quell the urge to break the offending hand, I stand up straight, dropping the pool stick so it clatters to the table. His uninvited hand rips from my pocket when I twist around, a speech about consent and how I will break every one of his fingers on my lips. But the speech dies when I find the space behind me, where I know he was just standing groping me, empty.

He's gone.

A commotion to my right drags my confused gaze in that direction. *Oh, right.* Not gone as in disappeared into thin air but being herded down the length of the pool table by a stalking SEAL.

I suck in a breath at the nearly feral look on Tony's flushed face. Feet cemented to the ground, heat rising beneath my skin, I watch in open appreciation as Tony continues until Tweedledum's back slams against the wall. Everyone around us stills, watching the encounter as Tony leans close, saying something I can't hear over the Creedence Clearwater Revival song thrumming through the speakers.

The groper's friends start toward Tony. Stretching backward, I

Chapter 8

grab the pool stick and swing it around, using it as a barrier. "I don't think so, boys," I say, rewarding me with a few death glares. "He started this. He can handle the consequences on his own. It's their fight now."

Their fight. It should be *me* putting him in his place and ensuring he never holds a fork the same way, but out of nowhere, Tony appeared to... what? Defend my honor? Stand up for me? Protect me?

He's well aware that I can handle myself, and have a knife secured inside my boot, yet he charged over here when he saw something he knew I didn't approve of.

Holy yarn balls, Catwoman, why the hell is that so fucking sexy?

I chew my lower lip, watching as Tony steps away from the douchebag with a single patronizing pat to the top of his head. With his furious gaze locked on me, what evaded me during the pool game comes flooding forward. My stomach tenses like I'm free-falling out of a chopper, and the heat building in my veins shoots straight to my core. The intensity behind his narrowed dark eyes is like a lightning bolt sparking every desire I tried to smother.

Feet planted, I follow his slow, confident strides with my eyes, tilting my face up to his when he stops where I lean against the edge of the table to support my weak knees.

"A word," he grits out.

"I don't—"

His eyes widen a fraction, the only warning before his palm dips beneath my loose hair and seals around the back of my neck, long thick fingers encircling and applying gentle pressure. Tony dips low, his soft lips brushing along the shell of my ear. I shiver in response to his closeness and the utter control he has over me like this.

"It wasn't a request, Elliot. It's an order."

9

TONY

I can't think straight as I guide her through the clusterfuck of high-top tables and drunks toward the front door. What the hell just happened? One second I was at the bar, blatantly watching her play pool while reminding myself that Elliot is the exact opposite of easy and how I should stop imagining her screaming my name. The next I was off the stool, barreling through the crowd, and literally stalking the motherfucker who dared put his hands on my girl.

At the battered front door, I give a little squeeze around her neck for her to open it. She doesn't hesitate, reaching for the metal handle. Surprise and excitement thrum through me at her obedience, and I brush a thumb along her soft skin in silent praise. The fact that she's allowed me to dominate her for this long is a damn gift. There are ten different ways she could break away from my hold, but she hasn't—yet. And what does it say about me that I'm turned on by the escalating anticipation for when she snaps?

A light cool mist sprinkles across my face, the little specks dancing in the streetlamp's warm glow when we step out onto the sidewalk. Instead of directing her toward the truck, I guide her toward a sheltered alcove of the neighboring building where an overhang protects us from the elements and prying eyes.

Heart thundering, muscles primed for anything, I slip my hand away. Elliot immediately twists, fists raised, but I expected her fight. Swaying back and to the side to avoid a swinging fist, I reach low and grip her hips. With a forceful shove, she stumbles back against the brick wall, my body following, sealing to hers. A surprised gasp escapes her lips, shooting a teasing tingle straight to my balls and making my rock-hard cock throb against the zipper of my jeans.

Not a great night to go commando.

Breaths labored, we search the other's face.

Her amber eyes follow the swipe of my tongue along my lower lip.

"What in the hell were you're doing in there?" I demand.

"I was going to ask you the same damn thing, Seaman," she spits back but doesn't move from where I have her pinned beneath me.

Gripping her hips, I dip both thumbs beneath her black tank top, finding her soft, hot skin. Almost panting with need, I trace circles along her skin, the tips of both thumbs dipping beneath the band of her jeans.

"I don't fucking know," I admit, surprising myself with my honesty instead of some dumb cocky comeback. "He grabbed you, and fuck if it didn't make me see red." I narrow my eyes at her. "This is your fault. If you weren't so you—"

"What's that supposed to mean?" she hisses, clearly pissed at what I'm mistakenly insinuating.

"You," I say, leaning closer, putting our lips a hairbreadth away. "You're my fucking kryptonite, Half Pint. A sexy-as-hell killing machine with an ass I itch to grab handfuls of and squeeze. Crazy but entertaining as hell, and don't leave out your defiance that turns me on so fast my dick's gotten whiplash since I've met you. That makes what happened in there, me snapping, your fault—"

"*My* fault?" she says with a fake laugh. "How is this my fault? You were over there all chatty with that... that...." She blows out a gust of air, sending a few strands of sweat-slick hair billowing upward. "You were clearly entertained elsewhere. Why the hell did you care?"

I open my mouth to defend myself, then shut it when I have no idea what she's talking about. "What the hell are you talking about?"

Chapter 9

"The beautiful woman with her perfect boobs who kept touching you." The venom in her tone shouldn't please me, but it sure fucking does. "And I needed to get away."

"Away from her?"

"From you, you bastard," Elliot yells and shoves both hands against my biceps. Prepared for the attack, I hold my ground. "I couldn't just sit there and watch it."

I search her eyes, too stunned at the gorgeous, volatile woman I can't get enough of, and then the obvious smacks me in the face. "You were jealous of her?"

"Was not," she spits, looking to the sidewalk.

"Half Pint." I groan and turn her head, forcing her attention back to me. "You're bad fucking news for me, you know that?"

She huffs. "And you're not for me? Distracting me with this," she hisses and waves down my body. "And the protective crap. Why the hell was that hot? I had it handled, but... ugh." She groans, pitching forward and slamming her forehead to my chest. "Just because you're good-looking, deadly, and actually fun to hang out with doesn't mean you get to do this to me."

I cock my head to the side. "Do what?"

"Make me feel." The words are so quiet I almost miss them when a truck rumbles by. "I can't afford that, Tony." She gazes up through her long dark lashes, slaying me with the vulnerability I find in her eyes.

"Then I guess that's settled," I mutter, inching closer. "Whatever this is between us won't happen. Neither of us can allow it to happen. We're stronger than this insistent pull."

"Stronger," she whispers and tilts her face up to my own, putting us nose to nose. "Can't allow any of this. Too dangerous for us both."

The slight squeeze of her thighs catches my eye. With a devilish smirk, I maneuver my knee between hers and lean forward, pressing my thick thigh against her pussy. An all-consuming fire flashes behind her eyes, making them almost glow in the dim light. I grit my teeth, holding back a groan when her slight weight settles on my thigh. The heat emanating from her core seeps through my jeans.

The flash of pure lust through her hooded gaze makes every reason I stick to easy pussy vanish.

With a possessive growl, I slip a hand into her hair, grasping a fistful. Her lids flutter shut, and a soft gasp escapes when I tug, forcing her face to tilt to mine. I crash my lips to hers, my hand in her hair keeping her under my control as I adjust the angle to take full advantage of her parted lips. Her tongue meets mine, both of us fighting for dominance in the kiss.

A groan vibrates in my throat as she shifts along my thigh. A flash of cool air floats beneath my T-shirt when her fingers slip beneath. Her cold palm sizzles against my too-hot skin, making me hiss into her mouth as she brushes her hands up to my pecs. Fingernails scratch along my abs, not hard enough to break skin but teasing me with the sting. Up and down her fingers explore before slipping around my sides.

With only lust and pussy on the brain, and me struggling to maintain that last ounce of willpower to not rip her pants off and fuck her against this building for all to see, I'm not prepared for the sparkle of nerves that flares with the brush of her fingertips. I go completely still, a massive wave of icy dread clearing my sex-focused brain. Elliot doesn't notice my shift, just continues exploring my back with her nails and fingertips. My heart stutters to a stop when a finger pauses on one of the larger patches of skin grafts.

Kicking back into overdrive, my heart races for a different reason. Untangling my hand from her hair, I rip our lips apart and tug her hands away from my body. Shuffling back, I don't stop until my back hits the opposite wall. Disgust and anger at myself and my reaction sink in my gut like a lead weight tied to my feet in the middle of a pool.

The dim light highlights Elliot against the wall, bent forward at the waist with her hands on her knees. Sheets of long dark hair sway in the cool breeze.

"Fuck," I curse and grip the back of my head to keep from charging across the small space and wrapping her back up in my arms.

"Exactly my thought." Flipping her head back, she stands and crosses both arms over her chest. A pink flush tints her cheeks, her lips swollen. The tossed hair, desire still pouring off her, and that sultry look almost make me forget why I ripped myself away from her in the first place.

I point at her chest, determined to ruin the moment to help me hold strong. "Not happening again."

She lifts a shoulder like she could give two shits if I ever touch her again and cuts me with a sharp smile. "Fine by me. Wasn't that great anyway."

"Is that why you dry-humped—"

I jump an inch at her rapid response, closing the few feet between us in a blink. Only years of training help me block her attempt to crush my trachea. Guess I took my comment a little too far. Stopping her fist with one hand, I spin us around with the momentum, slamming her chest to the wall. A mix of anger and desire swirls in the glare she sends over her shoulder.

My dick pulses at the unspoken threat. Great. *Now all she has to do is look at me and I'm ready to fuck her senseless.* Not really fucking convenient, considering we're about to go out on a mission together. I'll need to get this... effect she has on me under control before we leave.

Elliot thrashes, but I keep her secured until her fight dies.

"Just stay away from me, Seaman. You'll end up dead if you don't."

"Is that a threat?" I say into her dark hair.

Breaking out of my hold, she steps around me and whirls back, shoving me. My palms slam to the rigid brick before my face can collide with the rough surface.

"It's a promise."

From her ominous tone, I'm inclined to believe her.

The tense drive back to the apartment feels fifty miles longer than normal, the previous easy banter gone, silence vibrating between us instead. The tires splashing through standing water and the occasional squeak of the windshield wipers are the only sounds. I don't even glance her way, not ready to see the shift in the way she looks at me.

It's my own doing, but that doesn't make it any easier to swallow that I've possibly lost my chance with the one woman who wakes a part of me I'd long assumed was damaged, if not broken altogether.

Outside my building, fingers wrapped around the key, Elliot bolts out the door before I cut the engine. Cursing under my breath, I twist the key, shove the door open, and race after her. When she disappears around a corner, fear sneaks in that I've somehow lost her forever all because of my own dumbass insecurities. I have to set this right, have to tell her before it's too late to make a difference.

"Elliot," I call as I round the corner. "Listen, I—"

My words freeze, my senses snapping to high alert when I find her standing ramrod straight just outside my door. Creeping up behind her, I scan the area for whatever triggered her odd reaction. She startles, face whipping around to meet mine, hair fanning around her with the movement when I grip her elbow.

At the fear pouring through her normally defiant eyes, I pull her closer, ready to use my body as a shield against whatever has her afraid.

"Tonight didn't happen," she whispers quickly as she pushes out of my hold. Smoothing down her tank, she focuses on the ground. "You hear me, Hackenbreg? Tonight, whatever that was, didn't happen. There is nothing going on between us, not now, not ever."

I force my features to relax into a blank mask so she doesn't see how her words feel like a physical slap.

Before I can respond with something I would no doubt regret the moment it left my lips, she spins around and throws open the apartment door. A boom echoes when it slams against the inside wall.

"Hello, boys." I hear her call out in a sappy singsong voice.

Confusion pulses through me, fogging my thoughts. *She's in my apartment. Who in the hell would she be talking to?*

I hurry through the door, pausing for a beat to assess the situation, and immediately deem the two fuckers on my shitty couch as a threat. In two strides, I situate my larger frame in front of Elliot's and widen my stance, crossing both arms over my chest.

"The fuck are you two?" I demand. "You know what? I don't give a fuck. Get the hell out of my apartment."

"We're here for her," one asshole says as he stands. "And we won't leave without her."

I monitor the way he observes my every twitch and breath. His predatory stillness, the keen observation skills, and them only wanting Elliot make them one thing.

CIA officers.

"Why?" I ask, knowing I won't get a truthful answer, giving myself a second to come up with a plan to get Elliot out of here.

"For my operation readiness assessment," Elliot says, voice void of any emotion as she steps around me and continues toward the men.

I reach out and snag her arm, wanting to pull her back around me to keep her out of their hands. The way she acted outside the door, that fear was real, directly affecting my rash need to protect her at all costs.

"New friend of yours?" the one still sitting says, a smug look on his ugly-ass face. "Think you can keep your legs closed this time around—"

Before he can finish, I yank Elliot backward, almost sending her flying to the other side of the room, and take a calculated move toward the soon-to-be dead man.

The man laughs. "Oh fuck, it's too late to warn this poor dumbass—"

"Enough," Elliot commands. We all fall silent, minus my ragged breaths from holding my rage in check. "He's nothing." That boiling rage turns cold when her cruel words register. "Just a means to an end. Now stop talking like this is some damn teenage girl sleepover and let's get this fucking over with."

I'm still too stunned to react when she strides past me, slamming a shoulder into my chest, knocking me off balance. "Some guy at the bar left me desperate for a good fuck. Would either of you gentlemen mind helping me with that problem once we get to... which black site are we going to again?" Her voice fades as they walk down the hall. "This shit is always worse when you have the equivalent of lady blue balls. Would that be blue clit or blue ovaries? I'm not really—"

The ominous slam of vehicle doors signals they're headed out. All I can do is stare at the empty open doorway. A dull ache radiates from my chest, spreading through the rest of my body. I press a fist to my sternum to ease the growing pain.

"He's nothing. Just a means to an end."

Isn't that a fucking punch in the balls when it's said from the lips of the woman you're without a doubt falling for?

I curse myself for letting her inside, for allowing her smart mouth and crazy antics to sneak past my defenses. Stomping to the front door, I grip the edge and slam it closed. The desperate need for a drink drives me to the kitchen. Glass bottles rattle against one another when I yank open the fridge door. Grabbing the first brown bottle, I twist the cap off and take a long pull.

Her words don't matter. She doesn't matter. Where they're taking her and what will happen to her is not my concern. I will not allow myself to get caught in her web. I've witnessed firsthand what happens when you fall in love and lose all of yourself for the other person.

I won't make the same mistake as my father. Even for someone who's the embodiment of perfection, like Elliot.

She said tonight didn't matter, that I'm nothing but a means to an end. It shouldn't affect me.

So why the fuck does it feel like she's ripped my heart out of my chest?

"It's been three damn days, Lucia," I state, annoyance clear in my tone as I pace the short length of her and G's condo. She lounges on the small couch, gossip magazine forgotten on her lap, not bothering to respond as I continue my rant. She's used to it, considering I was here yesterday doing and saying the same things, when my worry

Chapter 9

and impatience were on the verge of making me do something stupid, requiring me to find an outlet. "You're CIA. Can't you ask someone when she'll be back? Three days is a long fucking time—"

"It's curious how concerned you are about her well-being. It's almost as if you care about her as more than just a potential mission partner."

My steps stutter. "Do not."

She snorts. "What are you, three?"

"Am not," I say just to get under her skin.

"Stop being an ass," Gabe says when he emerges from another room. Blue paint sprinkles an old Naval Academy shirt and streaks across his face and arms. He holds up the paint can and roller brush and winks at his wife. "Done. Told you I could do it in one day."

"Such a handy husband I have." The two hold a look, grinning like fools. I shift on my feet, feeling like I'm intruding on their odd, sappy moment. "So what if you did?" she says, turning back to face me.

"What if I did what?" Unable to keep still, I go back to pacing the living room. Out the massive wall of windows, the streets of downtown San Diego sit in gridlock, and pedestrians hurry along the sidewalks to avoid the harsh afternoon sun's heat.

"Cared about Elliot. I think you two are each other's match, if you ask me."

"Nothing happened."

Lucia perks up on the couch, tossing the magazine to the stack on top of the glass coffee table and sitting up as straight as she can with her round belly. "Interesting choice of words, Anthony. That's not what I asked." Ignoring her like the mature adult I am, I continue pacing, keeping my attention out the windows. "Obviously something happened the other night to push you to this obsessive state. Hell, you're acting like a panicked overprotective water mammal."

Pausing, I lean a shoulder to the window and scrub a hand over my face. "Nothing happened. It's nothing. We're nothing. I'm only worried because of the impact on the mission is all. If she's not back to get a read on Rico, then no one can."

Not a lie, but not the whole truth either. Hopefully she'll buy it. Sure, I'm worried about getting my revenge on that bastard Rico, but most of the worry stems around Elliot the woman, my friend, not the officer and what she can do for me.

Three days. Three days with no communication to me or Lucia.

The ball of dread that's been there since she left swells in my stomach.

Where the hell is she, and what is she going through without me there with her? I know I can't protect her from everything, though I will try if—no, *when* she comes back. I'll be okay just being there with her so she doesn't have to go through anything alone ever again.

"At least tell me if she's close," I plead, turning to face Lucia. Maybe if I know I can get to her fast if she needs me, that will soothe the nervous energy thrumming through my veins.

Her lips press into a tight line. "I don't know."

"What?" I exclaim, and push off the window. "Yesterday you said—"

"I told you what I know. The agency needs to ensure her mental health for the operation, but I don't know *where* exactly they're running those tests."

The corners of her lips dip in a frown, and she shifts her eyes, avoiding me.

"Lucia," I warn. "What aren't you telling me?"

"It might be nothing, but she said something odd the other night after the drowning event. She blew it off, saying it wasn't the first time she's had to be resuscitated."

"She said something about that before the swim. Said she almost died on an operation or something in the water."

Lucia's dark hair swishes from side to side with the shake of her head. "When she was talking to me, it was regarding her training with the CIA. I think... I think what she went through—hell, maybe is going through right now—is worse than I ever had. I knew the agency went to great lengths to ensure they prepare officers for anything, but now I'm wondering if they sometimes cross the line."

Inhaling a calming breath, I hold it to keep from storming out the door and setting fire to the entire country in order to find where they're holding her. Yes, she can take care of herself, but that's not the point. The point is I want to protect her. I want to be there for her. I want to throw myself in front of a bullet for that crazy-ass woman to show her how important she's become to me in our short amount of time together.

"There's nothing we can do," Lucia adds, caution in her tone, "except wait for her to come back. The agency wants Rico as much as the Navy, so I'm almost positive they'll send her back soon."

"Right."

"What are you scared of with getting close to her?" The innocence in her voice keeps me from lashing out for her to mind her own business. "Is it because she's difficult? Not throwing herself at you?"

"Sweetheart," G cuts in, stepping back into the room, rubbing a damp paper towel over his clean hands. He cuts me a concerned glance. G knows it all, knows why I do what I do and who molded me into the jackass I am today. "Back off a bit with the interrogation."

When Lucia winces, I shoot her a sad smile, letting her know there's no offense taken.

Grumbling something about being hungry and needing a drink, Lucia hauls herself off the couch and disappears around the corner into the kitchen.

"Elliot isn't your mom, Flakes," G offers the moment Lucia's in the next room, his gaze still trained in that direction. "You deserve this." He turns and hooks a thumb toward the kitchen area.

"What, a nice condo?"

"You know what I'm fucking talking about."

I do. Doesn't mean I want to sit here and talk about it. Not now, not ever. That one drunk night when I opened up about my abusive mother is coming back to bite me in the ass.

"She said I was just a means to an end," I admit. Falling into the leather chair, I groan and allow my head to flop backward. "Why do I even care?"

"When did she say that?"

"To the agency dipshits at my apartment when they were making remarks about me and her."

Gabe eases onto the couch and props both feet up on the coffee table. "Two things. First, I'm willing to bet she said that in front of the other officers to save face because you're more to her than she lets on, or she's trying to protect you from the agency drama."

I give him a "That's the stupidest thing I've ever heard" look. "I'm a damn SEAL, for fuck's sake. What the hell would she be protecting me from?"

"From what Luce referenced just now, maybe a lot. We've always known active officers are on the crazy side. Makes me wonder what that damn agency puts their people through."

My stomach churns. "If that's the case, what does that mean she's going through now?" The grim look that washes over G's face doesn't help my unease. "Alone." The word hangs in the air. "Fuck, get my mind off that. What's your second thing?"

"You care about what she said because you care about her. Don't deny it either, asshole. I've never seen you this worked up about a woman or as protective. It's not a bad thing, Flakes."

"Yes, it is," I grunt.

"Can you actually see Elliot being as cruel and demeaning as your mom?"

"No." Despite the conversation, my lips tug upward. "Maybe to someone who pissed her off, but no one she actually cares for."

"What about wanting to dominate you and make you dependent on her?"

"I think she might consider offing me if that happened. She likes control, but I've seen her bend when I take the reins too. It's not one way or the other with Elliot."

His blond brows furrow, forming a deep line between them. "Then what the hell are you so damn scared of?"

"I don't know." And that's the truth. "It's too much, too fast, and I already feel myself changing."

"For the better," Lucia calls from the kitchen.

I shoot an annoyed glare at G, who just raises both hands in surrender.

"Well, none of this matters if she doesn't come back," I say to no one in particular.

And dammit to hell if that thought doesn't make me want to punch a few holes in the wall.

10

ELLIOT

Despite the pain radiating from my abused and bruised body, I lift both middle fingers high in the air in a goodbye salute. I watch until the black Suburban's red taillights disappear down the deserted road. At one in the morning, only a few residents linger along their balconies, watching my display of hostility toward my colleagues.

My muscles quiver from the dwindling strength keeping my hands raised. Lowering my arms, I walk in a small circle, too injured to make a quick twist, toward Tony's apartment door but don't make a move forward. Unease at the unknown of what I'll find once I enter that apartment, how he'll treat me after my cruel departing comments that night, grew with each day I spent in that tiny interrogation room.

How many days? Two, three, ten? I'm still not sure how long they locked me in there trying different tactics to break me, to prove to all those who want me to fail that I'm officially broken—or can be. But I held my head high, steeled my spine, and vanished to that corner of my mind where I keep my happy memories for the worst of times.

I found that space full of new, more recent memories of a cocky seaman alongside the few good times I still remember from my childhood. That's why the agency can't know about Tony, why I said all those horrible things. If my associates knew how important he's becoming to me and my sanity, they'd use him to break me by threatening to break him. I've witnessed firsthand how far those bastards will go to ensure you're not a liability to the country or the agency.

A bright full moon shines overhead, silver light dancing along the damp asphalt. Shaking off my nerves, I take a hesitant step, then another until I'm standing in front of the peeling red-painted door. Instead of knocking, I reach for the knob. If it's locked, that will be the first sign that things have changed. And I guess it has. Even without those terrible words I said to protect him, things changed that night when he kissed me.

And kissed me good.

My breathing picks up just recalling the memory of his dominant lips on mine. The way he fisted my hair and held time in place as he devoured me. My entire body lit on fire under his touch, the way he controlled me. I'm so used to dominating weaker men that having Tony take what I was freely giving was beyond hot.

An inaudible whimper passes through my lips when the dull silver knob twists with no hesitation. Not locked. Pushing it open an inch, I scan what I can see of the living room, only stepping through when I find it empty. A familiar smell, Tony's unique spicy musk, filters through my nose. My entire body shudders with relief.

Immediately, my body and mind know I can lower my defenses, that I'm safe here. With him, I'm protected from anything the world or my employer can throw at me.

A shuffling noise from the bedroom has me pausing in the middle of the living room. Twisting the hem of my tank, I wait. The bedroom light flicks on, flooding the hallway with artificial light, highlighting the same jeans and tank top I wore the day I was escorted to the black site. Checking the hall, I do a quick stench test, sniffing my armpit. Ah shit. I smell and probably look like hell run over.

I sure feel like it.

A bulky frame steps into the hall and moves on silent feet toward me.

Chapter 10

The moment he finds me, I'm frozen. Face darkened in shadows, I can't get a read on what he's thinking or feeling. My pulse races as I wait in silence. Palms sweating, I swipe them down my jeans.

What will I do if he turns away?

I don't have to wait long.

With a soft curse, Tony crosses the room and wraps his arms around my shoulders, yanking me against his bare chest. Not expecting the force of his embrace, a hiss of pain from my various injuries whistles through my teeth. He eases his hold, moving his large hands to engulf my shoulders, angling me slightly away from him.

Those dark eyes scan my face. "What's wrong?"

I bite my lip to keep from vomiting up everything that happened the last few days. He doesn't need to know, but the words keep forcing their way up my throat.

"Elliot, so help me, if you...." He adjusts his grip on my shoulders, fingers flexing and straightening over and over. "Are you hurt?" I shake my head. "Don't fucking lie to me."

"Fine." I sigh and immediately regret the large exhale. My brows pinch and my face scrunches as a bolt of pain sparks through my ribs. "Maybe. I need to look."

A flash of fury sweeps across his tight features. With a stiff nod, he trails a single hand down my arm until two of our fingers hook together.

Without another word, Tony leads me to the bathroom and flips the light on. Keeping his back to the wall, he gestures for me to go first. When I turn back around, he's gone, the sound of drawers slamming shut banging through the small apartment. Tugging the hem of his Navy T-shirt down, covering the abs I so want to discover, Tony steps back into the bathroom.

My gaze snags on the gray sweatpants hanging off his hips. I can't look away.

"Take your clothes off."

"Hmm?" I say, still staring at the fantastic way the soft material hugs his thick thighs and tapers down to his bare feet. His words finally register, breaking through the mental pause his sweatpants caused. "Huh?" Surely he didn't just say what I think he said.

"Take your clothes off." Okay, yep, he said what I thought he said. "You said you're hurt. We'll take care of that first, and then we'll discuss where the hell you've been the last four days and what the fuck that was when you left."

I don't hide my cringe. "Yeah, about that—"

"Wrong order," he grumbles. Clearly having had enough of my stalling, he steps closer and reaches for the hem of my tank top. The graze of his fingers along the sensitive skin reminds me of that night he had me pinned. I hold in a groan as his fingers trail upward, dragging my shirt until it's gently tugged over my head.

The dirty fabric floats in the air and lands in the corner. Falling to his knees, Tony wraps both hands around my waist, holding me in place. Eyes narrowed in concentration, he scans my stomach with a calculated gaze as he searches for injuries. Only for a brief second does he linger on my black lace bra and the way my shallow, quick breaths push my breasts against the delicate fabric.

Why is he doing this again?

Nothing hurts with him looking at me like this. Everything about my job, the mission, the pain fades to black with the simple touch of his skin to mine. And I want that touch—everywhere.

Placing his hands on my hips, he twists me around.

"What the fuck is this?" I turn my head, twisting at the waist to check out whatever he's tracing along my lower back, but the movement has me sucking in a breath. "Your lower back is fucking black and blue, Elliot." There's no accusation in his tone, just pure unfiltered fury. And I know deep within me that his anger isn't directed toward me but the person responsible for inflicting my injuries.

The many injuries.

I open my mouth to tell him it's nothing, that I just need to jump in the shower and I'll be right as rain. But I can't get the lie out; instead a pitiful whimper escapes. I close my eyes, hating the vulnerability I'm showing, but I can't stop. Everything about his presence tells me I'm safe and that, for the first time in my life, I can let go of the control.

"Damnit, Half Pint."

I immediately miss the feel of his calluses scraping along my skin. When I start to ask him where he's going, I find the answer to my unspoken question as he kneels by the small bathtub. The roar of water fills the tiny bathroom area. I can only watch in pure fascination as he waggles his fingers beneath the streaming water, twisting and turning the knobs until the water is the temperature he finds acceptable.

I snap back to myself and icy fear coats through my veins.

"No," I rasp, lunging for the knob to shut the water off. "No bathtubs." Hands fisted by my side, I tremble like a leaf caught in a turbulent storm. "Please."

Tony twists on the balls of his feet to stare up at me. He takes me in for a minute and slowly nods. "Just thought it would help—"

"If I wasn't terrified of any type of body of water, big or small, it would help." Reaching down, I place both hands on his shoulders for balance. "Can you help me get in the shower?" He doesn't move, just continues to stare me down with purpose. "Fine," I mutter, utterly defeated.

"I didn't say I wouldn't help. But it comes at a cost, Half Pint. You talk, and I listen."

Strands of dirty dark hair fall over my shoulder as I hang my head and give him a reluctant nod.

Once again, his hands are on me, offering a soothing touch only powerful hands can offer someone like me. My stomach twists when he flicks open the top button of my black jeans and works the zipper down. For half a second, I have a total girl moment, worrying if my panties match.

Hooking two thumbs into opposite belt loops, he eases the material over my hips, slipping them down my thighs until they pool at my feet, then helps me step out of one boot, then the other. While I stare at the top of his head, whatever's been brewing and building for this man swells as he works to help get me undressed without really looking at me. By the flex of his jaw muscles and the strain in his neck, it's taking every ounce of willpower to not look, which makes the effort even more special.

"Do you want to sit to get your jeans off or hold on to me?"

I grip his shoulder in response and lift my left foot off the floor. After tossing them aside, he turns his focused attention back to the faucet and cranks the shower on. "Let me know if you need any more help. I'll be right outside—"

"Stay," I blurt. "Just stay in here? Talk to me?" I chew on the corner of my lip and look everywhere other than him. "I don't want to be alone."

And there it is.

Open, all-out honesty. Words I've never ever spoken out loud, even though they've festered inside me since I was a little girl. If he turns and walks out that door, I'm not sure I'll ever recover the sliver of vulnerability I've allowed him to see in the last ten minutes.

Gripping the edge of the tub, Tony stares at the white tile lining the shower wall. "Is there more?"

I rack my brain, trying to decipher his cryptic question. "More?"

"Bruises, injuries, shit I can't see." Spinning around, he levels a hard look up at me. "Because I'm hanging on by a motherfucking thread right now, Elliot. If I see more... trauma once you take the rest of your clothes off, I'll lose it. There won't be a damn person who can stop me from finding those bastards and beating them until they're eating out of a straw for the rest of their shitty lives."

His hard chest heaves up and down, shoulders taut with tension. Despite the pain and the acts of violence he described, my body reacts, warming me from the inside out. Heat rises beneath my cheeks, and my own breaths turn quick and shallow.

"Nothing like that," I say quickly, knowing what other trauma he's referring to. "The agency has unique ways of ensuring I'm mentally strong enough to go out into the field, but never that. I've been drowned, beaten, starved—"

"Not. Helping." Tony grits out. Closing his eyes, he saws his jaw back and forth, lips moving like he's counting. "Do you need help getting the rest of your clothes off?"

Could I do it? Sure. Would it hurt? Probably. Do I want him to do it so I can feel his touch again? Absolutely.

"A little help would be nice," I rasp, my voice weak. "Especially with the bra."

He crooks a single finger until I close the distance between us.

"Distract me," he says to my pussy. Literally to my crotch, since it's at his mouth level with him kneeling and me still standing.

"From the bruises—"

"From you being nearly naked standing in front of me." Slowly, those dark eyes sweep up my stomach, pausing at my breasts and then meeting my own. "You're injured, have a shit ton of explaining to do, and yet all I can think about is ripping this lace off your body and burying my face between your legs."

"You were never just a means to an end," I say in response instead of screaming a yes like I desperately want. We need to clear the air before anything happens between us. We're both holding back. That's clear as day. Maybe if we both open up, then we both have a shot at having something more than a one-night easy lay that takes more from you than it gives. "Even from the beginning."

As I talk, the thin fabric of my boy shorts slips down my thighs. Lifting one foot, he helps me step out of the black lace before moving on to the other.

"Everything I said outside your door and the moment we stepped into your apartment was to protect you."

"Protect me? You realize how crazy that makes you sound." I suck in a breath when the clasp of my bra releases. His fingers hook around the straps and slowly ease them off my shoulders. "Elliot?"

"Hmm?" I lock my gaze on the ceiling to keep from attacking his lips with my own.

"Why are there bruises on your arms that look a lot like fucking fingerprints?"

Instead of responding, because I for sure know he won't like the answer to his pointed question, I step around him and into the warm spray. I catch his eye for half a second before I yank the clear shower curtain across the metal bar, effectively putting up a flimsy see-through barrier between us.

With the adrenaline waning and exhaustion quickly setting in, I sink to the tub floor. Knees bent, I press my face to my thighs, allowing the water to pelt the top of my head. Soon water cascades down my saturated strands, providing a thick curtain of hair as an extra layer of concealment.

"They use people in our lives against us. Various ways, so you never know how they'll use your family or friends, but they will. It's why I'm like this." My tone drips with disdain. "No family, no friends, nothing and no one. Somehow they found out a weakness of mine and they used it—hell, still use it now—every chance they get to find that line where I break. But I don't because I don't have anyone they can use against me." Turning, I place my cheek on my knee and stare through the curtain to where Tony now sits beside the tub. "Until you. I didn't want them to know about you. To know that whatever is going on between us is more than just work."

"So it's more about protecting you than it is me," he states. "That, I'm good with. Do whatever you have to do, say what you have to say, be as fucking batshit crazy as you have to be to protect yourself from those fuckheads. But, Half Pint?" I smile at the nickname. I hate it so much that I'm starting to like it because only Tony would have the balls to keep using something I hate. "Don't ever think I need protecting. I'm not that guy. I'll never be that guy."

"I'm sorry you had to hear it though," I admit.

"Yeah, that sucked, but what really felt like a punch to the balls was what you said when you were leaving, about being left unsatisfied and needing their help."

I groan and tap my forehead to my knee. "Sorry. My go-to defense mechanism is to joke around about stuff like that."

"But it was my fault you were pissed off when we got to my place. I'm the one who pulled back outside the bar that night. Not because I didn't want you but because of something else, and I hated myself for being a damn coward. I wanted to explain when we got back home that night, but then they were here, and...."

I wait, not sure if he's done or not. It sure sounds like he still wants to tell me. I thought I was the reason he pulled away, but the way he's talking, it might be more about him. Which is great since I'm still slightly embarrassed about straight-up humping his leg outside a bar. The memory of it all sends another wave of intense heat to my stomach and lower.

"And what?" I prompt as I reach for the men's three-in-one liquid concoction that's the closest to where I sit. Before I'm even halfway, the stretching motion shoots a bolt of agony down my back. "Fucking pathetic," I grumble to myself.

The screech of metal has me tensing, but I don't dare move too fast. That damn pressure chair they had me in while asking question after question put my body through the ringer. That's what the back bruises are from. The fingerprints along my arms, well, the reason for those might need to stay hidden to protect both of us.

A scarred, callused hand blindly sweeps through the inside of the shower. The gray bottle I was reaching for tumbles into the tub, followed by a curse. A tentative grin tugs at my lips as he pats blindly around the tub, searching for the bottle.

"We have two options I can see. Either I pull this curtain aside to help, ensuring you get clean with minimal pain and before the water runs cold, or you can do it yourself with me offering blind, limited assistance. Your choice, Half Pint."

My answer feels like a pivotal point, as if whichever I decide will alter the course of whatever messed-up attraction we've built to this point. Which is why my answer comes quickly and with minimal thought to the repercussions.

"Your help. Clothing optional."

11

TONY

Seriously? I'm hanging on by the dismal remains of my willpower to not strip naked and jump in with her, and then Elliot goes and says *that*. I swear the ceramic tub cracks beneath my grip as I hold myself back.

"You can't say shit like that," I grumble. "Not when you're not in any condition to do anything but get clean and in bed."

Shit, even that sounds bad.

Complaining under my breath, I tug the shower curtain back even farther. Back curved as she hugs her shins, the bruises along her lower back stand out even more. Several other purple spots that I didn't see during the initial inspection dot along her spine but don't look nearly as deep. "What the fuck did they do to you?"

I didn't mean to say it out loud, but now that it's out there, I need an answer.

Everything in me tells me to take care of Elliot, make sure she's safe and comfortable, then go hunt these CIA bastards down. Whoever laid a hand on her will lose said hand, and more if it's up to me. I know it's not responsible, or legal, or even moral, but my mind can't see it that way when staring at her abused body.

"Can you start with my hair?" she asks instead of answering. "I haven't had a shower in…. How many days was I gone?"

I swallow back the bellow of anger vibrating in my chest. "Four days. You were gone for almost exactly four days." Movements stiff and robotic, I squeeze half the contents of the bottle into my palm and work the soap into her long dark strands. Pressing my fingertips to her scalp, I draw tiny circles, massaging the top of her head while working the soap into a thick lather.

"Oh hell yes," she says with a breathy moan and tips her head all the way back, eyes closed, mouth slightly parted.

I stare transfixed at the look of bliss on her petite features. Beneath my gray sweatpants, my rock-hard cock twitches, sending a bolt of sensation along the tip each time it brushes the soft material.

"How do you do it?" I ask, trying to distract me before I yank her out of this tub and fuck her on the bathroom floor.

"It's all I know," she says, face still tilted to the ceiling. "I wasn't the most well-behaved kid. Got into a lot of trouble, and by the time I reached high school, it was jail or enlist. So I enlisted, and caused trouble from day one." I huff a laugh at that. Of course she did. "The authority part, people yelling at me for no damn reason, really pissed me off, but they had cool toys. I'd never been around guns before, or been taught how to fight. Because of my discipline issues, they would have kicked me out before I even finished boot camp, but *they* came to get me first."

"Scoot forward to rinse," I mumble. She does as I ask, sitting there beneath the spray until I can work the massive amount of suds from her saturated hair. "What happened after that?"

"They took me to some nondescript building, asked if I wanted to be a spy—okay, they didn't use that exact word, but I'm summarizing here—and I said sure. There was nothing to go back home to if the Army kicked me out."

Lathering up another layer of soap between my hands, I wash her shoulders and arms with more care than I give my cock.

"I grew up on the streets," she says after a moment.

I bite my tongue to keep from interrupting, but damn, that's a big bomb to drop, and I really hope she plans on explaining.

"I really didn't know any different growing up. My parents were amazing, just very antiestablishment of any kind. Well, I guess at first they were wonderful parents. They gave me what they could, made sure I was safe, that kind of thing. When it came time for me to go to school, it was difficult for them, but they figured it out. Any time a teacher suspected we were homeless, I'd move schools. It wasn't too bad at first, but when kids noticed my clothes and that I wasn't as clean as them, everything just got harder."

My hands stilled along her back, my fingertips now just brushing up and down the knobs of her spine as she opens up. I know this is rare, that everything she's telling me right now is a fucking gift.

People like Elliot, like me, with scars so deep and raw, we don't share how those wounds were inflicted because if someone knows how to reopen those wounds, they have all the power. So this right here, what she's sharing with me, is her giving me the power to rip her apart to the core if I choose to. But I never will. No, I'll keep this information hidden deep within me so no one can use it to hurt her.

"You said your parents were good at first," I say after a few seconds of heavy silence, as if she'd gotten lost in her own memories. "What happened?"

"Drugs. They made friends with some of the wrong people, and bam, they were hooked. Instead of their time and what little money we had going to me for school supplies and clothes, it all shifted to keeping up with the meth habit. I was in third or fourth grade when I started fighting for money. It was something others did to stay entertained in our little encampment. The first time, I got my ass handed to me and no money. I quickly learned if you didn't win, then you got nothing despite the toll on your body."

"Holy shit," I whisper. "Elliot—"

"That went on until I was in middle school," she says, cutting me off. "Then one day, I came back from school and they had evacuated our entire encampment. Every single person gone. I never saw my parents again." There's a finality in her tone. No sadness, no emotion, like she's just reciting facts instead of traumatic incidents through her life. "I had nowhere else to go and was underage, so child protective services took me in. I bounced around a few places until they found my dad's brother, my uncle."

Dread builds in my gut at the sheer hatred that's physically making her body tremble. For the first time in my life, I wonder if I'm strong enough for this, strong enough to hear what else she's about to reveal.

"It wasn't a good situation from the beginning. Though he never sexually abused me, so I always saw that as a win." The familiar tang of blood coats my tongue as I bite down hard to keep from shouting and demanding she give me this motherfucker's address. I'll hunt him, and I'll kill him. There is no negotiating on this. "But he had unique… unorthodox, I guess you could say, ways of trying to keep me in line. I was feral, really. Living in a small apartment, being watched and questioned daily, had me pushing back on everything. So he started disciplining me after I got kicked out of a third school."

Turning for the first time since we started the shower, she places her chin on her shoulder. Those long dark lashes, now dripping with water, flutter open. "It's why I can't do baths," she whispers, almost like she's afraid anyone else might hear her weakness. "Or pools." My shock must register. She offers me a sad smile and nods. "I didn't pass out from exhaustion. Anyway, my uncle was so much bigger than me. I tried fighting back, but…. Honestly, I think he got the idea from some movie. Holding me underwater until I stopped fighting, then doing it again to prove a point. Sometimes I'd black out and wake up on the bathroom floor soaking wet, alone in the dark."

"All I need is a name, Half Pint," I say, leaning in close. So uncharacteristic of me, I place a soft kiss to her shoulder. "There won't be anything left of him."

"Thanks," she whispers. Glassy eyes meet mine. "That's the nicest thing anyone has ever said to me."

My returning smile is all menace. "It's a promise, Elliot. Him and anyone who's hurt you."

"That's a lot of people, Seaman."

Chapter 11

"Good thing I'm great at killing, then, isn't it?"

Her eyes widen a fraction, and for half a second, I worry maybe I've pushed too far. Allowed her to see too much of the bloodlust that constantly thrums through my body, made worse since Colombia.

"Fuck, that's hot." She blinks, scanning my face. "So why did you? Why did you push me off that night at the bar? I just assumed it was me."

I really want to shift this conversation back to her. Learning about her life is terrifying but fascinating, but she deserves to know what really happened.

"Why in the hell would you assume that?" I say into her hair. The streams of warm water beat down on top of my head, soaking through my shirt. "You're—"

"Crazy, cold, unemotional, hard to be around, a bitch, controlling, overbearing, batshit crazy." She rattles off the list, ticking up a finger with each inaccurate description like they're things she's repeatedly heard about herself.

"I was going to say dangerously perfect for someone as fucked-up as me. I'm no saint, Elliot. I have fucked-up views of relationships stemming from years of watching my mother abuse my father until he couldn't take any more and killed himself. I expect every woman to take and take and take until there's nothing left. Then you walk in like a fucking grenade to every idea I had about strong, confident women. You're the counterpart to my crazy, and I don't... I don't know what to do with that. I'm fucking lost in you, and I'm not sure I ever want to be found."

I suck in a breath and press my forehead to her shoulder. My fingers tremble with fear, heart slamming against my ribs. I've never done this, shared so much. Given a piece of my soul away to someone who deserves it, who will understand every fucked-up scar and still-healing wound.

"That night, I was lost in you. In your touch that drove me insane, your delicious flavor I couldn't get enough of, the way your body molded beneath mine. It was like I was drowning in you." I jolt when her fingers slide around my bicep and squeeze. "I was injured on a mission. It's why I was sidelined to paper pushing. It's... it's my back. They repaired what they could, but there's still some nerve damage where they had to graft some skin over the worst parts." I want to tell her more, tell her the truth, but I hold back the rest of the details for now. "I haven't been with anyone since."

"We all have scars," she says. "Some of them visible and others so deep it's almost as if they're carved into your soul. If anyone can understand either, it's me. You don't have to be embarrassed. Those scars are just proof of the shit we've lived through, things we've survived to come out on this side." Reaching up, she traces the long, thin pink scar along the column of her neck. "It's a reminder of how strong we are, to keep living when others can't. But if it's still too raw, if me touching those reminders is too much, I get it. Just tell me, guide me to what's safe."

I nod, the skin of my forehead sliding up and down her slick shoulder. I slip my hand around her trim waist, brushing my thumb along the underside of her breast. At her gasp, I bite the soft flesh where her shoulder and neck meet. The gasp turns into a needy moan.

"Tony." Her voice is breathy. "I think my back is clean." I hold a breath, every ounce of focus on her next words. Shifting, she pushes back, moving me out of the way to carefully lie against the slope of the tub. "How about starting on my front?"

Forearms pressed to the edge of the tub, I take my time studying every inch of her beautiful naked body. Undressing her earlier without looking was one of the hardest things I've ever done, but now I get to look my fill with her permission.

Pebbled nipples beg for my mouth as her chest heaves up and down with her labored breaths. Faint scars litter her golden tan skin. I choke on air, nearly blowing my damn load like a thirteen-year-old when I reach the apex of her thighs, finding a shaved mound. There's a soft thump and a subtle vibration when her knees collide with the ceramic walls of the tub, legs spread wide, putting her perfect cunt on full display.

Movement draws my heated gaze to her busy hands. One reaches up, cupping her tit, pinching the tight bud, while the other slips along her stomach, moving toward her pussy. Reaching out, I capture the roaming hand around the wrist and place it along the edge of the tub.

"Keep it there." I hitch my chin to the other hand. "Same with that one, Half Pint. This body is mine until I'm done." Her lack of response has me shifting my gaze from her body up to her face. "Say it," I order.

Her brows rise a fraction, and I have half a thought that she'll push back, but her lids droop and her lips part. "Yes, sir."

I squeeze my eyes shut and tip my face to the ceiling to keep from coming in my damn sweats.

Once I have my shit under control, I refocus on the beauty sprawled in the bathtub for me. The warm water pelts her skin, turning it pink along her stomach and chest. Her fingers curl, nails scraping along the smooth surface, but don't move off the edge.

Using the tip of a single finger, I trace the outer edge of one nipple, never touching the peak. I repeat the motion on the other side, savoring the way she squirms under my touch, sending water sloshing. Without warning, I pinch the tight pebble between two fingers and tug.

Her screamed curse shoots a bolt of lust straight to my balls. Panting harsh breaths through my clenched teeth, I tug harder. Her back arches off the smooth surface, her moan changing to a painful whimper. I mentally curse myself for getting carried away. We can have fun, but I have to stay in control to ensure she behaves. Shifting my torment to the other side, I grab a handful of one breast while I play with the other.

"More," she begs, the earlier flash of pain gone. "Please, Tony."

"You have been a good girl," I muse, smirking like a damn kid in a candy shop. Slipping one hand down her toned stomach, I pull the other from the spray to palm my aching dick over my sweatpants. A hard squeeze and stroke does little to suppress the painful throb, only making me desperate for more.

A groan catches in my throat as my exploring fingers slip between her slick folds. Heel of my hand pressed against her swollen clit, I tease her entrance, pushing a finger inside to the first knuckle before pulling back. Her hips lift, seeking more, but a responding hiss of pain has her settling back against the tub.

I still my movements. "Half Pint, if you want this to continue, you have to stay still. I like to play the thin line between pleasure and pain, but messing with an injury is not on the table. Understood?"

"Yes," she rasps, her wide eyes pleading.

"Yes, what?" I correct.

"Yes, sir."

"Good girl." Without warning, I dip two fingers deep inside her warm pussy. "Holy fuck, Elliot." I shove my hand beneath the elastic waistband of my sweats and grip my cock, thumbing the swollen head to spread the drops of precum.

I pump my fingers at the same rhythm as the hand squeezing the life out of my dick.

Her cries for more fill the bathroom, echoing off the tile. Sweat beads along my forehead and neck.

"Fuck," she cries out, muscles tensing and fingers clutching the edge of the tub like a lifeline. Her pussy squeezes my fingers like a fucking vise, a torturous preview of what it will be like when I'm balls deep between her thighs.

Unable to hold back another millisecond, I grunt through my release, hot streams of cum coating the inside of my pants and slicking my hand.

Pitching forward, I catch my weight with a forearm to the edge of the tub.

Nostrils flaring, I breathe deep, coming down from the best fucking orgasm I've had in months.

Lifting my head, I meet her shining amber eyes. Gone is the edge, the suspicion that's always lurking there. Instead, something scarier shines through. And I have a terrible feeling that she sees the same in my own.

Hope.

Trust.

Fear.

And for the first time, I'm good with a woman seeing this deep into my broken soul.

Correction, good with *this* woman, this fighter and survivor who can still laugh and joke despite it all. She's who I want seeing this side of me, because I know she'll keep it safe.

Maybe I was wrong earlier. Maybe there is a part of me that needs protecting.

12

ELLIOT

Bladder on the verge of rupturing, I still don't move from of the cocoon of warmth encircled around my back. The worn pillowcase shifts beneath my cheek with my growing smile despite the discomfort.

A genuine smile.

Not one edged with craziness that I show the world to scare them away. Not fake or forced or sad.

A real, content smile.

Well, maybe not fully content if the demanding throb between my thighs means anything. The orgasm he wrung from me in the shower was beyond anything I've felt in years, yet here I want more. A delightful quiver hits my shoulders at the memory of his commanding tone. I want more. More of him dominating, more of his touch, and hopefully the next time, all of him. I press my thighs together to ease the emptiness.

His skin heats my fingertip as I trace the outline of the hand gripping my hip, imagining it wrapped around his cock as he guides it toward my parted lips.

Those long, thick fingers curl, applying pressure to my full bladder. With an annoyed huff directed at my impatient body, I lift Tony's heavy-ass arm off my waist and scoot off the bed. Tiptoeing as best I can with my injuries, I awkwardly creep my way to the bathroom through the dark. I flip the light on after closing the door. The brightness blinds my unprepared eyes, making me blink past the sudden intrusion to see.

I gaze at the tub, replaying last night's fun while I relieve myself. Before I flush, a reddish tint of the water has my fingers hovering over the lever. It's not from my period, thanks to the IUD the agency required after the Colombia incident. That means the blood is coming from somewhere else. Considering Tony's explosive reaction to the bruising along my lower back, it must be from damage to my kidneys.

"Motherfuckers," I mutter and flush the evidence. Instead of returning to bed, I make my way down the hall, fingers trailing along the smooth walls as a guide to the kitchen, and then tug open the fridge. Not sure what I expected, but the wire shelves stacked with healthy premade meals, bottles of water, and multiple containers of fruit come as a shock.

A looming presence at my back has me grinning into the fridge as I grab a bottle of water.

"Did you keep up with the running too while I was gone?" A few glass bottles rattle together when I slam the door shut. Turning, I carefully lean back against the cool metal.

"I did," he says with a yawn. His sleepy eyes flick to the clock on the microwave just over my shoulder. "It's four thirty. What the hell are you doing up?"

"Had to pee." I twist off the cap and chug half the contents before taking a breath.

His attention sharpens at the movement. "You feeling okay?"

I nod. Just because I opened up last night doesn't mean he needs to know about everything in my life. Like the minor detail that my kidneys are bleeding, my brain feels like it's swollen and pressing against my skull, and my lungs are burning from the inside out. That seems a little TMI for this budding relationship.

Relationship?

Chapter 12

Whoa. When did this make the leap from lust to relationship?

Maybe it was when he fingerfucked me, sending me over the edge in record time.

Yeah, that was probably it.

Tony scrubs a hand over his face. "I don't believe you, but okay. Just give me a heads-up before you pass out or die."

I smile around the plastic lip before taking a drink. "I'll take your request into consideration, Seaman."

"You do that, Half Pint. Come on," he says and holds out his hand. "We have another hour before I go run. Let's go back to bed."

"*You* go run? Don't you mean *we* go run?"

He shakes his head with a pointed look that even the early morning darkness can't hide. "You're not running."

"I'm not?"

Giving up on waiting for me to come to him, he steps into the kitchen, moving closer until I'm pinned to the fridge.

"Give yourself twenty-four hours."

"Why should I?" I press even though he's right. The thought of running makes me want to curl into a fetal position.

"Because I'm sure there's more damage than what I saw. Tell me I'm wrong."

I pop my mouth open, ready to contradict his statement, but snap my lips closed when nothing comes out.

"Want to talk about it?"

"Not really," I whisper.

"Will you tell me why?"

Leaning forward, I press my forehead to the center of his chest. "To ensure their secrets are safe, that I'm not a liability if Rico catches me."

He steps back and tips my chin up, forcing me to meet his steely gaze. "If you're with me, he won't lay a hand on you."

I offer him a sad smile. "That's out of your control, Seaman. Besides, I got the impression that the agency expects me to get caught." I turn my unfocused gaze lower, staring at the yellow lettering on his blue T-shirt. "It's like they were preparing me for *when* it happens, not if." I shrug. "I don't know why, and maybe I'm reading too much into it."

"You're thinking they know something we don't."

I nod, sinking deeper against the hand cupping my cheek. "Maybe, maybe not. Maybe they're covering their bases, or they're still concerned about my mental stability after the failed operation." I swallow down the lump forming in my throat. "See, my partner died that night. Rico shot him when I wouldn't give up the password for the drone's information. I killed him to—"

The next words are swallowed by lips pressing against my own. Twinges of pain radiate up my back when I wrap my arms around his neck, but instead of pulling away, I tighten my hold, relishing the pain. A hot palm slips beneath the hem of my sleep shirt and grabs a handful of my ass. The sharp ends of his buzzed hair prick into my fingertips as I rake my fingers up and down the back of his scalp.

A pitiful whimper climbs out of my throat when he pulls back just enough to break the kiss.

"I wake up every day with the guilt of those who died under my command. It weighs on me until I don't think I can fucking breathe. It takes me remembering two things to get out of bed every morning, to keep doing what I do as a senior officer."

Curling my fingers, I gather a handful of the back of his T-shirt. "What's that?"

"First, they had a job where they knew each mission. We have a greater chance at dying in the field than coming home." I swallow and nod, acknowledging the truth in that statement. Kurt was an officer just like me. He wasn't an innocent civilian. "And two," Tony continues. "We weren't the ones to pull the trigger."

A single hot tear escapes the corner of my eye, streaking down my cheek.

"You didn't kill him, Half Pint," Tony says as he wipes away the evidence of my weakness with a swipe of his thumb. "He died serving his country, and that's an honor many of us will succumb to. Don't carry what that bastard Rico did on your conscience. There was nothing you could do."

Chapter 12

When I don't respond, he forces my face back up to his by pressing that wet thumb beneath my chin.

"Say it," he commands.

"There was nothing I could do," I whisper. Another tear leaks out. "I still don't know what happened that night. Why everything went to shit. I don't think... I don't think I can really let it go until I know. Until I know why... know why he had to die." It almost comes out. I almost let it slip that he wasn't the only one I lost that night. But I catch myself at the last second.

Why would he care? I was no one to him when I lost the baby. He's a damn Navy SEAL with emotions of steel. Telling him would only solidify in his eyes that I'm a fucking idiot for sleeping with my partner. And what if he thinks what we're doing, whatever this is, is how I felt about Kurt?

Kurt was just sex, a way to relieve the tension of the operation.

Tony... my seaman, he's so much more than I ever expected to feel or connect with. He's changing me because he sees the real Elliot Smith. He sees me as an officer and as a woman. And that combination is everything.

"We will get your answers," Tony says with conviction in his tone. "We will both get our answers."

It hits me that he never explained why they chose him for this operation.

"What answers do you need?" I ask, my eyes flicking between his, searching for clues.

His lips press into a tight line. "I—"

A pounding on the front door cuts him off. Whirling around, he rips open a drawer and retrieves a nine-millimeter Glock. My breath catches at the snap of the slide engaging. Sealed against the fridge, I watch in lustful appreciation as he stalks to the front door.

Fucking hell, that's hot.

Officers have surrounded me for years. I've watched them move through training exercises and seen them in action on an op and never had this kind of reaction. But my seaman stalking across the living room with his gun at the ready? So fucking glad I put panties on after that shower.

"Open up, Anthony."

At Lucia's voice, I push off the fridge, grab the water bottle I dropped to the floor, and head toward the living room just as Tony opens the door. She arches a single brow at the gun in his hand and looks back to him.

"Seriously?"

Tony scoffs. "You're one to talk. Pretty sure you and G have guns stashed all around that condo."

"He likes to be prepared with multiple in one area. It still rubs him that one time I had a gun and he didn't." She steps across the threshold, and my attention zeroes in on her pink fluffy slippers. She follows my gaze and shrugs. "My feet are swelling, and it's way too early to force these sausages into heels."

In a quick movement, Tony releases the clip and empties the chamber before tossing both to the couch. Holding out his hand, he flicks his wrist. "Come on. Sit down before even those things don't fit."

Lucia narrows her eyes, and I cover my mouth to smother a laugh.

"I can talk about my fat feet, Anthony. You cannot."

"Women are nuts," he mutters under his breath. "Either way, sit your tiny ass down."

She presses her hand over her heart, and her eyes go misty. "You think it's tiny?"

"Holy fuck." Holding up both hands in surrender, he slowly backs away until he disappears down the hall.

"Anthony, get your ass back here," she yells.

At this point, I'm crying. Tears from holding in my rolling laughter pour down my rounded cheeks.

"Not happening, crazy pregnant lady," Tony yells from the back room.

"Look at that, Lucia," I say on a hiccup. "You made a SEAL retreat."

"I'm not retreating," he bellows.

Chapter 12

"I'm here about the mission." Heavy, quick footsteps sound down the hall. He stops at the entrance and braces himself with a forearm pressed to either wall. With a satisfied nod, she turns to me. "First, good to see you back in one piece." I wipe my leaking eyes and give her a thumbs-up. "Because the agency and the Navy have cleared you, Tony and Lovall—"

"Who's Lovall?" I ask, finally regaining some semblance of composure.

"Lieutenant Brandon K. Lovall, aka McLovin," Tony explains. "One of my men. A good SEAL."

"Is he hot?" I ask just to poke at the SEAL now hovering near my back. Lucia laughs, holding her belly while a scoff sounds behind me. "Kidding, Seaman. Don't get your skivvies in a bunch."

"You're scheduled for a briefing at 0800." I snap my head toward Lucia, who now holds my full attention. "After, you'll grab whatever gear you need and bug out."

Renewed energy courses through my veins. I bounce slightly on the balls of my feet, suddenly unable to keep still. "Do you know what they're thinking?"

"Basics. We're keeping this small, need-to-know only since we still haven't identified the mole. From what I understand, you'll depart immediately from the base in Cartagena for whatever coordinates you suggest, Elliot. You do your thing to locate Rico with the SEALs as backup. You won't get carte blanche on how to draw Rico out but pretty damn close. We want to get you guys in and out of Colombia as fast as possible."

A wash of relief settles over me at hearing that. I'm not mentally prepared for another long-term operation.

"Air drop or chopper?" Tony asks.

"Not sure. Our hopes are you can locate Rico before he knows Elliot is back in Colombia."

"But if he knows I'm there, he'll find me," I interject. "Why not just let me parade up and down the streets naked, firing off a few rounds and yelling for him to come and get me?"

"That's very specific," Lucia says with a chuckle. Tony shoots me a glare from the corner of his eye that clearly states "over my dead body" before she continues. "As entertaining as that might be, we'd like to catch Rico unaware if we can. He's less likely to disappear again if the attack is a surprise."

"She's injured." Whipping around, I slam a fist into Tony's rock-hard bicep. "Just calling it like it is, Elliot. Nothing personal. It's an assessment I'd give of all my men before a mission."

My lip curls in a snarl. "I'm fine."

"They informed me that she incurred a few bumps and bruises during their assessment but gave no details, just that she was fine and cleared for duty." Lucia's brows dip in concern. "What's the injury?"

"Bruising to her lower back," he replies. "I'm assuming there's some corresponding kidney damage as well."

Fucking SEALs. So damn perceptive.

Lucia turns her full focus on me. "I don't care what my supervisor says. If you're hurt, I'll pull you unless you tell me otherwise. So be straight with me, Officer Smith. Are you good at moving forward?"

"Yes," I hiss. "Despite what my nanny here says."

She responds with a reluctant nod. "If you get a damn kidney infection or your organs shut down because you're lying to me and are about to step into a damn petri dish, I'll kick your ass in the hospital."

"Pretty sure either of those would cause death in the middle of the jungle."

"Which is why I mentioned it," Tony says under his breath.

"Then I guess I'll have to beat up your dead body," Lucia states at the same time.

I tilt my head to really study the woman. "I think we should be friends."

"Now *that* just sounds like a lot of mayhem." Tony stretches his arms high overhead and yawns. "With this news, I'm going back to bed, considering it might be a while before I'm sleeping in it again. Thanks for letting us know. Good night, Lucia." Stepping forward, he gives her round belly an awkward pat. "Night, baby."

Once he's disappeared into the bedroom, I turn back to Lucia and shake my head. "He's an odd one."

Her eyes narrow, making me retreat a step. Fucking hell, she's scary when that ire is turned on you.

"Here's the deal, Smith. I might think he's a jackass and an idiot most days, but he's a good man. Lost and a lot broken from his past, but he's one of the good ones. If you hurt him, I will kill you and feed your tiny body to the sharks."

I swallow hard and nod.

"Great," she exclaims and claps her hands. "Now that that's covered, I'm heading home. I agree with Tony's take. Might as well try to get some sleep in our own beds because it will be a while before we get another chance."

Fear slithers through me. I shift my panicking gaze from her face to her belly. "You're coming too?" *Please say no.* I'll need my full focus on finding Rico and not dying myself, not on protecting my new friend and her unborn baby.

At the door, she turns, hand resting on the doorknob. "No, but I'll be here monitoring your positions and updates while you're in the field. I won't rest until you three are back home and we lock Rico in some black site."

With a wave, she leaves, quietly shutting the door behind her.

After grabbing another bottle of water, I find Tony in the bedroom, lying on his back and staring wide-eyed at the ceiling.

"You nervous?" I ask. Placing the bottle on the floor, I crawl under the covers and mirror his position, keeping a foot of space between us.

"Nervous? No. Feeling underprepared? Yes. I sure as hell hope they give us more details than that before we bug out. I don't enjoy going in with a hazy-ass plan." He turns his head to face me. "It puts you in danger as well as me and McLovin. The more information we have, the better."

"See, I'm thinking the opposite." Licking my lips, I turn on my side and tuck both hands beneath my cheek. "We had all the information eight months ago, and look what that got me. A murdered officer and several dead SEALs." My heart hurts saying it out loud. "I'd like to know who they were," I say more to myself. "Pay my respects for their sacrifice. They were there because of information I passed through the proper channels. That's why I think going in blind is better. I'm not sure if there's a leak somewhere in the information stream or what, but not having a plan means Rico can't plot against us."

He blinks, staring at me like he's seeing me in a new light.

"What?" I ask, moving back an inch. "You're looking at me strange."

"You really want to visit them? The fallen SEALs?"

"Well, yeah. I don't carry their deaths on my shoulders like I do Kurt's, but yeah, I do. I can't do anything about what happened that night. I can't apologize, but I can at least pay respects to their graves and maybe their families too, if they're open to it."

Twisting, Tony lies on his side and stretches across the bed, cupping my face with such tenderness my heart swells.

"You constantly surprise me."

"Then I guess things will never get boring." His hand slips to cup the length of my neck, his thumb brushing the still-tender scar. "We'll be fine," I tell him. "I won't let anything happen to you."

His returning smile is genuine. "I think that's my line."

I shake my head. "Nope. Your line is 'Let's ease this pre-operation stress by fucking until it's time to leave.'"

He lifts a challenging brow. "Oh, is that my line?"

I nod and bite my lower lip.

"Sounds like a shitty line." My shoulders slump in defeat. *Shit, what if he thinks differently about me because of what all I revealed? Maybe he sees me as this fragile little thing running high on emotions.* "But the premise is solid."

With a hard tug, I'm gliding across the sheets. Tucking me against his chest, Tony hovers a few inches above. "If I get too rough—"

"I like it rough," I rasp. Fingers curling into the sheets, I fist handfuls to keep from reaching up and yanking his lips to mine.

Chapter 12

"You're injured." He silences my protest with a hard kiss. "Not negotiable. Tell me when you're in pain and I'll ease up."

"Okay," I relent.

His grin turns sharp. "Okay?"

I swallow hard. "Yes, sir."

The words barely pass my lips before he's on me. Rolling on top, Tony cages me in with both forearms pressed to the bed beside my head.

"Good girl."

That praise really shouldn't make me happy.

But it sure fucking does.

13

ELLIOT

Tony's lips seal against my own, his tongue slipping between and demanding entry, which I gladly give. Shifting his weight to the side, he supports himself on one arm while the other shifts lower, his hand dipping below the hem of my sleep shirt. My abs flex beneath his warm palm as he moves higher.

A low groan rumbles in his chest when he cups my entire breast and squeezes.

My back arches off the mattress, making pain flare from my bruised body, but I shove it away, too focused on the growing desperate need for his rough touch. A burst of pleasure-filled ache zaps from where he's pinching a tight bud all the way down to my core. I squeeze my thighs together to ease the building throb.

"Let's get rid of this," Tony says, his lips brushing against my own teasingly. In a smooth move, he has the shirt over my breasts, his greedy eyes taking in my naked chest. Bending forward, he sucks a peaked nipple between his lips while he pinches the other.

My head thrashes from side to side as the all-consuming need for him grows beneath his ministrations. With more gentleness than the moment deserves, Tony helps me out of the sleep shirt, studying my face for any signs of pain.

"Seaman," I whimper. "Get on with it." His responding chuckle against the sensitive skin of my neck shoots another bolt of desire to my core. The soft material of his T-shirt rubs against my pebbled nipples. "Take it off," I beg before thinking of my words.

Tony pauses, pulling back an inch to search my now-wide eyes.

"Sorry, I wasn't—"

"Just don't ask to see the damage," he grits out. His focus goes to my hands. "And we'll have to do something with those tiny hands of yours."

The "tiny" part should piss me off, but I'm too turned on to give a fuck. He can call them tiny, massive, or purple if he hurries this along and climbs on top of me. The bed shakes when he pops off and stalks to the dresser. The wooden furniture shudders with the force of Tony ripping the drawer open, tugging two shirts free.

When he turns, there's a fire behind his brown eyes that spikes my pulse even higher.

Grabbing one wrist, he pulls the arm to the side. "This hurt?" he asks as he ties one end of the shirt to the bedpost and works to secure the other end around my wrist.

"No," I say breathlessly. The knot is loose enough that I could slip my hand through with ease, but that's not the point. This is for him, and, to be honest, for me too. I've fantasized about situations like this, when a man was strong enough to dominate me instead of the other way around.

When he's done, he stares at me, eyes trailing down my naked body, pausing on my boy shorts.

"Those need to go, and then I need to taste that sweet pussy of yours. Understood?"

"Yes. Fuck yes, please."

His eyes flick up to mine, eyebrows raised. With a massive hand wrapped around my thigh, he rolls me to the side. The sting of his hand connecting with my ass registers after the loud smack vibrates through the room.

A moaned string of curses falls from my lips, eyes squeezing shut.

"Understood?"

"Yes, sir," I plead. "More."

His wide palm caresses over the spot he slapped. "After my snack, baby. I've wanted to sink my tongue deep into you since you walked into that damn office."

With utter reverence, he hooks two fingers into my cotton panties and tugs them down my thighs.

Completely naked and needy as hell, I watch as he wraps a hand around his thick cock over his boxers. Stretching to the bedside table, he tugs the drawer open, reaches inside, and tosses a strip of condoms onto the bed.

My core clenches as I count the individual packets.

One, two, three, four. Holy shit, tonight might be the best night of my life.

The mattress dips beneath his knees as he crawls onto the bed, positioning himself between my legs. His hot palms sear against my inner thighs when he pushes my legs wider.

One hand with a death grip on his cock, he trails a finger of the other between my slick folds, eyes devouring the movement. That finger floats in the air before slipping between his lips. Tony moans around the single digit, eyes fluttering closed.

"Sweet, just like I knew you'd be." Lying on his stomach, he slips his wide hands beneath my bare ass, fingers flexing as he lifts my lower body with ease to his waiting lips. "Holy fuck, you smell just as good as you taste, baby. I want this fucking scent all over me so I can smell your cunt on me for days."

"Stop talking, Seaman," I grit out and draw my knees up, giving him better access to eat his fill.

"Yes, ma'am."

At the first swipe of his tongue from my entrance to my swollen bud, my back bows off the bed, pain flaring, but I cover the cry of discomfort with a desperate moan. Tony's tongue swipes up and down as if my pussy is his favorite ice cream cone. Flipping my hands around, I grip the soft cotton T-shirts to give me something to hold on to.

Like he promised, his curled tongue spears my center, plunging in and out just enough to tease me to the breaking point. I feel one hand slip away from my ass. The next moment, two fingers replace his tongue, plunging in and out while his lips seal around my bundle of nerves.

Unable to stop, my hips flex, thrusting against his face, desperate for more. Then his teeth nip and fingers plunge in deep, curling to hit a sensitive spot, shoving me over the edge. Pleading for more, urging his fingers harder and faster, I explode around his fingers, clenching down hard. His curses and praises fill the room as he sucks and teases my pussy until I lie limp on the bed.

Panting, I stare up at the ceiling, smiling like a damn fool. His hard body moves up mine, slick lips from my release kissing a trail up my stomach, then the tip of each breast before continuing higher.

Hovering over me, he licks his lips before dipping lower, sealing his mouth to mine and forcing his tongue inside. My eyes roll, lids falling shut at the salty taste of my release mixed with his unique flavor on his lips and tongue.

"Tony," I plead when he pulls back an inch. "I need you." He reaches for the condoms, but I shake my head. "Here first." I slide the tip of my tongue along my upper lip for emphasis.

"Not if you want me to last longer than thirty seconds." He chuckles and grabs the strip of condoms. Reaching lower, he tugs off his boxer briefs, his hard cock popping free. On his knees, he strokes himself, grip tight as he takes in his fill of me. "You're beautiful, Elliot."

Only he would say that, because he has scars of his own from battle. My golden skin is marked all over with thin white scars and a few larger ones from healed bullet wounds.

"Shirt," I say, hitching my chin toward his chest. "I want to see you, Tony. Want to feel your skin against mine."

A flash of vulnerability flashes across his face. Reaching back, he grips the soft cotton in both hands and tugs it forward, slipping it over his head in one smooth motion. He tosses it to the side.

"Holy hell," I say in awe. "I want to touch you so bad." I tug on the restraints, but not hard enough to disturb the loose knots.

"I know," he says, sadness in his tone. "Maybe someday, baby. But not—"

"Just get the fuck on top of me and stop teasing me with that cock of yours."

Just like I hoped, the sadness vanishes, replaced with pure male pride.

"This one?" he asks as he continues to stroke himself. He pinches the swollen head, his lids fluttering closed. "I think I like your idea of letting you have a taste before I fuck your pussy raw." My shoulders shake in a full-body pleasure-driven shudder. "You want that, don't you, baby? Want me deep in your throat before I'm buried between your thighs."

"Yes," I whimper, licking my lips in anticipation. I follow his slow movements as he crawls up my body before hovering over my chest.

My still-damp strands cling to his fingers, pulling and tugging as he weaves them into my hair. I lift my head, and a flash of confliction passes his face. I know what he's thinking, wondering if this is a good idea because of my condition.

Well, fuck that.

Pushing through the pain, I lean up farther and lick from base to head with the tip of my tongue.

That does it. All doubts about this being a terrible idea vanish from his pinched features, shifting to a feral grin. I gasp at the pain radiating from my scalp when he tightens his grip and pushes past my parted lips. We groan at the same time, mine stifled with his cock pushing deeper.

He stares down at me, a terrifying look on his face that only inches up my need. Slowly, he pulls all the way out to rub his slick head against my lips before pushing back in, hitting the back of my throat. Eyes watering, I swallow past the gag reflex, taking him even deeper.

With a harsh curse, he pulls all the way back, popping out from between my pressed lips.

"Fucking hell, Half Pint. Your mouth was made for taking my cock. I think I just saw heaven." He eyes my mouth like he wants to dip that thick cock back in, then shakes his head. Reaching over, he rips open a condom packet and rolls it down his twitching dick.

The hold on my hair lessens as he shifts back down my body, shoving my thighs apart with one knee, then the other. I hold a breath when he presses against my entrance, teasing with just an inch before pulling out.

"Tony fucking Hackenbreg," I grit out through clenched teeth. "Fuck me or die tomorrow. Your choice."

He presses his forehead to my own. When I peel my lids open, his brown eyes are staring down into mine. "I think you mean that," he says, still not moving.

"It's a promise."

"Well, then." His smile widens, turning sharp, my only warning before he thrusts forward, spearing me with his thick dick.

My hair tugs in his hold when I dip my head back, a hiss of pleasure whistling through my clenched teeth. I focus everything on the delicious burn of the stretch. The fullness with him bottomed out deep inside me. His bare chest presses against my own, tickling my peaked nipples with each of his heavy breaths.

"Elliot," he whispers like a prayer before easing back. I whimper at the loss, only to gasp when he thrusts back inside harder than before.

The bed shakes with his powerful thrusts, each one sending a shooting pain up my lower back, but it only drives my pleasure higher and higher. Hands tied, his massive body moving over mine, all I can do is take everything he's giving, loving every damn second.

Tension builds in my lower belly. His thrusts shift from smooth and deep to short and erratic, nailing that special spot over and over in quick succession.

"More," I beg. "Harder, please. Fuck." I can't form a sentence; all I can focus on is the build of my orgasm.

Panting above me, Tony moves lower, sealing his lips against my neck.

The sharp sting of his bite triggers my orgasm with the delicious mix of pleasure and pain. Crying out, I arch off the bed, damning the pain, sealing my chest against his.

A grunted curse brushes past my ear as he finds his own release, only stilling when we've both fallen from the high. Still deep inside me, his cock twitches, shooting bursts of tingling pleasure through my core.

Pressing his weight onto one elbow, Tony stares down at me, eyes flicking between my own, asking a silent question.

"I'm better than fine," I say, knowing he needs reassurance that he didn't make my injuries worse. "Don't worry, Seaman. I'm tougher than I look."

His features soften. "I know, baby, but with me, you don't have to be." My muscles relax, sinking me deeper into the plush mattress. "You up for doing that again?"

A soft gasp escapes me when he pulls out, leaving me feeling empty and somehow wanting again. Stripping off the condom, he ties the end and tosses it into the trash can by the door. Wrapping his hand around his still semi-hard dick, he gives it a tight squeeze. He catches my focused attention on his cock.

"Because I am. As long as you're not in pain and are begging me for more, I can do this all damn night, baby, and plan to if you're willing."

Was that a trick question?

Even if this causes more damage to my already battered body, I don't give two shits. This with him is beyond anything I've felt, anything anyone has ever wrung from me. Of course I want more. I'll take everything he's willing to give.

"Hell yes." I sigh and close my lids, savoring the feel of his hand skimming up my ribs toward my breasts. "Hell fucking yes."

The chopper lurches, prepared for the landing impact. I barely sway when we touch down. Tony swirls his finger in the air in a "let's go" signal. The other SEAL, McLovin, and I remove the straps keeping us secured to the bench and stand in unison, grabbing two duffels from the pile of gear as the door slides open.

Heat and humidity flood in from the force of the still-rotating blades. The thick air coats the inside of my throat, making every inhale labored as I jump out, staying low, following Tony's boots. Memories of doing this same thing infiltrate my every thought. The whirling helicopter blades swallow the stomp of my black combat boots.

Keeping one step behind Tony and McLovin, I take a few moments to collect myself from the sudden onslaught of grief and panic this country invokes. With a military base teeming with alpha males, I can't show one ounce of weakness or they'll be all over it like sharks on blood in the water.

Sweat already coats my bare arms and drips down the back of my neck. The sensation of hateful stares from those watching makes my skin itch, but I maintain the outward cocky bitch attitude I've honed over the years. Adjusting the thick canvas strap of the heavy-ass duffel, I grunt through the sharp pain that radiates from my lower back to the rest of my body.

McLovin glances over his shoulder, the sun glinting in his dark sunglasses. "You good back there, *gato montés*?"

I huff a laugh at the handle he gave me on the trip here to Cartagena. Apparently I'm hilariously crazy, warranting the Spanish name for wildcat as a nickname. Tony didn't disagree, finding it just as funny as McLovin, or seem concerned at the other SEAL's friendliness.

"All good, merman."

His head tips back, and his deep laugh fills the air. Tony shoots a smirk over his shoulder.

Pausing a respectful distance from the chopper, Tony looks around the base. "We need to find the command center," he says to no one in particular.

Catching up, I tap him on the shoulder and point toward a plain green-painted metal pod. "It's that one. At least it was the last time I was here."

Chapter 13

His brows rise above his sunglasses. "You started your original mission here?"

"Yep." I bite my lip to hold back a mischievous grin. I should tell him about the bad blood between me and the base commander, but where would the fun be in that?

"That look scares me," Tony says cautiously. "Shit, you blew something up, didn't you?"

Oh yeah, and there was that too. Forgot about that incident.

"It was one small canvas shelter. They shouldn't have gotten as mad as they did."

We turn as one unit in the direction I showed, this time walking side by side.

"Now this I have to hear," McLovin says, bumping me with his shoulder in a friendly gesture.

"I was testing a chemical mixture with the materials I'd have access to down here and I...."

"You what?" McLovin asked, clearly amused.

I toss my hands in the air in exasperation. "I sneezed, okay? I sneezed, and a little too much ammonia spilled over, and boom." I flare my fingers out and make an explosion sound.

"So you're warning us that you have jungle allergies." Keeping my gaze on the metal pod, I let loose the smile I'd been holding back. "And made a few enemies in the short time you were here."

I nod, agreeing with Tony's assessment. "That's a good summarization. Though enemies is a strong word."

Just as the words leave my lips, the metal door of the command center pod slams open, banging against the outside wall. A familiar slight frame storms through on a damn warpath. I wince at the sheer hate radiating off the base commander. "Except for maybe him. But he deserved it, I swear."

"Officer Smith," the base commander snaps, his boots clomping down the three metal steps, making it tremble beneath him. "What the hell are you doing on my base? I told you if I ever saw you again, there would be dangerous consequences."

I lift a shoulder in a dismissive shrug. "What can I say? I was in the area and thought I'd stop by to check in, see how your recovery is going." I dip a pointed gaze to his crotch and arch a brow.

I smirk at his tiny hands curling into white-knuckled fists, a laugh slipping out when he takes a challenging step closer.

"You fucking—"

"Base Commander Hank," Tony says, stopping Handsy Hank in his tracks. "Hackenbreg and Lovall." He taps his chest first, then nods toward McLovin. "Per my orders, you were expecting us. Officer Smith is here as a part of our covert team, though her arrival was on a need-to-know basis. Clearly you weren't on that list. Careful with your next words."

I want to clap. Like a good slow clap for the anger vibrating through his tone, making his words cut like a knife through the heavy air.

"Right," he hisses through his clenched jaw. "Mess hall is still serving lunch. I'll have someone show you where you can stash your gear until you leave." His gaze slides my way. "By nightfall."

"That was the plan anyway, so good thing we agree that the least amount of time my team spends here is for the best. I have a feeling once Officer Smith here tells me what you did to direct her crazy toward you, I'll need to be as far away from this base as possible."

The two men stare each other down, Handsy Hank shrinking by the second.

Whatever dominance battle this is, I'm digging it. I can't look away from Tony. His stiff posture, hands casually clasped in front, oozing confidence in his ability to kill the base commander in five seconds flat. And there's something else that makes it all even better. Tony's standing up for me while not standing up for me. Which is so fucking amazing. He's not showing off, just defending me like he would any of his men.

Maybe we could find a storage shed or dark corner somewhere so I can show him just how appreciative I am for how he handled this awkward encounter.

A young grunt steps away from her commander's side and instructs us to follow her to the storage area for our gear. Several feet away, unable to hold back, I twist around to send Handsy Hank a one-finger salute.

"You're taunting him back there, aren't you?" McLovin asks. Slowing down, he maneuvers his two bags into one hand and hooks an arm around my shoulders. "I feel like that's another delightful story I need to hear."

"What did he do for you to pull whatever shit you did? There was legit fear in his eyes, Half Pint. Hate, sure, but a lot of fear, and that wasn't because of me." Tony lifts his chin to the female enlisted soldier, dismissing her after she points out the shed.

She doesn't leave but turns to me. "Ma'am." I shrug out of McLovin's hold and drop the duffel to the dirt. "Permission to speak."

"Granted."

"Thank you. On behalf of every female on this base, anything you need, today or in the future, just find one of us. You had our back, and we will forever have yours."

With that, she offers a salute and turns on her boot heels, disappearing around one of the storage container metal walls.

"Ah hell. Now I really need to know," Tony demands.

With a groan, I pick up the duffel and toss it inside the container. It booms when it lands on the metal floor. The other four bags fly through the air, followed by our packs.

"Well," I say, wiping the sheen of sweat from my forehead with my just-as-sweaty forearm, "he thought he could take advantage of the situation by suggesting an inappropriate way that I could repay him for accommodating agency personnel on his base."

"I don't like where this is going," McLovin whispers conspiringly to Tony as we step out of the container.

"Ten bucks says she ripped it off," Tony announces with a smirk.

"I'll take that bet."

They both turn, Tony gesturing for me to finish the story.

"Well, technically, you both win. I didn't rip it off." McLovin starts to protest, but I hold up a hand to stop him. "But not for lack of trying." Both men wince and cup a hand over themselves. "I let him think I was on board with his plan, then just...." I curl my fingers like

I'm holding an air dick and jerk my hand down while bringing up the other hand, fisted, to where Handsy Hank's face would be. "I heard through the grapevine that he had internal stitches to support the damaged muscle."

"Gato montés," McLovin says with a rolling laugh. "That's justice served, if you ask me."

"That's what I thought too." We high-five and turn to Tony.

Tony shoots me a wink as he tosses a six-inch knife into the air, letting it spin twice before catching it midair. "He's on that growing list." He taps the razor-sharp tip against his temple. "That's a promise, Half Pint."

That should not make me damp between my thighs.

Shit, I did *not* pack enough underwear for this mission if he plans to keep doing things like that.

"You two need a damn room," McLovin grumbles and turns to leave.

"What?" Tony and I question innocently at the same time.

"The sexual tension on the chopper was so thick I debated jumping out and hitchhiking to Cartagena."

I consider that for a second. "Is that why you've treated me like your little sister? Don't get me wrong, I love it since one SEAL is enough for this girl. Just wondering."

He gently pats the top of my head and starts to respond, but Tony's words shock the hell out of both of us.

"It's because he's gay," Tony says nonchalantly while rocking back on his heels, scanning the base.

"What?" McLovin says, disbelief dripping into his deep tone.

"Yeah, well, I just assumed." Tony shrugs. "It's not an issue, so I never brought it up."

McLovin leans heavily against me, vibrating with restrained laughter.

"What made you come to that very wrong conclusion, T?"

Tony's features soften in confusion. "Someone mentioned you dance professionally, so I just assumed ballet or something like that. Plus, I've never seen you at any of the meet-ups with a girl or taking

Chapter 13

one home after. Like I said, it doesn't affect your role as a SEAL or as my friend, so I never brought it up. Figured you would tell me when you were ready."

McLovin hunches over, laughing so hard he has to support himself with his hands pressed to both knees. When he looks up, his cheeks are flushed and his eyes are watery from laughing so hard.

"T, we've known each other a while. Hell, you've been my platoon lead for a long time. You know I respect the hell out of you, so don't take offense when I say, what the ever-loving hell are you talking about? I'm not gay."

"You're not?" Tony questions.

"Nope. I'm a pussy man through and through."

"Gross," I interject.

"And the dancing thing, what you heard, was half right. I dance... at a strip club." The end of my ponytail whips against my cheek with how fast I swivel to face McLovin. I eye his lean body, imagining what's beneath those loose fatigues. "A ladies' club outside San Diego."

"Huh," Tony says and shrugs at the same time. "Cool. You guys ready to eat? I'm fucking starving."

McLovin smacks Tony on the back and grips his shoulder.

Joking about Tony's misunderstanding and McLovin's dancing hobby, we head for the mess hall. I nod to the few soldiers we pass, finding myself smiling for no reason. The comfort of being included, like I belong with these two, is amazing. It makes all those nights alone, both while on assignment and not, feel that much more hollow.

How will I ever be able to go back to working alone after this?

First, I have to survive Rico a second time, then decide if this crazy career path I've been racing down my entire life is the one I want to continue on.

And if I do want to leave the agency... I have to figure out a way to do it while still breathing.

14

TONY

The butt of my rifle digs into my shoulder, the thick underbrush doing its best to trip me up as I stalk through the jungle with McLovin and Elliot at my back. Face covered in black and green paint, dressed in black tactical pants and a long-sleeve snug black Dri-Fit shirt, if anyone is on the lookout for us, they'll need night vision like us to track our movements.

Three quick taps on my shoulder have me stopping short. With her goggles tilted to the compass between her fingers, Elliot raises a flat palm and points due north before curling four fingers down.

One more mile.

Thank fuck. Give me the ocean every damn day over this swamp-ass place. If I didn't know better, I'd think just inhaling the thick air would keep me hydrated instead of doing the opposite.

There's an insistent urge to make sure Elliot is drinking enough water because of the climate and her injuries.

I adjust my grip on the assault rifle to hold myself back. What the hell did those CIA bastards put her through in their so-called operation readiness assessment? I'm no fool. I know there are other injuries that they inflicted on her without leaving a visible mark on her body, like her wheezing, as if her throat was shredded raw.

But of course, that didn't stop me from feeling every inch of her in the shower and then fucking her until we were both nearly too spent to make the mission briefing. Remembering her soft skin, those muscular legs wrapped around my waist, and her nails digging into the back of my neck makes my dick twitch against my boxer briefs.

Not now, damn idiot. Thinking about us will get us killed down here. I need to keep a clear head, all thoughts away from Elliot's perfect body and sweet pussy.

It takes longer than expected to reach our destination because of an active drug operation, several portable tents lined up in a small clearing processing whatever shit they're selling, that we had to skirt around to not draw attention to ourselves.

With the processing camp several meters at our back, I catch sight of a structure through the scope.

I drop to a knee, the moist soil leaking through my already damp pants, and hold up a tight fist. Elliot slides past me, now taking the lead as we creep closer to the shed.

The door, heavier than the outside rotten wood, doesn't make a sound when I pull it open for the other two to slip inside. Giving our surroundings one more survey, I follow, slipping inside the CIA safe house.

The crack of plastic sounds through the dark silence followed by a soft glow emitting from three military-grade glow sticks. Elliot tosses them to the dirt and strips off her gear. Hooks line the wall, offering the perfect place to hang our guns and goggles, hopefully helping it all dry faster despite the humidity. After stripping off my boots, I wring out my damp socks and switch them out with a clean pair from my pack. Across from me, McLovin does the same before moving on to his sopping-wet shirt. I glare in jealousy as he rips it over his shoulders without care of what we'll see beneath, wrings it out, and hangs it on a spare hook.

"We're less than two miles from a small town several of Rico's men frequent," Elliot starts. "And by town, I mean a shitty bar and brothel. I used this shed once or twice during the last operation to hide weapons, meet my handler, things like that. It's secure but not soundproof." McLovin and I both nod in understanding. "We'll sleep here tonight, head out tomorrow morning to see if we can gain any information on Rico's whereabouts."

"Sounds good," I say, pitching my voice lower than normal, even though the pounding rain on the roof will easily cover the sound of our voices. With a groan, I ease down to the floor, placing both forearms on my bent knees. "What will happen if someone recognizes you? Won't that tip off that bastard?"

She nods while stripping out of her long-sleeve black shirt before starting on her canvas pants. My teeth grind together, jaw muscles tense to keep myself from ordering her to hurry the hell up with the striptease and put some dry clothes on.

McLovin's foot kicks out, connecting with my shin. I snap my gaze from Elliot's glowing skin to the smirking SEAL I now want to murder with my bare hands.

He shakes his head. I narrow my eyes to thin slits. Tilting his head toward Elliot, he shakes his head again.

It doesn't take a rocket scientist to figure out what he's getting at. Yeah, yeah, yeah, I get it. Saying something about her being half naked with him in the room would reward me with a nearly ripped-off dick or stab wound. But holy hell, the need to tear off my shirt to cover her toned body is stronger than the morning tide.

I kick back at McLovin's foot. He grins and coughs into a fist pressed against his lips to cover a laugh.

Great. He's laughing at me.

I must look like a fool, but I find myself not giving two shits.

"I guess someone recognizing me could happen, but if they do, they're more than likely more scared of me than Handsy Hank and won't say anything that could spark my crazy into action. But just to be sure, I'll go incognito and wear a hat." Her dark brows bounce up and down her forehead.

"Please stop calling him that," I grumble. Every time she does, I swear my blood pressure spikes and heat builds in my bloodstream, making me boiling hot.

"Handsy Hank. Handsy Hank. Handsy Hank."

I flip her off and lean back against the wall, closing both lids. The sound of the rain lulls me to a half-asleep, half-awake trance. McLovin whispers something to Elliot about taking first watch, quickly followed by a cold drizzle blowing inside the dryish shed, coating my already damp arm, then quickly ceasing.

Hushed movements sound around the shed. I track her all around me while keeping my eyes closed. Soon a body plops down beside me and scoots closer, sealing our sides together. Something primal thunders in my chest when her head rests against my arm and a content sigh whispers through the silence.

"You good?" I ask.

"Yeah, just a lot of memories bubbling to the surface I'd rather not remember."

"Yeah, I know exactly what you mean." If I'm feeling the pressure of unwanted memories forcing their way to the surface, then she has to be too. "Let's get some sleep. If I've learned one thing in my years of service, it's to never pass an opportunity to sleep when you can."

"Such wise words," she says, snuggling closer. "Your clothes are soaked. Take them off."

"I'm fine," I snap with heat to the words.

"I have seen you naked before. Pretty sure McLovin has too."

I work my jaw, sliding it back and forth to keep from saying something I might regret. "I said I'm fine."

"You don't have to be embarrassed. Not with me," she whispers.

There's not an ounce of pity in her voice, yet still her words make me feel weak, pointing out my insecurities. She grumbles a protest when she topples over as I push off the ground to stand.

"I said I'm fine. I'm going to relieve McLovin." I don't wait for her to say anything or beg me to stay. Ripping the night vision goggles and my gun off the hooks, I forcefully shove both feet into my unlaced boots and head outside.

Heavy cold drops of rain immediately soak the top of my head and stream down the side of my face. I'm a coward for not facing her, for running instead of telling her what failed mission caused my scars. Something won't let me speak the words out loud to her, to

Chapter 14

admit what I've kept hidden since the day we met. She doesn't know it was my SEAL team or have a clue it was me who hauled her bloody body out of that damn house, keeping us both from dying that night.

What I can't figure out, the question I haven't been able to answer from day one, is why does it matter if she knows or not? I guess I don't want to see her expression when she finds out. Because no matter what, things will change between us; for better or worse, her perception of me will shift. I definitely don't want her gratitude or for her to feel like she owes me. I did my job that night, that's all. What happened that night is best kept in the past, shoved down deep into the back of my mind where the grief and feeling of utter failure can't overtake me.

"Figured you'd be balls deep the moment I stepped out," the asshole says without glancing my way when I step beside him.

I give the area a quick scan before bending down and lacing up my boots to keep the rain from slipping inside any more than it already has.

"We're on a mission." That's an accurate statement, and hopefully he'll buy it as the only reason I'm not still inside that shed with the only woman who can tie me up in knots like this. "You go sleep. I'll take this watch."

"What happened?" I turn my head and stare him down, though he can't tell considering the goggles. "Come on, T. There's only one reason you'd leave that woman in there alone."

"And what's that?" I grumble just loud enough to be heard over the rain slapping the fat leaves hovering high above our heads.

"Clearly, because you're a dumbass."

"Watch it, Lovall."

He shifts in place, adjusting the gun to rest across his chest. "I told you I respect the hell out of you, man. But whatever's going on with you since that mission is in your head and negatively affecting all aspects of your life. We all lost friends that night, not just you, but we're moving on like our brothers would've wanted. Hell, you're healed and still not back on active duty, for fuck's fake."

"Stay out of it."

"Fuck that, T. You're my friend and lead. I won't let you fuck up whatever you two have that seems to be a good thing for you both. I've been with you two for all of twenty-four hours now, and you're different with her around. Hell, maybe even when she's not. And that's a good thing."

"Is it now?" I tighten my grip on the gun, hoping the comfort of the weapon will ease my growing agitation.

"Fine. If you're not going to hit that tonight—"

I whirl around and grab him around the throat, choking off his next words. "Don't you fucking touch her. She's off-limits."

"Because of the mission," he mocks. I tighten my hold, but he just smiles like the crazy ass we all are. "Right." With a hard shove, he dislodges my hold. "Figure your shit out, T, or you'll miss out on something that some of us would kill for."

Keeping my focus on the dense jungle, I listen to his retreating steps and mumbled curses as he stomps back to the shed.

He's right, not that I'd tell him that. I need to get over whatever is holding me back from telling her everything and moving on with my life. Show her what I'm too disgusted to even look at in a damn mirror.

My stomach sours at the thought of her look of revulsion when I allow her to see the damage.

No. McLovin is wrong. What she and I have isn't special. It's a diversion. Whatever is going on between us will end the moment we return home with Rico in custody. Elliot will move on to the next CIA operation, and I'll go back to...

Nothing.

My heart gives a painful squeeze. I'll go back to the empty existence alone in my shitty apartment, eagerly waiting for the next mission to at least have something to fucking do—to be needed.

No matter how much the idea of going on without her in my life hurts, that's what will happen for her benefit. She's a rising star with the CIA, and I'm a damaged, broken sailor going nowhere fast.

Elliot and I are a flash in the pan. Burning hot and bright, but only for a split second before vanishing. It might not be what I want,

Chapter 14

the idea of Elliot walking out of my life and moving on hurting worse than a damn gunshot wound, but it has to happen. I have nothing to offer to make someone like her stay.

Divorced, cheating asshole, broke bastard with no family, and wounds so deep they might never heal.

Who would want that?

Elliot deserves better than me.

I refuse to drag her down to my level, holding her back from becoming all she can become.

A flash in the pan. That's all we are.

Even if I would give anything to turn our flash into an infinite blaze.

15

ELLIOT

I'm still gaping at the far wall, hurting in places I did not know could feel pain, when the door eases open. My aching heart leaps into my throat at the same time anger flashes only to vanish, leaving an empty feeling in my chest when McLovin steps through instead of my asshole seaman. He removes his gear piece by piece, sliding down the wall across from me once he's done.

It's in the silence that I know the two talked out there. It's too awkward, heavy between us when he's been all jokes and easy banter since I met him. My curiosity and desperate need for answers make every second seem like a year.

"So," I drawl, hoping I sound as casual as I do not feel, "everything good out there?" What I really want to know is if Tony mentioned why he overreacted and just fucking left me in here alone, hurt, pissed, and worried. The worried part is a new concept, a foreign feeling. Worried about us, if there's even an us to worry about.

McLovin grunts a noncommittal response. Making more noise than necessary, he adjusts his large frame along the dirt, grumbling about being uncomfortable, and leans back, eyes closed.

"Okay, fine. If that's the way you want to play it." Reaching forward, I grab one of the glow sticks and chuck it at his chest. "Level with me. What's his deal, and why is he being a fucking asshole?"

Straight to the point. Should've done that in the first place instead of acting all normal and nice.

When the hard plastic smacks his chest, he peeks one eye open. "Cut him some slack, woman. He's still working through shit from that fucked-up mission, gato montés. Give him some space and time to do it. I'm shocked you're pressing him, considering."

"Considering what?" I sigh. "That I'm as fucked in the head as he is?"

"Considering being back here must be hard for you both. I'm sure being back stirs up some agonizing memories."

My stomach twists in knots. "Right. Sure, it's difficult for me, but why him?"

Please don't say because he was in Colombia eight months ago.

"That mission here in Colombia." His other eye pops open. Raising both knees, he rests his forearms on top. "You didn't know?"

I shake my head. There are too many questions I need answered, but I can't ask a single one, my thoughts and words frozen.

"Dumbass. Figures he wouldn't tell you. T hasn't recovered from losing so many of his men." I swallow, my throat suddenly dry. "They were my friends too, but he's taking it the worst since he was the lead and only escaped dying with our brothers because of you."

My lungs seize. All I can do is blink at the confused SEAL.

"Shit," he curses. "You didn't know that either. He didn't tell you?"

My wet hair slaps on my shoulders with another quick head shake.

"Listen, it's not my place to tell." Reaching back, McLovin rubs at his neck. "He's gonna fucking kill me. I can see his vindictive damn smile now while he carves out my heart."

"Tell. Me." When he doesn't immediately give me the answers I need, I leap up from the floor and lunge across the small space. Knife in hand, I slam against him, following him to the ground until I'm on top and the tip of the knife is a hairbreadth from slicing his jugular. "Tell. Me. Now, merman."

"Easy there, gato montés," he whispers. "Now get off me before I toss your tiny ass across this shithole, pissing off both you and T."

Knowing he's right and that I couldn't hurt him even if he refuses to tell me all he knows, I climb off him, shoving the blade back into its sheath.

His dark eyes lock with mine, clearly annoyed at my aggression, while brushing the dirt off his arms. "T was the first one in the house that night and the one who found you. While the others cleared the place searching for Rico, he hauled you outside. Barely got out when the explosion hit—"

"Just as we exited," I say. The hazy memories from that night filter through. The feeling of the humid night air, the unbearable pain, and the intense heat mixed with the scent of burning flesh. "The SEAL who got me out, who saved my life that night. That was Tony?" McLovin gives a hesitant nod. "Oh my...." I cover my sob with the back of my hand. "His back."

No wonder he didn't want me to see his scars. He knew I would ask what happened, and he didn't want me to know.

"There was a lot of damage, plus the fact that they couldn't operate until he was back on the ship. The doctors pulled debris that was imbedded from the house and his gear from the muscle—"

I hold up a hand, stopping him. He relaxes like he's grateful I did.

"And burns." He dips his chin. I wipe the tears leaking from both eyes. Everything he hates about himself is because of me.

"You?" I rasp, unshed tears making my throat raw.

A sad expression washes away the look of concern on his face. "Wasn't there." He stretches out his leg and taps a finger on top of his knee. "Twisted it on a prior mission, so it sidelined me for Colombia." Tap, tap, tap goes his finger. "And not a night goes by when I don't lie in bed wondering why. Why I wasn't there with them. Why them?"

"I don't know," I blurt. "I don't know what happened that night. What changed? Everything was good. It's why I entered the password signaling the SEAL team. Then... then things went to shit, and Rico's men...." I'm a rambling idiot now as the words just come flowing out. "They nearly killed me. Rico nearly killed me. I almost died that night, but I didn't because he saved me." Out of nowhere, my confusion and grief morph to anger. "Do you know how many nights I lay awake wondering who carried me out of that hellhole so I could thank him? Why wouldn't he tell me?" I demand, pointing the knife at McLovin's face. "Why didn't he tell me?"

His face pinches in a grimace. "Not sure, gato montés. You'll have to ask him that to get your answer. But I have a theory if you'll calm down enough to hear it."

I slowly lower the knife and cross my arms.

"Because we're protectors. We save lives, and we also take them if needed. We've all had a civilian, or even other military brothers and sisters, hold us up on a pedestal after we've helped them out of the worst day of their lives. Maybe T wanted an even playing field. For you to not judge him or praise him for doing something he can't forget. He lost brothers in arms that night, and the way we're wired, we don't talk about it because when we do, we remember."

"But if anyone would understand, it's me," I whisper, allowing the hurt to bleed through my voice.

"Then talk to him. Not me, to *him*. Because I can tell you right now, he's so caught up in his head out there, he won't come in here on his own. You'll have to go to him."

Not wasting a second, I press my palms to the cool dirt to stand. My soaked pants refuse to pull over my clammy skin. With a string of curses in various languages, I give up on getting dressed and forcefully kick them off my feet until they fly across the shack, landing beside an amused McLovin.

Fuck this. We're in the middle of nowhere, and it's dark as hell out there. Clothing is a suggestion, not required.

With only a black sports bra, tiny matching boy shorts, night vision goggles perched on the top of my head, and an AK-47 slung across my shoulder, I reach for the door.

"Elliot." I glance over my shoulder, finding McLovin digging in one of the packs. "Don't take it personally. He had his reasons, and if I know T, it was more about something he's trying to work through than anything to do with you. And here." A can sails through the air straight for my face. I barely catch it before it breaks my nose. "The bugs in this place are prehistoric. Better lather up if you're going out there like that."

He's right. The mosquitos here will drain me dry if I don't put on a layer of protection. Rubbing the oily mixture onto my legs, stomach, and arms, I toss the can back to him with a retreating "Thanks."

The moment the door closes, all-consuming darkness swallows me whole. Slipping the night vision goggles over my eyes, I press the On switch. Instantly, everything previously doused in inky darkness shifts to gray. Touching another switch to add heat sensor, I search the area for my dumbass SEAL through the spitting rain.

I sigh a relieved breath, finding him twenty paces to the right, almost completely concealed by a massive tree's thick trunk.

He notices my nearly silent approach, just a tiny tilt of his head in my direction, but doesn't turn. My pulse races like I'm running from a live grenade as I approach with the worry that he'll tell me to leave, or worse, not acknowledge me at all. I won't force him to talk it through, make him relive those terrible memories and pain. It's fresh here, the smells and feel of the air, like I've been sucked into a time warp that shot me back eight months. So I get it if talking about it here, on our first night in the country where both of our lives changed forever, is too much.

But a desperate part of me wants him to talk to me, to ask me to stay out here even if it's just to stand in silence processing it all—together. I want to be his strength like he was for me two nights ago when I exposed my stained soul.

The rotting leaves and plants crunch under my boots. Stopping at his side, I give him a second to start the conversation, but he never does.

"Why?" I ask, jumping straight to the point.

His goggles turn my way. "Where the hell are your clothes?"

"Inside. Answer the question, Seaman."

"You'll have to be more specific than that, Half Pint."

A flood of relief washes away some of the hurt at hearing the nickname I used to hate.

"More specific, huh? Okay, how's this? Why the hell didn't you tell me?" A fresh rise of anger swells. Dropping the gun, which swings to my side thanks to the shoulder strap, I shove him with as much force as I can muster. Of course, the jackass doesn't even move. *Fuck him and his fucking gigantic body.* "You're an asshole, you know that?"

Whoops. There goes not taking his way of dealing with trauma personally.

"Oh, I'm well aware of my faults. Being an asshole is at the very top."

"He told me." I swear Tony stills, not even breathing as he stares down at me. Stupid jungle and its darkness. "That it was you who—"

"Don't," he growls. "Whatever you were about to say, don't. I did my job that night. I didn't save you. I did a job."

"Liar." I shove him again.

This time his hand snaps out and wraps around my bicep, keeping me at arm's length.

"Maybe I am. Maybe I was lying to myself thinking it would be better that you didn't know who I am, what I did so you wouldn't ask for the details that are still too difficult to say out loud or feel fucking obligated to me."

"Obligated?" I ask condescendingly.

"I'm not your hero, Elliot. I'm no one's hero. I'm a liar, a cheater, a fucking terrible husband, and an asshole to everyone who gets close to me. Those are not the qualities of a man to be put on a pedestal, not of the man you deserve."

"Excuse me?"

Tony's grip relaxes, his hand falling to his side. "I'm not your hero."

I wave a hand, dismissing this ridiculousness. "Not that part, you idiot. The part where you're standing there telling me what I fucking deserve. I'm a grown-ass woman who can make my own decisions. If I decide you're a fucking hero, then you're my fucking hero. You got that?" I ram my pointer finger into the center of his chest. "But you're not." His shoulders round inward like I just kicked the damn wind out of his lungs. "Because I don't need a hero, Seaman. If you haven't figured me out yet, I can handle most shit on my own. But after everything I've done and gone through, I can tell you one thing for certain: I don't deserve anything. I fucking take it."

His lips part, jaw going slightly slack.

"So here's where we stand. You will not decide what or who I deserve ever again. If you're questioning something, simply ask, and I'll tell you straight up what's copacetic and what's not. Am I thankful you dragged me out of that house? Hell yes. Do I see you as this perfect godlike hero? Not a chance. Not because you're not worthy of that title, Tony, but because heroes are boring with their perfection. Give me screwed-up, bloodthirsty, dominant alpha-hole all day, every day over those bitches in capes."

"I lost my men," he says so quietly I almost don't hear him. The brokenness in those words squeezes the air from my lungs.

"I know." I steady my voice, holding back the onslaught of emotions fighting to take control.

"I had to get you out. I don't know why, but you were just there, this beautiful bloody thing, and I knew I couldn't leave without you. I should've been in there with them, shouldn't have diverted from the plan—"

"And what would that have done? Would being dead make you feel better?"

"It would make me not feel this," he says, slamming a fist to his heart. I swear even the night insects and creatures still at the sheer devastation radiating off him. They too feel his pain and empathize with the grief of loss. "This constant thousand-pound weight pressing the will to keep going out of me. But I can't let it go. I can't let them go."

"Who says you have to?" Reaching high, I cup a wet palm to his cheek. "We don't get to choose when the memories release their claws, but we get to choose to keep living despite the guilt and pain. You told me yourself that I shouldn't hold myself accountable for Kurt's death because I didn't pull the trigger. Same goes for you, Tony. You didn't trigger the explosion. You did not know saving some random woman's life would alter yours. This is a fork in the road. You can either keep allowing yourself to dwell on the memories of that night or change course, to not forget about their sacrifice but to move forward and live with their memories."

"Why?" he asks. Dislodging my hold, he slips a hand around the back of my neck and pulls me to his chest. The goggles awkwardly dig into my eye sockets, but still I lean an ear as close to his chest as possible to savor the steady thump of his heart. "Why do you care?"

That's a loaded question I haven't even unpacked yet. I learned five minutes ago that the man I'm falling for is also the one who saved my life. That will take a bit to process through, but I will, just like I have everything else. Tonight is about him, to guide Tony through the maze of grief so he can find a life worth living on the other side.

Hopefully with me.

Holy fuckballs, Joker, where the hell did that come from?

Bad heart. Bad. Do not get attached to this amazing human who is a perfect match to us in every way.

"Silly seaman," I say, leaning back, realigning the goggles over my eyes. "I care, more than I should, because of *you*. Not the SEAL or the man who saved me, but you. Just Tony Hackenbreg. The man who lets me be me, who sees the hideousness inside me and smiles. And if you want to know the truth, I really, really want to be the woman who you trust enough to do the same with."

"For how long?" he asks, then slices a hand through the air, cutting himself off. "No. We're not having this conversation right now."

"Why not?" I demand.

"Because we're on an active mission and wearing night vision goggles." He bops mine with a hard flick of his fingers, making them shift on my face. "I get what you're saying, Half Pint. I do, and we'll finish this conversation another time. But tonight, we're just a SEAL and a CIA officer trying like hell to survive so we can get home."

I nod, tapping a finger against my cheek. "Okay, but, man, that's too bad for you."

He tips his head back and groans in frustration. "I'm afraid to ask." When I don't respond, he circles his hand, motioning me to continue. "Come on, out with it. I know you're dying to tell me."

He's right, but not because I want the last word.

"I was just thinking that it's a shame you feel that way because I know something you don't." I pause for dramatics and step closer, molding my body against his, and reach around, grabbing handfuls of his firm ass. "Heroes get kisses on the cheek from their girl. Alpha-holes get sucked off in the middle of the jungle."

Tony stops breathing, his chest completely still against my own. Slowly a hand slithers down my back, dipping beneath my boy shorts to grab a handful of my ass. I suck in a shocked breath when he squeezes hard enough to no doubt leave fingerprint bruises. His lips brush the shell of my ear. Heavy pants whisper past.

"Well, when you put it that way.... On your knees, Half Pint, because I invented the term 'alpha-hole,' and I intend to take you up on your offer."

With a hand pressed to the top of my shoulder, he slowly pushes me lower until my knees sink into the damp ground.

"Here, hold this." Unstrapping the gun, I pass it and the goggles into his awaiting hand. The jungle goes pitch-black the moment the goggles slip off my head. Blindly I feel up his thick legs, moving until my fingers skirt along a thick canvas belt. "Tony, I can't see shit." I swear I can feel his sinister smile. "If a snake gets close to me, you haul my ass off the ground and bolt. If I feel anything slither against me while your cock is in my mouth, I swear on everything that's holy that I will bite it clean off."

I tighten my grip on his hips when he takes a step backward. Making quick work of the utility belt, I pop the button of his tactical pants and ease the zipper down. His responding groan when I dip my hand into his boxer briefs sounds above the leaking rain, sending my anticipation into overdrive.

I've wanted this since he verbally bitch-slapped Handsy Hank earlier. Toss in the news revealed in the shed and I'm borderline desperate to show him how much I appreciate everything he's done for me that night and today. And maybe even beyond that. He's changing me for the better. I'm more stable, clear-headed, and less rash. I still want to blow shit up, but I'm actually thinking through the repercussions before acting.

Go me.

His hard cock is hot against my palm. Wrapping my fingers around it, I give him a hard squeeze, enjoying his hiss of pleasure as I work his pants down his upper thighs. Inching closer, I press the swollen head to my lips, sucking an inch before pulling back.

"Fucking hell, woman," Tony curses above me.

I do it again, hoping to push him to the breaking point. Never have I wanted a guy to take control when I'm the one in the driver's seat, but Tony is different. A desperate part of me wants him to slip his fingers through my hair, fist the strands until it hurts, and force his thick cock past my lips and down my throat.

Thankfully, Tony obliges my inner dark fantasy.

A stinging pain along my scalp has my lips parting on a gasp. Taking advantage of the opportunity, he holds my head in place and pushes deep into my greedy mouth. My teeth scrape along the sensitive skin, his hold in my hair tightening in response.

His thighs flex under my tight grip I'm using for support as he thrusts in and out, each time going deeper until he's tapping the back of my throat.

"That's it, Half Pint," he encourages. "Swallow me like a good girl."

Fuck.

A new rush of dampness soaks the crotch of my boy shorts. On my knees in front of this warrior, making his own quake with pleasure, and his dirty, praising words is too much for this girl. Prying one hand from around his thigh, I snake it lower, dipping inside my underwear.

The first brush of my fingertip along my swollen, slick clit has me moaning around Tony's dick, still pumping in and out. A low groan has my eyes peeking upward even though I can't see anything in the dark without the goggles.

"What's that naughty hand doing down there?" Tony asks. My

hand stills. I don't respond until he slides all the way out. A single finger presses beneath my chin, tipping my entire face upward. "I didn't say stop."

With a sigh of relief, I glide my fingers lower, pushing two deep inside.

"Is it enough, baby?" Fuck him, he knows it's not. "Or do you want what was in your mouth fucking that sweet pussy of yours instead of your thin fingers?"

Instead of answering, I stand in a single smooth motion, tugging my boy shorts down until they dangle around my ankles. All I feel is the quick brush of moving air before two hands grip around my waist, hauling me off my feet.

"Wrap your legs around me, baby, and I'll give you what you want."

Zero hesitation on my end. Wrapping both legs around his trim waist, I hook my ankles together, the move sealing my center to his thick cock. Unable to stop, I flex my thighs, slicking his dick as I grind against him. Shoving me back an inch, he positions himself outside my entrance and shoves me down until he's deep inside.

"Fuck yes," I groan and bite his shoulder, getting more T-shirt than skin. "More, more," I chant.

"Needy little thing, aren't you?" Tony grunts into my ear as he thrusts deeper than before. "Don't worry, Half Pint, I fucking love it. I'll sink my cock into your desperate pussy all day, every day. Holy shit, you're squeezing me like a damn vise."

With his hands gripping both hips, he lifts me higher, slamming me down at the same time he thrusts upward, hitting a new angle that has stars sparkling behind my closed lids. His grunts and praises drive my need higher, making me desperate for each hard thrust.

Too soon, from the pent-up need that drove me wild all day, I explode. Crying against his shoulder, I bite down again, harder this time, as the intense orgasm shakes me from the inside out. Before I can come all the way down from the high, I'm yanked upward and slowly lowered back down until my knees once again sink into the moist jungle floor.

Knowing what was coming, I immediately parted my lips just as his slick head pressed against them. Fisting my ponytail, Tony wasted no time thrusting deep.

"Swallow for me, baby. Work that throat around—"

His words cut off the moment I did as he asked. With a curse, he pushed in deeper, my nose hitting his stomach. With no warning, he exploded, shooting hot spurts down my throat. I swallowed every drop, loving the unique flavor of his release mixed with my own.

Sitting back on my heels, I wipe my mouth with the back of my hand. Tony snatches the two fingers that had been inside me and hauls them higher until both slick fingers dip into his mouth, his tongue flicking the tips.

Unable to see a damn thing, I can only offer a sated grin into the inky darkness.

Seems I've met my match in every way.

And I'll do anything to keep him safe, even if that means giving up my own life for his.

So maybe this is love. An explosive, edgy, bloodthirsty type of love.

Not an ordinary love, but an unusual perfect for us kind.

And that's perfect enough for me.

16

TONY

Discreetly, I rub my ass against the top of the wooden bar stool in hopes of relieving an insistent itch. I hold back a throaty moan from the brief relief before the itch fucking comes back more intense than before.

"You look like you're humping the stool," McLovin says, the brown beer bottle edge pressed to his lips suppressing his smile. "Though, I'd say that's what happens when you get head in the middle of the motherfucking jungle. What were you thinking?"

"That I was about to get head in the middle of the motherfucking jungle." I rotate on the stool, desperate for a damn second without my ass feeling like it's on fire. "Damn jungle mosquitos ate my ass." I take a quick sip of my beer—no way in hell would we drink anything that isn't bottled in this shithole—and shrug. "Still worth it."

McLovin's deep laugh echoes in the bottle as he downs the remaining liquid. With a swipe along his lips, he turns, directing his attention to Elliot, who's currently working her female magic at the opposite end of the bar. A round of boisterous laughter from the small group fills the area. Yesterday we played it safe, kept Elliot hidden while trying to learn anything about Rico's current whereabouts. When that was a bust, Elliot suggested we try this place, where Rico's men frequent.

"Hope this works, T. I'm ready to get out of this humid hellhole and away from this constant case of swamp ass."

I dip my chin in agreement while keeping half my attention on Elliot. Focusing on the weathered wooden plank that makes up the bar top, I try to dislodge the ominous feeling that won't shake. The crisscross of thin white scars stands out against my tan skin as I flex and stiffen my fingers into tight fists.

"Something doesn't feel right," I say out of the corner of my mouth to McLovin. The moment I voice the unease, my pulse jumps, ticking higher, as if saying the words made the dread real. I survey the shitty bar, taking in every occupant and memorizing the details.

"T," McLovin curses, waving a hand in front of my face. I blink, not realizing my vision had turned unfocused. "We're all good, brother."

Air wheezes down my dry throat, burning in my lungs with every rapid breath. My fingers wrap around the edge of the bar, knuckles going white. "No, you're wrong. There's something—"

His large hand cups my shoulder and squeezes—hard. The discomfort snaps me out of the downward spiral. "T, we're fine. Your crazy-ass girl down there is fine. I think it's all in your head."

"You don't know that," I say, jaw locked, teeth grinding together. "Any second this place could go up, shit could go down, and—"

"That's the case for every fucking mission we go on. T, you're working yourself up because this is your first time back in the field, and if that wasn't bad enough, you're here in the same damn country where it all happened. Being back here must trigger PTSD." I huff and try to shrug out of his hold, but he doesn't let up. "Yeah, yeah, I know we're the baddest badasses on the planet, but what you went through, that shit will affect everyone, even us."

The sharp ends of my short hair prickle along my palm as I scrub the top of my head, thinking over what he said. It makes sense, but does that mean I'm broken forever?

"If that's true, how can I trust my gut again? What if I'm this fucked in the head—"

"First off, you're not fucked in the head. Like I said, it's a total shitty hand that your first mission back in the game is in the same place you almost died and lost several good SEALs. That would mess with anyone, even me. I'm not worried because I wasn't with you guys that night. If I had been, I'd probably be in the same boat as you right now. Hell, maybe worse. Talk yourself off that ledge, man. Take a second to really look around to pinpoint what's off, not just the feeling in your gut. Then point it out to me, and I'll give it a quick check with a clear perspective."

I scan the bar, taking in every detail from the patrons to the exits.

One older male bartender is more focused on the rowdy bunch of three in the far corner than our empty beer bottles.

The three who are clearly hammered, slurring, and yelling, allowing all to hear their conversation.

Two exits, front door and one in the rear. That will be our safest exit if shit goes down.

Out of the few patrons, only three are carrying small handguns, nothing larger.

Two fuckers corner Elliot against the bar, growing closer by the second. I expect to feel a rush to storm over there and rip them away from my girl. Only pride rises in my chest as I watch her work. She's in complete control and can handle herself against the two if needed.

That leaves me and McLovin as the only others to be suspicious over.

My chest rises and falls with a heavy breath. "You're right," I admit. Rubbing a hand over my face, I pinch the bridge of my nose to refocus my damn mind. "Fuck, this sucks."

"Yep. But we are human, T."

"Shut your hole, Lovall," I say with an annoyed huff. "We're more than human."

His head tilts one way, then the other, as he considers my very accurate statement. "Maybe, but in this type of situation, we're just as human as the rest of them. Let me know if it gets to be too much again. I'll help free you from the past."

I try to offer some smartass, cocky comment about not needing help, but the words catch in my throat.

Shit, did a moth fly into my mouth, or is what's blocking my throat emotional shit from the heaviness of the conversation?

"Thanks, man," I say, clearing my throat.

Movement at the end of the bar snags our attention. My half pint pushes off the bar, says something to the two men, and starts our way, the locals watching her sashaying ass the entire way.

"Hello, boys," Elliot says in a too-chipper voice that immediately raises my suspicion as she wedges herself between our two bar stools. With a conspiring glance down the bar, she hangs an arm on each of our shoulders and leans in even closer. "So I have good news and bad news. Which do you want first?"

"Ah hell, Half Pint." She shoots me a glare at the same moment she smacks the back of my head. My smile widens even though I should be pissed at the reprimand. "Come on now. I thought the name was growing on you."

"Yeah, when we're alone, Seaman." I snarl at the name, and she lifts a single dark brow as if I just proved her point. She tips her head toward McLovin. "This big guy needs to be afraid of me, not think I'm some harmless bite-size person who won't retaliate if he gives in to the urge to pat me on top of the head." That hard glare releases me to swing toward my fellow SEAL. "And just as a friend-to-friend public service announcement, if you ever pat me on the head like a child, I will slice off your hands and shove both up your ass."

"Noted," McLovin says with a nervous chuckle. "Now go on, gato montés, share the good news first."

Her small fingers tap along my shoulder in rapid succession, the only outward sign of her tension. "They gave me a very generalized locale where our little asshole arms friend has shifted his operations."

"Nice work," I murmur.

A sudden shift in the air, the talking and laughter from earlier silenced, has the hairs on my arms standing on end. The bar's edge presses against my ribs when I pitch forward to see what changed in the last three minutes. I play it off, pretending to not notice or care about the glares and hostility radiating off the other patrons and even the older bartender.

"Based on the assholes staring us down like they want to kill us, I'm afraid to hear the bad news," I murmur.

"Oh, right, that. You're correct in reading the room, Seaman. Ten points for the Navy." I don't even ask what in the hell kind of scorecard she's keeping up in that mind of hers. "They want to kill us. Well, me," she says with way too much fucking glee, bouncing on the toes of her boots. "The idiots I was talking to said if they gave me the information I wanted on Rico, then they'd have to kill me. Which, let's be honest, is ironic since that's my agency's famous line, but anyway—"

"Elliot," I warn, cutting her off. Movements casual, I slide both hands from the bar and rest them on top of my thighs in case shit goes down in a rain of bullets. I want my weapons easily reachable. "What did you do?"

"Oh, right." She gives my shoulder a soft pat. "My response was 'Have fun trying and dying.'"

McLovin's deep laugh booms through the space while his palm slams to the aged bartop, making all the drinks tremble. The other men in the bar tense, hands jerking to their sidearms.

"Well, then." McLovin's dark brown eyes shine with excitement when they meet mine. "Let's have some fun, shall we?"

"Yay," Elliot exclaims, wrapping her arms around his shoulders for a hug. "I knew you would be the fun one."

Pushing off my friend, Elliot twists toward the men itching to kill us, a Glock already clutched in each hand. Our stools tip back, slamming to the ground from the quick action of McLovin and me standing, more than ready for the fight.

McLovin goes for his gun while I reach for my knife, sliding it from its sheath. A quick flick of my wrist and it rotates through the air, finding its mark deep in the bartender's throat. Eyes wide, the man stumbles backward into the shelf of cheap liquor bottles. The shotgun in his hands, aimed at my girl, tumbles to the ground.

Pop pop pop.

Alarmed shouts blend with the rapid gunfire. The captivating scent of used gunpowder engulfs the stale air, combining with the sharp tang of fresh blood. My tongue darts out, slicking my dry lips as my excitement skyrockets, chasing away my earlier uncertainty.

Less than a minute after the fight began, only our combined deep breaths sound. Tendrils of smoke rise from the barrels of Elliot's guns, still raised and ready. Stalking forward, I keep my awareness sharp on the off chance she missed the mark, only wounding one of the men lying on the ground. Elliot toes the side of one body with her blood-splattered combat boot. She catches me watching her with rapid fascination and raises both brows.

"What?" she questions, holding up both hands, careful to keep the gun barrels pointed away from me and McLovin. "They started it."

With a small head shake, smirking, I use the bar as leverage and hop over, the wood groaning and cracking beneath my heavy weight. Avoiding the massive crimson puddle, I wrap my hand around the hilt of my favorite knife and tug it free from the bartender's throat.

"You think they *all* work for Suarez?" I ask no one in particular.

"Him or maybe the cartel we avoided, who don't like strange Americans snooping around town."

I absentmindedly nod, agreeing with McLovin's assessment as I survey the room. "Sucks shark balls that it came down to this, but we knew we'd run into resistance asking questions."

"Which is why we brought all the toys," Elliot chimes in from where she's picking over the dead men's guns.

"Guns," McLovin corrects. "They're guns, not toys, gato montés."

"Tomato, tomahto. And here I thought you were the fun one," she grumbles loud enough for both of us to hear. A burn flames in my cheeks from smiling so damn much. "As much fun as this is standing around the carnage, I suggest we haul our cute asses out of here. Others would've heard the gunshots by now, alerting their shitty version of a cavalry to come back up their boys."

"Let's try the back door," I suggest and turn to start that way.

"Sure, I'm down with ass play," Elliot chirps. I spin on the heels of my boots, a cloud of dust floating up from the fast movement, to shoot her a blank stare. "What? Oh. Right, you meant back door as in exit, not a sexual innuendo. Sorry, all this is a turn-on, and my mind is in the gutter apparently."

"Holy fuck," McLovin states, nearly choking on the words. "I think I'm in love with your crazy ass."

"Watch it," I command with enough bite in my tone to stop laughing. "Yes, Half Pint, I meant where we should exit this crime scene. The other—" I shoot her a wink, "—we'll discuss later."

"Oh goodie," she responds, sounding legit excited. She holsters her guns and starts for the door, smacking me hard on the ass as she passes.

Holy fuck. How in the hell am I supposed to focus on our safety and catching Rico after that? Now all I can think about is her offering that fine ass for me to sink into.

This amazing woman will be the death of me, but considering the new take on life she's breathing into me, she's worth it. Never have I had this, the tightness around my heart when I looked at someone. In this violent moment, surrounded by death, I know she's the only one for me. Elliot Smith in all her strange, sometimes volatile glory is worth living for. No more wallowing in my grief, or hiding behind a psych eval keeping me from active duty, or avoiding my best friend and wife to not feel the stab of jealousy.

Elliot, as good as she is at taking life, somehow saved mine.

We don't dick around long, narrowly avoiding a heavily armed group of hostiles that rumbles down the road seconds after we exit the bar. Barked orders and the slam of doors hit my ears just as we duck into the heavy cover of the nearby jungle. Careful to keep our movements hidden, we crouch low, weaving until the sound of voices fades. At a small clearing, we squat low in a tight circle.

"What are the coordinates of the potential new Suarez location?" I ask Elliot. After wiping some jungle shit off my hand, I reach out and clean off a smudge of blood from her right cheek.

"Thanks. And he gave nothing specific like coordinates, just vague directions." She points to my right, then left, then behind her. "He said a mile or so whichever way is southeast." A line forms between her furrowed brows. "Now that I have a second to process what he said, it's odd."

"What do you mean?"

She shifts back and forth on the balls of her feet. "Because the dead asshole talked like it's a new operation altogether, not just a new location for Rico."

I hum my agreement. "You're right, it sounds suspicious. I wouldn't put it past Rico to plant those shitheads hoping to capture you when we came sniffing around for information."

"Possible. Or one of those drug operations we passed on the way to the agency shed is Rico's and he's venturing into the drug trade."

"There are too many questions we can't answer without intel," I cut in. "Let's find the operation and do some recon, then decide what to do from there."

We all nod in unison.

"Great. Now." Elliot looks at me and cringes. "Which way is southeast again?"

Despite the danger of drawing attention to our location, I can't hold back an answering boisterous laugh.

I'm in deep shit. How can I not fall helplessly in love with her?

If that bastard at the bar wasn't dead, I'd kill him. A mile southeast, my ass. After walking a grueling three miles in the direction he showed, circling back, and splitting up several times to cover more ground, we find the camp: several ten-by-ten pieced-together metal buildings scattered around a decent-size natural clearing deep in the Colombian jungle.

Squatting low, rifle poised and ready, I monitor the activity through the scope from my position while Elliot does the same on the other side of the camp, McLovin stationed somewhere in

Chapter 16

between. The afternoon's sun cuts through the jungle canopy, heating the air to the point of suffocation.

Knowing water is key to survival here, I set the gun down and take several long pulls from my canteen, processing what I've seen the last hour.

There only seems to be a handful of females. A few young-looking girls were here already, and once, an incoming truck unloaded five to seven more, herding them into a metal building. One thing is clear: this definitely isn't a drug operation like we assumed. And it probably isn't Rico's, or at least not something our intelligence office knows about. Rico Suarez is an evil bastard who deserves a slow, gruesome death, but from what we know, he's never dabbled in this, which I can only assume based on what I've seen is human trafficking.

The buzz of several mosquitos hums in my ear, but the heavy-duty repellent we brought keeps them from biting every inch of exposed skin. Wish I would've thought about applying that shit to my exposed ass last night, though most would agree I was within my rights to have forgotten, considering the circumstances. A knowing grin spreads as I scratch the multitude of bites along my ass while remembering the best damn blow job ever. Maybe it was the danger or watching her pouty lips wrap around my cock through the night vision goggles, but fucking hell, it's an experience I'll always remember.

I'm almost certain every moment spent with Elliot will be a memory I'll never forget. That's my girl, unforgettable in a crazy, sexy-as-hell way. Vulnerable in the right moments and tough as diamonds the next. How she switches it off and on is damn amazing. She reminds me so much of Lucia in that way it's scary. But Lucia only shows that softer side with G, and it seems Elliot only does the same with me.

A swell of male pride fills my chest.

I offer her the safety net she needs to let go—no one else, just me. Divorced, broke, asshole me. And she knows it all now. Knows what I offer, and for some fucked-up reason, she still wants me.

How in the hell I got lucky enough to land in her path is beyond me. I'm already in deep, which will suck when she leaves, but I can't stop myself from falling for her. It would be like asking the ocean to stop the tide or the moon to not give way to the sun.

"Fucking hell," I mutter to myself. "What am I, a damn poet now? Grow a set of steel SEAL balls, Hackenbreg."

Movement in my periphery catches my attention, but immediately I relax at the familiar gait and frame.

"You seeing this shit?" McLovin asks as he squats beside me, balancing on the balls of his feet.

"Yeah. What the hell? This can't be Rico's operation, right? I've heard no one mention he was into trafficking on top of arms dealing. You?"

McLovin's shoulders rise and lower as he tips back his canteen. "I don't know, man," he says in a rush after chugging his water. "Things have been quiet for eight months. Who knows what other revenue streams he created as a side gig while he felt the heat of the CIA and Navy on the arms dealing side?"

"True," I acknowledge. "But this?" I discreetly point toward the camp. "Human trafficking is a long way from selling guns and shit."

"Not really." Lovall and I both swivel, guns raised. Not concerned at all about the two rifles aimed at her head, Elliot smiles and sinks to her knees beside me. "He already has trade routes established. It would be easy for him to just reverse it all."

"In what way?" Fuck, why does she have to be brilliant too? Well, besides the directionally challenged issue, which is cute as hell.

"Studies show most of the girls come from poor families in South America and Central Europe. Those are two areas where Rico sold guns, which means he had to get the guns from the US, where he's buying them, to here and farther south somehow. If he reverses the trade route, brings girls from here to be transferred through Central America along the previous routes taken for guns coming from the States, then it would be easy. He would just need a partner who has contacts in the skin trade."

"Fucking hell," McLovin says, disdain dripping from the two

words. He adjusts his grip on his rifle and stares down the scope. "Can we kill them all now?"

"No," I say at the same time Elliot gives a "Hell yes." I shoot her a side-eye glare. "Not yet. We need to—"

"Oh," Elliot grimaces and shifts her weight.

"Oh hell, what did you do?"

"I really thought you would say yes to killing all those bastards and getting the girls to the Cartagena base."

"Elliot," I grit out. "What did you do?"

A loud explosion rings in my ears and vibrates the ground. Black smoke billows up, rising higher and higher toward the other end of their camp. The same area Elliot was monitoring.

McLovin and I both stare her down.

"It was just a small bomb," she says, already checking the magazine of her Glock before moving to the one on her assault rifle. "One of you stays out here to offer coverage. I'd suggest Seaman over here, but I have a feeling he won't want to miss out on the fun, so that leaves you, Merman, as our sniper and backup."

"Hold on just—" Another explosion, slightly smaller than the last, booms through the jungle. Screaming and the sound of gunfire fill the air as the smoke and dust settles.

"That was the last one, I swear." She holds up her hands, smiling like a fool. "Now, let's go with my plan, yeah?"

Not waiting for a response, she leaps to stand and dashes through the heavy foliage, her short stature coming in handy and helping her move quickly without crouching.

"Good luck with that one," McLovin says while he adjusts the gun on his shoulder and leans forward to look through the scope. The gun shifts with his first shot. "Go. I'm covering you both."

"We don't have authority to do this."

"So? This shit isn't right. We can always say we thought we saw Rico if that makes you feel better."

My smile widens, and I smack him on the shoulder. "It really does." Grabbing my M4A1 assault rifle, I shove it against my shoulder and stand to follow Elliot's path.

I don't think, just fall back on my training and instincts as I race into the smoke-filled war zone. Elliot runs ahead, firing off a few shots as she steps out into the clearing. From my vantage point, I catch a group of three armed hostiles creeping along the opposite side of a building, their intent clear on sneaking up behind her.

Not today, motherfuckers. Never with my girl.

With silent steps, I follow the three around the metal building, staying hidden until they move away from their cover. Three ARs rise, one yells in Spanish for Elliot to stop but doesn't get to finish before I pull the trigger.

Three bullets, three dead sex trafficking bastards.

Good fucking riddance.

With that threat down but more to go, I step around the building to find Elliot. I'm not surprised when I spot the end of her rifle is pointed between my brows the moment I round the corner.

"Nice shot, Seaman. I think I'll keep you." She lowers the gun enough for me to catch her manic grin. "I've taken out two, plus your three. Oh, and the guy who was in the latrine when I blew it up. So that makes six. I counted at least ten minus the girls during the recon. Four more to go."

Moving as one unit, we continue to clear the camp, her at the lead and me covering her back.

"You blew up a guy on the shitter?" I ask when we duck behind a building for cover to miss a rain of bullets.

Elliot falls against the flimsy metal, smiling, her lips parted with her rapid breaths. "Yeah. It was the only place I could think of that wouldn't house women."

"Smart, Half Pint."

"You don't sound surprised."

"Of course not. On your right," I say. She swivels the barrel of her gun and fires off two rounds, taking out the man who'd somehow gotten past our earlier efforts. "Come on, there can't be that many assholes left."

"Then we take the women back to base—"

Keeping our steps steady, we shuffle down another row of sheds.

Chapter 16

"Half Pint, these women aren't you and are probably scared shitless about now. We'll need to radio the base to come get them from this encampment. There's no way they can make the trek through the jungle to get to that shit shed, and that's five miles from here, then another few to the base."

"Shit, you're right."

"You don't sound surprised," I say, smirking.

"Of course not."

I catch the movement on my right too late. But of course she doesn't. The deafening boom of her rifle rattles my teeth, vibrating along the foam ear protection stuffed down each ear. When I turn, a filthy asshole lies in the mud, a shiny silver revolver on the ground beside him. "Sorry, on your right."

A soft chuckle vibrates in my chest, and I bump her shoulder with mine before motioning to continue forward.

It takes another ten minutes to double-check the area is clear before we open the locked doors and guide the terrified women out into the fresh air. My stomach churns with disgust at the filth they were forced to live in for who the fuck knows how long. Several cringe away from me, huddling deeper into the corners. Leaving the comforting and hand-holding to Elliot, I station myself outside the buildings as she works to keep them calm.

Once every shed is emptied, Elliot urges the women to stand in the center of the camp and explains in Spanish who we are and what will happen next. Her long dark hair secured high on her head sways in the wind, the setting sun sending beams of soft light that highlight her beautiful face and intelligent amber eyes.

Fuck.

Today proved two things in my mind.

Elliot is more of a badass than some SEALs I know.

And there will be no coming back from her. She has set a bar no other woman can reach. I'm ruined by Elliot Smith, and I'm good with that. Because I'd rather have had her and my heart be left in pieces when she leaves than to have never had her at all.

17

ELLIOT

After sunset, when the darkness blankets everything it touches, the jungle comes alive in the most beautiful way. The hum of various insects and nocturnal predators prowling the night would terrify most, but not me. I smile at nothing in particular from where I lean against a thick tree trunk, watching the jungle's activities through the goggles. The smile plastered across my face hasn't dropped since we left that damn holding camp.

Whether that encampment is part of Rico's operation or someone else's altogether, I don't give a shit. I'm glad we shut it down despite the hell we might catch back home. Twenty-eight trembling, scared, and filthy women were loaded into military trucks and driven away from that hellhole. Some couldn't remember how long they'd been held at the location; others said they were occasionally released from the shed only to be loaded on the back of a truck and driven around for a few hours before being brought back.

That struck me as odd, especially since none of them could remember a woman leaving and not coming back.

If that was a human trafficking operation, well, whoever ran the logistics really sucked at the trafficking part. Transporting those women up to the States would be where the money was, not keeping what they considered inventory here in the middle of the jungle.

My head thumps back, hair catching in the edges of the rough bark as I rack my brain to recall any details Kurt relayed regarding the agency-directed operation he was assigned prior to the one with me. He'd surveyed a known trafficker for almost two years in Honduras, but I can't remember if he ever mentioned anything about the normal ins and outs of a trafficking ring.

Maybe this was normal? Keeping some backup women hidden to ship up when needed? Or maybe their trade routes are blocked, and that camp was just a temporary holding center?

It felt off.

All of it, but I couldn't put my finger on why.

A hush falls. Immediately I'm on alert, scanning the area. It's small, but movement in the distance has the hairs along my arm rising. On silent feet, I rush to the shed where McLovin and Tony should be sleeping. I don't even open the door all the way, not wanting to waste any precious seconds, before whispering for them to get geared up.

Both leap to stand in one motion, going from asleep to not only awake but alert in a blink. They move stealthily, pulling on their long-sleeve shirts and strapping on their weapons.

"What is it?" Tony's voice is low, barely audible over the pulse pounding in my ears.

"Not sure. Felt weird, then movement." I step out of their way and they both file out with me ready to fire off a few rounds for cover. Then we make our way to the jungle's camouflage. No one speaks as we hurry deeper into the darkness. When Tony holds up his fist, we all drop to a low crouch.

"Where did you see the movement?"

"I was leaning against that big tree a few yards from the shed when I saw it on my left."

Tony nods. "Were you facing the shed?"

"Yes."

"Then I'm assuming you saw the movement northeast."

Chapter 17

I nod like I have any idea if he's right or not.

The snap of a twig has his lips sealing shut. We all sink lower in hopes of staying below the small saplings and lush plants.

"Maybe it's the cartel doing a wide perimeter sweep," McLovin whispers while checking his gear.

"But if it's Rico's guys, they probably have thermal imaging on their goggles," I add.

"At least we have ours too." I nod at McLovin and adjust my goggles, switching on the thermal sensors. Red blobs in the shape of bodies flare to life. He points upward. "We need to gain some elevation to see how many we're dealing with."

"We're sitting ducks all together," I point out. "If we spread out, we can separate their little hunting party." I turn on the balls of my feet to face Tony, totally expecting him to want to keep me close but hoping I won't have to shoot him to make him realize that's a terrible idea.

"Good idea."

My jaw drops in shock.

Muffled voices float through the stale air. I sigh in relief at the wickedly smart SEALs beside me who also speak Spanish, so I don't have to translate what we're all hearing.

Based on the commands and directions of the shed, this isn't an unknown cartel doing a perimeter sweep but the worst-case scenario: Rico Suarez's minions.

"Seems like the CIA's safe shack isn't so safe," Tony grumbles.

I offer a reluctant nod. He's right. These fuckers could only find this location if they had the exact coordinates. But we kept this operation as only need-to-know, so how would our mole have known we'd be here? That I would be here?

"I don't like this," I caution as unease grips my stomach and twists. "Something isn't right."

"Agreed, but we don't have the luxury of figuring it out now. Split up, defuse the threat, then meet back here," Tony orders. "Fuck, I wish we had our radios."

The radios that are sitting in the shack slowly being surrounded by glowing red figures.

Without another word, McLovin and I split off from Tony, McLovin heading one way and me the other. Keeping as low as possible in case the fools surrounding the shed don't have thermal imaging, I hurry through the underbrush.

Keeping the shed within view, I haul ass for a minute before squatting down low in the brush. Breathing labored, throat and mouth as dry as the desert, I pitch forward, only catching myself with a hand to the moist jungle floor. Something runs across my hand, and I bite my lip to not shout a curse and gun down the offending insect. My back throbs from exertion and the need for water, but I can't worry about that now—though I think I've said that at least four or five times already today.

Blinking away the sweat dripping from my brows, I secure the butt of my gun against my shoulder and shift to get comfortable with my stomach pressed to the ground.

Now if a snake slithers across any part of my body, I will give up my position to everyone within a five-mile radius with my uncontrolled scream. Hopefully, everyone will understand, and we can just hit a reset button and go back to the regularly scheduled program.

Huh. Wow, guess I lied to Tony. I have two faults. The directionally challenged thing and being afraid of snakes. But so is half of America, so that's more of like a minor fact about Elliot Smith than a fault.

Whew. Still only have the one fault.

Winning.

Quick, rhythmic bursts of gunfire erupt through the jungle along with the sound of the bullets pinging off metal. A few fall to the ground when the ricochet bullets come back and hit the idiots. Of course a CIA safe shed is bulletproof. Clearly Rico didn't know everything about this spot. Hopefully the other secret about the shed wasn't exposed as well. We might need it to escape this shit show if more of Rico's men show up.

A flash of sparks and another from the depths of the trees. Two of

Rico's glowing red men slump to the ground, killed by my two partners before the others even know what's going on. Furious and chaotic shouts echo as they spin around, guns raised.

But they don't fire blindly toward the shots that killed their buddies. They just stand there, guns pointed.

Odd.

This is too many oddities for one day. It feels like....

Bile surges up my throat when the words clang in my head.

A trap.

The soft damp earth molds beneath my elbows and oozes between my fingers as I push to stand, its lingering moisture soaking through the sleeves of my long black T-shirt.

But I don't get far.

Something heavy slams against the back of my skull, ripping the goggles off my face and forcing me forward until my nose buries in the rotting leaves.

I struggle with every ounce of fight I have in me, shoving against the ground, kicking blindly. Bits of dirt and plants clog in my nose as I desperately try to inhale. What feels like a knee slams into the small of my back, making the pain from earlier feel like a fucking tickle. Jungle debris fills my open mouth as I scream from the pain and frustration.

I scrape my nails along the ground, catching and ripping plants and roots as I fight to dislodge the weight from my back.

Then I feel it. A knowing sharp pinch along the back of my neck.

I instantly go still, not because of the drug's immediate effect but because I know what it means.

Within seconds, my fingers and toes tingle, the sensation rushing up my appendages and racing toward my torso. Tears leak from my closed eyes as the inky darkness of the night somehow becomes darker.

Soul-crushing sadness floods through my veins and squeezes my heart in a death grip, though not because of the unknown of what's coming.

I'll never get a chance to say goodbye to the one man who allowed me to be both Officer Smith and Elliot. Tony will never know what the last few days have meant to me—to feel normal and loved and cherished. I know he and McLovin will do everything they can to find me, but it will probably be too late.

My employer was clear during their operation readiness assessment.

They would ensure Rico's capture, no matter the cost.

Even if that cost is me.

Before everything fades, a tight hold on my hair yanks my head backward, lifting me until a few chunks rip from my scalp. My back hits a hard body, head lolling forward as an arm tightens around my waist, holding me firm.

"Welcome back, Elliot."

As if that were the cue to douse me into unconsciousness, the drug takes hold and pulls me under to blissful oblivion.

18

TONY

It's like shooting fish in a barrel. Sweeping my gun an inch to the right, I line the crosshairs up with another glowing red figure and pull the trigger. *Three to go.*

Another shot rings out, leaving two idiots now standing. I glance in the direction Elliot headed but can't find her glow through the trees and heavy foliage. Everything in me demands I stop what I'm doing and check on her, make sure she's okay, but I can't. At this moment, I'm a SEAL, not a boyfriend. I'm to hold my position until we neutralize the threat like planned.

But I fucking hate the nerves fighting through the excitement of the conflict.

The pop of unfamiliar weapons snaps my attention back to the final two idiots. A machine gun in each hand, they both let loose a spray of large-round ammunition.

Rolling to the side, I take cover behind a narrow tree trunk. Bark splinters inches from my head, imbedding sharp remnants into my cheeks. I grimace, grinding my teeth when one round slices through my shirt and cuts into my bicep. Warm liquid immediately seeps out, the already sodden material of my T-shirt soaking up what it can.

What the actual fucking hell is going on?

They let us pick their friends off and now open fire around the entire jungle? That makes little sense.

Something doesn't feel right. I hesitate, wondering if maybe my instincts are off because of the last mission, but I shrug off my doubt. None of this is normal combat. I'm missing something. And I'll be damned if I let anything happen to the two who are here under my command.

Gun ready, I count the seconds, waiting for the lull in rounds to make my move. When the gunshots slow, I assume to reload another magazine, I take the few-seconds break in live fire and spin around the tree, gun raised and ready.

Two bullets. Two dead fuckers.

Surveying the area through the scope, I find a small red blob to my right. McLovin. Swinging the other way, I scan the underbrush, searching for Elliot and any lingering hostiles to take out, but don't locate either.

Dread hits me like an open-palm slap to the ball sack.

Steps calm and careful, I cover the short distance to where I assume Elliot went to hunker down. Nothing. The farther I tromp, the harder it is to breathe through the suffocating fear. Not finding her location, I circle back and race toward the shed, hoping maybe I'll find her there waiting with that wide smile of hers.

My nostrils flare with each deep inhale as I desperately suck down air to keep me calm and levelheaded. There's no need to assume the worst.

Yet.

McLovin leans against the shed, gun casually hanging by his side but still close enough that he can use it quickly. I don't even acknowledge him before I stalk around the small structure. Desperation shoves up my throat, making it hard to swallow. The door lets out a small protest when I yank it open. Using the goggles, I scan every dark corner of the place.

Empty.

"Where is she?" I snap when I storm out of the shed.

He stands straight and flexes his fingers around the hilt of the gun. "What the fuck do you mean, where is she?"

I clench my jaw so tight it's a wonder my teeth don't shatter. "We find her. Now."

His responding nod is clipped, clearly as tense as I am at the idea of Elliot not being with us. Together we start toward where we both assumed she would post up earlier when we split up.

What if she's hurt, injured from the damn rain of bullets? Fuck, I didn't see her drink a lick of water today. What if she's passed out somewhere, organs slowly shutting down from dehydration?

Or worse, dead?

A pitiful whine scratches up my throat at the thought, but I shove it out of my mind. I can't think that way until I find her body. Until I know for certain she's no longer with me, I can't afford to let those soul-crushing thoughts slow my search for her.

Using the barrel of the gun, I move leaves and stalks of thick greenery out of the way, all while keeping my head on a swivel and thermal sensors turned on. My movements turn frantic, my steps no longer calm and controlled as the minutes tick by with no sight of Elliot.

"Over here," McLovin calls. I'm at his side the next moment, nostrils flaring with each deep breath. "There."

I follow his pointed finger to something on the ground hidden in the rotting leaves.

Squatting low, I pick up the discarded goggles lying in the dirt.

Elliot's goggles.

I curl my fingers around the strap. Its hard plastic digs into my palm, breaking the skin as I continue to clench it tight.

"It was a motherfucking trap," I growl. "I'm so fucking stupid."

"Neither Elliot nor I figured it out. It's not just you, T." I reach up and palm the back of my head. "Listen, calm the hell down. You're no good to her or me with you desperate for bloodshed."

"We will get her back," I say, my tone cold.

"We have to find her first."

I rack my brain, trying to think of a way to track her. Then it hits me.

McLovin shouts my name at my back as I race to the shed and throw the door open so hard it breaks, now standing half open with the top part ripped off its hinge. Digging through the supply duffel, I feel for the secure satellite phone we were to use to reach Lucia if shit hit the fan.

I don't turn at the presence of someone coming up behind me, knowing full well it's McLovin.

"What are you doing?" he asks, stepping inside. Digging around the bags, he changes out his spent magazines for fresh ones.

I mutter a curse as I wait for the damn thing to turn on. "Calling Officer Wilcox."

"Ah shit," he curses. "That woman scares the hell out of me."

Normally I'd find that hilarious, but not now. Not until we find my half pint safe and she's back in my arms. "She can help us find Elliot."

"How?"

Not responding to his question, I dial the number that will connect me directly to Lucia.

"What's wrong?" Lucia says, not bothering with a greeting.

"An ambush, a trap to split us up. I need Elliot's tracker information."

"A tracker," McLovin grumbles as he moves around me and begins digging through another duffel, setting out more guns and ammunition. "That agency sucks."

"She was taken?" Lucia asks.

"Yes," I say. The word tastes sour.

I failed her. I failed this mission. I failed everyone.

"Damnit," Lucia yells on the other end of the line. "We were fucking set up, weren't we? Again."

"I don't know."

"Take a guess, Anthony. Did I send you guys into a damn trap?" The pain and guilt in her voice, something I'm very familiar with, are like a knife to my heart. "Please don't tell me I got my new friend killed."

"The tracker, Lucia," I order, voice strong and sure. "Give me the information. We'll find Officer Smith and bring her home. Alive." I'm

Chapter 18

not sure who I'm promising that to, her or me. "But I can't do that until I know where in the hell they took her."

"Working on it," Lucia says, sounding a little stronger.

"And whatever happens, Lucia, it's not your fault. We all knew the risks of bringing Elliot back down here, that she could be his primary target all along. Now we just use what's happened to our advantage to find that bastard and save Elliot."

"Got it. They're still on the move."

I circle a finger, showing to McLovin it's time to bug out. "Bring it all," I tell him, nodding to the stacks of full magazines and other weapons. "We'll need it."

After piling everything back into the duffels, I turn toward the door. Solely focused on what needs to happen next, I don't check outside first. A ping next to my head has me cursing and diving back into the shed, pulling the door closed with me.

More pings pelt the sides of the bulletproof shed but don't penetrate the metal.

"Fucking surrounded," I shout to McLovin and Lucia, who's screaming in my ear.

Lucia repeats my name several times, but my mind is racing, trying to figure a way out of this shit show to get to Elliot.

Motherfucker had this planned the entire time. Take her, then take us out so we can't come for her.

Too bad Rico messed with the wrong motherfucking SEAL.

"Tony," Lucia bellows, finally gaining my attention.

"What? Trying to figure—"

"Are you in the shed?"

"Yes, surrounded."

"Use the tunnel."

I turn wide eyes to McLovin. "What tunnel?"

"They instructed Elliot to only disclose that safety measure if absolutely necessary for survival."

"Well, shit." I point to the ground. "There's a tunnel." Immediately he drops to his knees and begins feeling around. "Where's the door?"

"The plans say opposite side of the door in the north corner," Lucia explains. I relay the information to McLovin, who shifts around to search there. "It's not big. Straight drop down. Wide enough for you to crawl through."

"We have gear, weapons."

"Then push them in front of you. Come on, SEAL, you scared of a cramped space?"

"Fuck you, Lucia. Not the time."

"Here," McLovin calls. The sound of groaning metal fills the shed among the ping of bullets still spraying the protective metal.

"Found it. Going in. Call you on the other side to get her exact location."

"Stay safe."

Ending the call, I help McLovin toss the second duffel down the hole. "She said it's narrow."

"How far?"

"Not sure." The ground vibrates beneath us, and flames shoot through the gap in the broken door. "Shit. They're tossing grenades. We need to get the fuck down there now."

He's already dropped into the hold before I finish. Once he calls the all clear, I hook a finger around the metal ring attached to the cover and jump. The door slams above me just as my feet hit dirt.

Using the goggles, I take in the tunnel. A few feet ahead, McLovin is already army-crawling through the small passage, only his feet visible.

Narrow, sure. But we've been through worse—underwater.

Kicking the last duffel forward, I push it as far as I can before lowering myself to the floor to crawl. Dirt rains down from the crude tunnel, making me wonder what Rico's men were doing up above outside the shed. Each inch of skin is slick with a mix of sweat and blood. The wound across my bicep burns, ripping open wider each time the muscle flexes to drag my lower body forward.

The idea that Rico's men might also wait for us on the other side has me plotting a backup plan to get us out of this mess alive. I have to. I have to get to Elliot. She knows I'll never stop until I find her.

Chapter 18

Anger burns in my veins, pushing me faster at the thought of that bastard having my girl.

One thing is for damn certain: when I find her, save her, and get home, I'm never letting her go. Elliot is it for me in every way. Without her, what would be the point? I don't want to go back to my desolate life. I want what she brings, hand grenades and all. I'm not sure if she feels the same way or will even want me at the end of all this, but I'll try no matter what.

I'll do everything she wants, anything she needs to make her forever mine.

I just have to find her first.

My muscles burn with exhaustion by the time we reach the end. Keeping the duffels in the tunnel, McLovin and I maneuver to stand, our noses almost touching. It would be awkward if we weren't SEALs, but this is normal for us.

"I'll go first," I state with zero room for argument.

McLovin nods and laces his fingers together. He holds my weight with practiced ease as I stretch high to unfasten the heavy steel bar across the metal lid covering our exit. Bones pop and skin splits when I ram my shoulder against the metal. I groan in relief when whatever sits on top outside this tunnel shifts, allowing the hatch to open an inch.

Shifting the goggles to thermal, I peek out the small slit to scan what I can of the area.

Nothing.

Well, except the large glow prowling on all fours several feet away, but I'll take a hungry jaguar waiting for us over Rico's army any day.

Opening the metal lid farther, I wrap a hand around a wide root to leverage myself out into the open. Rolling to my back, I angle the gun high for another sweep of the area. Three breaths is all I allow myself before rolling back toward the tunnel entrance to open the lid all the way. Gun at the ready, I reach down into the hole, hand open. A canvas strap brushes against the tips of my fingers. Fisting the duffel's handle, I yank it out of the hole and toss it behind me before reaching for the second and doing the same.

After helping McLovin out, I slam the door shut and lock it from the outside.

"They're prepared for everything," I say, covering the metal with nearby debris with my boot. "Like the bulletproof shit shed."

I catch the canteen of water McLovin tosses my way and take a long sip, still staring at the tunnel entrance.

Something doesn't fit.

"Why didn't Rico's men know about the escape tunnel?" I ask and take another drink. Fuck, I'm thirsty. Kneeling, I zip open a pack and feel inside until I find what I'm looking for. Ripping open the package of gel, I ooze the contents into my open mouth. It helps with dehydration, infusing your body with a burst of electrolytes and salt.

"Clearly they have a leak somewhere in the CIA," McLovin responds between gulps of water. "Like last time, but not one who knew about the tunnel."

"Which excludes Elliot."

"You're kidding me," he says, shocked. "You couldn't actually consider her as the CIA mole. You fucking love her."

I lift a shoulder, not correcting his assessment regarding my feelings for her, and take another drink before tossing it back to McLovin to shove into the duffel.

"I don't, but you have to think from a broader perspective. She was the only one on both missions, so she would be the first suspect. But since we know she's not, who does that leave?"

"Analysts, maybe. Coordinators, though that's Lucia this time, and I know she's not a traitor. She might be scary as hell, but she's a good one through and through."

"Agreed. I just keep thinking we're missing something."

"Worry about that later. We need Elliot's coordinates."

I respond with a solemn nod while I reach back for the phone in my side pocket. We need Elliot's location, but we also need to understand the full scope of what's going on. Something tells me if we don't, this mission might end up similar to the one before.

And I can't survive that again.

Especially if Elliot's death is one I'm responsible for.

19

ELLIOT

Crude words spoken in Spanish from somewhere close filter in and out as I slowly fight off the groggy effects of whatever shit drug that bastard injected me with, which is my first signal that I have in fact been captured and am in deep shit. Every thought is layered in fog as I try to lie as still as possible to not indicate that the concoction is wearing off. I focus on the two distinct voices, one discussing his girlfriend's problems while the other offers horrible advice in return.

Breaths labored, my entire body aches, and goose bumps rise everywhere as if I'm cold, yet beads of sweat travel over my cheek and neck. I try to swallow to soothe my burning throat but can't. My swollen tongue sticks to the roof of my mouth. Add in the pain radiating from my lower back, which tells me the bastards didn't see the need for an IV or liquids while I lay unconscious on the dusty floor for who knows how long.

Has it been a day, two?

Lids still lightly shut, I focus all my energy on moving a single pinkie finger along the ground, shifting a thin layer of dirt with the tiny movement. Dirt floor, Spanish-speaking guards, and the stench of body odor, human waste, and mildew indicate I'm in a cell or basement. I strain my ears, holding a shallow breath to listen for anyone else.

A familiar anyone else.

My heart kicks into overdrive at the thought of my seaman and McLovin being captured too.

Tears well as I listen for any sign of those two being close. If Rico took them when he did me, who knows what he's doing to them? Or has already done? Just like he did Kurt. Or maybe he'll hold them, making me watch as he hurts the two men until I'm willing to do whatever he wants to end their torment.

Like give him the password that will open access to the drone information.

My stomach sours, bile creeping up my throat, but I force it down. Throwing up would be a sure signal to the guards that I am, in fact, conscious. I can't give up this one minor advantage yet.

Several minutes pass with me listening for any sign that the boys might be with me. Coming up empty, I force myself to relax. If they're not here, that means I won't be forced to witness their torture and it be used against me.

I'm alone, and that's for the best. Even if thinking the word makes loneliness cover me like a weighted blanket. With the unknown of what's to come, I long for Tony to be here with me, want his stubborn, cocky ass telling me it won't be that bad. Before, doing all this on my own was a breeze, but now... now I feel alone and forgotten.

Shoving those dangerous thoughts aside, I narrow my focus on the issue at hand.

Like getting the fuck out of here before Rico's men use me as their personal punching bag—again.

Shifting my focus to my wrists and ankles, I twist them back and forth in short, slow movements, testing for bindings.

None. Hope flares, but considering last time I killed four men and escaped, there's not a chance in hell these fools would leave me unbound without being confined in a cell or cage.

Please don't be a fucking cage.

An uncontrolled shiver races down my spine at the thought. I've seen enough at our black sites, used for the more unruly guests, making me never want to be held inside one myself.

Only after taking ample time to process everything without my vision do I peel my lids open. Blinking rapidly, I clear away the layer of gunk and dirt to study my surroundings.

I nearly let out a heavy breath of relief when I see a single row of bars in front of where I lie and stone walls on either side. A cell, then, not a cage. The stone walls rise from the brown dirt floor outside the bars and where I can see without turning my head. The guards' back-and-forth conversation continues as I search the area for vulnerabilities but come up empty. To really see what I'm working with, I need to move, but the longer they think I'm drugged, the longer I have to come up with a plan.

If there is a plan to create. If Rico did all this just to capture me for whatever nefarious reason, then there's no doubt he's made this cell Elliot-proof. My only sliver of hope is if—and that's a big if that I'm not willing to dwell on for my threadbare sanity—my seaman and merman are still out there, they will find me.

When the CIA initially embedded the tracker between my shoulder blades so I couldn't dig it out like the first one, because apparently I'm a flight risk, I resented them. Right now though, I would high-five the shit out of whoever's idea that was. Now the boys can zero in on my exact location. If not Tony and McLovin, then someone. Hopefully lots of someones.

Not that it helped last time.

My heart hurts knowing my capture will put Tony right back in the same position as last time. Hopefully he'll be okay, be able to push through the memories and focus on getting out of this alive and unharmed.

Holy crazy train, Harley.

I'm more concerned about my seaman, his trauma, and what all this will do to him than my captured self. I endured some pretty traumatic shit too last time Rico Suarez held me captive, but here I am, lying in the dirt, possibly dying from dehydration, worrying about

Tony and hoping he's safe. And not because I hope he's solid for my sake.

No, it has nothing to do with my well-being. It's because I love him. Somehow in all this shit, between the banter, soul-revealing moments, and life-changing orgasms, I've fallen for that asshole. His health means more to me than my own, his safety my priority instead of first assessing my surroundings.

I'm in love.

Isn't that the shits? I'm in love with a man who's in as dangerous and demanding of a career as I am. How in the hell will that work? If I make it out of here, that is. Which I should probably try to figure out instead of dwelling on the fact that I, CIA Officer Elliot Smith, am in love with a hot-as-hell, caring, protective, pouty, asshole Navy SEAL who sees me for me and supports my crazy while managing me somehow.

My heart swells every time I think about those three words.

I'm in love.

I'm in love.

I'm in—

"I know you're awake in there, Officer Smith." My heart drops at the familiar deep voice. "You're not restrained. Sit up and face me like the bitch you are."

Well, when he puts it that way.

Instead of acknowledging Rico, I raise a too-heavy arm, flipping my middle finger in the air toward his grating voice. Fear travels through my veins, chilling me to the bone when Rico gives an order in Spanish to make me cooperate.

Before I can prepare for their attack, a shocking sensation fires through my thigh, burning at the initial contact and electrifying my veins. My body convulses along the dirt. Gritting my teeth, I hold in a scream of agony and rage.

Even after whatever prodding rod is yanked away, I can't stop twitching and my bladder from releasing—the only time dehydration is a win because of the small amount now soaking my pants.

Chapter 19

"Now," Rico says way too cheerfully, "let's try this again. Sit up and face me. We have some things to discuss, you and I."

My palms slip in the dirt, almost sending me crashing forward, planting my face in the ground, but I catch myself on an elbow. Muscles tremble with the effects of the electric shock as I tuck my knees under my torso and sit back on my heels. Vision blurry and jumpy—that can't be good—I zero in on the bastard who ruined my life just eight months ago.

Rico stands on the other side of the bars, smiling while chewing on that damn toothpick I've always wanted to stab into his eye and pull out like a gruesome hors d'oeuvres.

Huh. Maybe the agency was legit in sending me to that anger management facility. Clearly I have a few areas of concern in that category.

Removing his white fedora, he runs a finger along the brim as he watches me fight to stay upright. Dressed in white linen pants and a black silk long-sleeve shirt, he looks like the picturesque arms dealer. Dripping with money and zero morals.

"Nothing to say?" he asks, clearly a rhetorical question. "You were more talkative last time."

"Not the way I remember it," I say through clenched teeth. My jaw might never come unlocked after those electric bolts. My gaze slips to the guard standing closest to the bars and the long prodding stick with metal prongs on the end clutched in his hand.

Rico follows my gaze and gestures toward the implement with his hat. "It's quite impressive. It comes from my South African clients. They use it to tame their... what do they call them? Oh yes, inventory."

My upper lip pulls up in a snarl. "And here I thought you couldn't sink any lower."

He laughs. "A new friend opened my eyes to the revenue stream, and it's paid off nicely. I still have the weapons side, but this new skin trade is even more lucrative."

My stomach tightens as unease makes it churn. Not with disgust but something else, like my body knows what's going on but my mind hasn't pieced it together.

"What do you want with me?" The words hiss through my clenched teeth.

"Ah, that's for after we add your two new partners into our little game."

"No," I whimper.

The bastard smiles wider, clearly enjoying my distress. "You didn't think I'd let them go after I had you, did you?" He clicks his tongue. "You've lost your edge, Officer Smith, if you think I'd let such a valuable asset just slip through my fingers. Oh, don't look so frightened. I promise you it'll be worse than you expect."

"I'll give you what you want," I state, my jaw finally opening enough for the words to make sense. "Leave them out of this. This is between you and me, no one else." My training is screaming at me to stop talking, to stay strong, to deny that the men mean anything to me.

Rico shakes his head and repositions the dumb hat back on top.

"This is no longer just about the drone, Officer Smith, though I will get that information from you eventually before you beg for death. This is about reminding those who come after you what happens when someone dares fuck with me and my operation. You will pay for deceiving me, and now I know the best way to do that is to start with your friends."

"If you hurt them, I will kill you. There's not a person on this planet who will stop me from ripping you apart piece by piece."

"We'll just have to see about that, won't we?" He turns and walks to the only exit I can see from where I kneel. "Oh, and I hope you enjoy the surprise we have. You're here because of him, and I know he's just dying to see you." His deep chuckle follows him as he disappears through the arched doorway. "Sedate her."

The second Rico's fading words reach my ears, I push off the floor to leap to my feet. But my legs collapse beneath me. My shoulder slams against the ground, followed by my side, which jolts my aching lower back.

Chapter 19

Nails digging into the dirt, I pull my dead lower body toward the far corner, hoping that will somehow save me from whatever injection Rico just instructed the guards to administer.

A fist slams into my thigh, making my arms give out, leaving me stranded in the middle of the cell. Rolling to my side, I stare at the thick metal dart sticking out from my left thigh.

"Ah, fuck." The effects of the tranquilizer flow through my bloodstream, numbing my leg up to my pelvis, spreading along my lower belly before engulfing my chest. Damp cheek in the dirt, eyes wide open, I memorize the guards' ugly-ass faces for when I wake up and will make them pay for this.

I continue to stare them down until the drug's effects swallow my brain and drag me back into the dark abyss of unconsciousness.

20

TONY

Even my sweat has sweat.

My skin stings like a thousand ant bites from the small lacerations along my face and arms from limbs and small trees as I race through the dark jungle. I don't slow my pursuit as I barrel through the underbrush toward the coordinates Lucia sent half an hour ago. It's slow-going moving through this jungle shit at night, but it's better than being spotted on a road.

By now they will have realized we weren't in that shed, which means not only do we have to find Elliot, but we also have to keep our head on a swivel to ensure we're not spotted. Which is fine—this is just a day in the life with our job—but just because we're used to it doesn't make any of it less stressful or easy. Never let your guard down. Always stay vigilant. That's how you come home in one piece. And now more than ever, I have a reason to come home.

A small clearing opens up, easing our resistance. We need to continue on, but first—water. Pausing, I rotate around, drop the duffel bag filled with our weapons to the ground, and unzip the heavy metal zipper. McLovin does the same just a foot away, knowing exactly what this brief pit stop is for.

I twist off the top of my canteen, rip open a package of super juice powder, and dump it in. After a few swirls, I press the edge to my lips and tip it all the way back, chugging the entire contents in one go. Breathing deep, I wipe away the remaining drops from my lips with my sleeve. The taste of copper lingers on my tongue. Looking through the goggles, I scan up my arm to where the bullet grazed my bicep. Dark thick liquid continues to seep from the wound, but overall it seems to be clotting, which is ideal. The last thing I want in this place is an open wound that can get infected just from the stagnant air or the danger of having the scent of fresh blood attract predators of the four-legged sort.

The grind of the two zippers sealing shut is absorbed by the active nocturnal insect life. With a clipped nod, I drag the duffel back up over my shoulder and start running again. We've covered ten miles and have twenty more to go. Getting there before dawn would be fucking fantastic. With only the two of us—for now, at least—against all Rico's men, we need the cloak of darkness on our side for this fight.

Hopefully it won't just be us for long. After zeroing in on Elliot's coordinates, Lucia activated another SEAL platoon that was waiting on a carrier close by just in case. I've never been more appreciative of her over-planning than now. Could McLovin and I do this on our own? Sure, but it wouldn't be easy. With Elliot in the mix, I want every man our country offers on this. Fuck my pride and the need to do this alone to prove some dumb point.

She's all that matters now—getting her out of Rico's grasp unharmed and back stateside where I can do my best to convince her to somehow stay with me. There's a chance she'll reject me, say I'm too damaged for someone like her, too poor, too below her level. But I will try. Only death will keep me from begging that woman to be my forever girl.

Twice we're forced to double back and find a less direct route because of a turbulent river and a gorge too wide to leap across. It kills our time, but we still make it within half a mile of Elliot's tracker location in a little under two hours.

My muscles tremble and ache, but I press forward toward the

goal, though now instead of racing as fast as I can push my body, I'm strategic with each step to ensure there aren't concealed warning sensors or traps. At my back, McLovin steps exactly where I do so we leave as few tracks as possible.

Muffled conversations, the rumble of large trucks, and the scent of diesel mixed with cooking meat signals we're close. An opening in the thick leaves has me stopping, holding up a fist for McLovin to do the same. Movements smooth, I withdraw the sat phone and press the Call button.

"We're here," I murmur. "Tell the next team to watch for traps. Lovall almost got his foot snapped off in a rusted iron trap on the way here. Not sure if it was Rico's or left over from some other cartel asshole."

"Noted," Lucia replies. "Do you see either target?"

I know what she's doing. She's removing all things personal by not using Elliot's name. And it works—kind of.

"Not yet, moving in closer. What's the ETA on the other team?"

"Heillo will drop them ten miles from your location at 0500. They'll make their way to the target's coordinates and rendezvous with you. The lead will fall to you on commands."

"Moving closer now to get an idea of what we're up against."

"Stay safe."

Ending the call, I slip the phone back into a side pocket of my fatigues. Knowing McLovin will follow, I stalk toward Rico's estate.

A two-story stone house sits in the middle of the clearing. A wide patio extends off the side, bright lights illuminating the various potted plants scattered about. Guards stalk the edges of the manicured lawn, all with high-powered assault rifles strapped across their chests. A few stand close, talking and laughing, while those nearer to the house stand at full attention. Fires burn along the perimeter, keeping the concealing shadows to the adjacent jungle.

Staying low, we stalk around the entire estate, searching for the best point of entry. Toward the back, one fire is dimmer than the others, not as well-kept as the ones toward the front, and appears to be our best option for converging on the estate without notice.

Sneaking back around, we carefully step out of cover, guns pressed to our shoulders, ready to fire if needed. Hopefully we can get in, gain some intel we can pass on to the other platoon, and get out.

That's if everything goes as planned.

Which, in Colombia, hasn't been the case when I'm involved.

Thankfully the guards are too focused on their phones, watching what sounds like some sports game, to notice two massive shadows slinking across the yard. My heart thunders a steady beat, fueling the adrenaline pumping through my veins.

The house's rounded stone presses between my shoulder blades and ass when we seal ourselves against the structure. In quick smooth movements, we inch down the wall toward an open window.

The bright light pouring through makes the infrared on the goggles useless. Shutting off the night vision, I twist to peek through the window. A sheer curtain waves in the gentle breeze, blocking half my view, but the other half I see crystal clear.

Rico fucking Suarez.

He paces in front of an unlit fireplace, talking to someone I can't see. A portrait of a saint hangs above the mantel, almost like he's praying over the arms dealer. Angling an ear, I focus on the private conversation.

"... not sure how," the man I can't see says. His tone is tense. "We move on as planned."

"I will make her bleed," Rico says with clear, barely restrained anger.

"If she declines my proposition," the other man says. "You made your point last time when you fucking shot her."

"You know the bitch won't choose you," Rico says with a scoff. "You're a damn fool thinking this'll impress her." He waves a hand around the house.

So this isn't Rico's new place? Then whose?

I need an unobstructed view of the man to hopefully identify him later, but that would jeopardize my position. Not worth the risk.

Though if they're talking about Elliot this way, that means she's still alive, unharmed.

"Yes, she will, when she realizes she doesn't have a choice," the other man growls. "What do we do about the rogue fuckers? They'll come after her. Those bastards always want to be the hero." The clear disdain and hate in his voice makes me want to laugh.

Poor guy feels inferior. That's the only reason others hate us. They want to be a SEAL and couldn't muster up. That will make killing the guy easier. He thinks he's smarter and better than us.

So he'll die a fool. That's his bad, not mine.

"If they come, my men will take care of them. Remember our deal, my friend. I get the password no matter the method, even if she accepts your proposal. If she doesn't, I'm the one to put her down." The man's response is too muffled to understand. "Yes, yes, I won't break her beyond repair. But I will be the judge of when to stop. She must pay a price for disrupting my business, to show others we aren't to be messed with, and I will get the *real* password I was denied."

The way he says *real* makes me believe it's a point of contention between the two men.

But why?

"Yes." Shadows shift across the floor along with shuffling noises. I seal my back against the wall in case he moves this way. "Where is she?"

"In the cell, still knocked out from the tranquilizer." My blood boils at the image of Elliot hurt, unconscious in a cell. I really can't wait to make these two bleed. The one I can't see will die. Rico, well, he might be sent back to the CIA black site missing a few appendages... maybe organs. Haven't gotten that far yet.

Shit, I really am becoming as crazy as Elliot.

And funny enough, I don't mind it one bit. Her version of crazy is my kryptonite, it appears.

"I have something we use on the girls to keep them awake. We don't have all damn night to wait for those fuckers to find her."

The girls.

So that dirty douchebag is the one responsible for that shithole we cleared out earlier. It all fits now. The rats at the bar telling us the exact location of the site, the girls having been there for weeks without being transported north to be sold—it was all a part of his plan to know when Elliot was in Colombia. How did he know about the CIA shit shed though? And how does he know Elliot, anyway? Clearly he doesn't know her well if he thinks he'll be able to convince her to be his human trafficking partner, if I'm accurate in the assumption based on their conversation. I've only known her a little over a week—albeit an intense week stuffed with months' worth of shit—and I know she'd rather kill herself than have anything to do with all that.

Hell, the woman shot herself in the shoulder to shoot the guy behind her.

Who does that?

Elliot fucking Smith, that's who.

My crazy-ass soul mate.

"Get the shot ready. We'll secure her before waking her up. I'm partial to the men guarding her this time. I don't want them to end up like the last three responsible for restraining her."

The two talk a little more about new trade routes before leaving the room, with me only glimpsing the other man's back.

Tall, dark hair, lean, but by the way he holds himself, he's trained.

CIA maybe? A rogue officer would make sense. It's how he'd know about the shit shed and Elliot. Maybe the answer doesn't matter now, or maybe it's the key to everything.

Pulling out the phone, I hand it to McLovin and motion for him to hightail it back to the jungle's depths. I know he heard the whole exchange too, so there's no need to possibly give our location away by repeating it all.

With a clipped nod, he's gone, disappearing through the darkness.

Now all I can do is wait to see if they bring Elliot here or drag her to another area of the house.

Or... I could sneak in through the window and find Elliot before

Chapter 20

they shoot her up with who the hell knows what drug they've concocted.

Before I can act on the suicidal plan, someone walks back into the room. Not daring to peek around the edge of the window, I get as close as possible to hear every word.

"... soon." Rico's voice floats out the window. I snarl into the darkness. "We have to wait until we get that password. Then we take out both of them."

My brows jump up my forehead. He's not talking to his new business partner but someone else, maybe a guard or general of his small army. "The whore routes are secure. We know what we need to know. He's no use to us after we get what we want from her."

It shouldn't surprise me that Rico is double-crossing the other guy—no loyalty among thieves and all that shit. But it seems the other guy isn't smart enough to realize Rico is a shady fucker and willing to do anything for money. If his new partner set up this new revenue stream, laid out the plans and details, well, then the fool deserves to die.

But what I don't like about Rico's plan is he said to take them both out. That means Elliot too, which won't happen. I won't allow it.

Their muffled voices grow distant, along with their retreating footsteps.

This rescue and capture mission just became more complicated.

Just the way we SEALs like it. Just like G said last week, easy is not in our vocabulary.

My smile is full of teeth and menace.

Now to plot various plans of attack for all potential outcomes while I wait for a hint of Elliot's location.

Then we act, and I get my girl home.

21

ELLIOT

My lids pop open, blinking rapidly as I somehow go from unconsciousness to alert and jittery in an instant. The rapid thump of my heart, desperate to beat out of my chest, and the sense of my nerves on fire signals a blaring warning that something is really wrong. I can't think straight. When I go to shake my head, the room spins, making my empty stomach roll. Heat builds beneath my skin, making it feel tight, my body achy at the cellular level.

Blips of the electrocution in the cell and tranq dart sticking out of my thigh flip through like a movie put together by a crack addict after 720 cups of coffee.

Tongue dry, I try to lick my lips, but the ache in my jaw has me stopping the slight movement. The throb in my head continues to escalate, feeling like my brain might ooze out of my ears.

The room around me comes in and out of focus. I slam my lids shut over and over to clear my vision. Rough fabric beneath my fingertips feels like shards of glass, my skin overly sensitive.

What in the hell did these bastards inject me with?

That question swims in my groggy thoughts before flittering out. Twisting, I cry out in agony at the pain roaring from my lower back. Slouching back, I hiss when the cushion molds around me. With my hair hanging in front of my face like a curtain, I use the concealment to figure out where the hell I am. Between the greasy strands, I locate a vintage-looking green velvet couch under me, Saltillo-type square tiles beneath my bare, bound feet. A plain dark wood coffee table clear of anything I could use as a weapon sits a few feet from me, and beyond that an unlit fireplace and some dude in a white gown with a strange halo over his head, hands together in prayer. Some random saint Rico prays to, no doubt.

Is there a saint for bastard arms dealers?

I feel like everyone in the world deserves a saint but him. But who am I to judge? I want to murder him in various excruciating ways. Does that mean I don't get a saint?

Not that I care, because I have something better than some painting. I have two badass SEALs on my side, out there looking for me.

The memory of what Rico said right before one of his fuckers shot me with a tranquilizer flashes through my mind, but it doesn't hold the same terror as it did before. Not because I care less but because I know something Rico doesn't. Those two men, Tony and McLovin, are smarter than him. They won't get caught. They'll fight their way out of whatever trap Rico planned and will make their way to me.

I hope.

An open window to my right is the only viable exit to the outside world I can identify, but by the sounds of echoing voices, there must be a door somewhere at my back.

The looming presence over either shoulder signals I'm not alone.

"The hell did you idiots give me?" I say, words slurred.

Restraints bind the tops of both arms, pinching my shoulder blades together, and at the wrists.

Smart fuckers. Guess they learned their lesson last time when I broke free and killed their little friends. With this type of binding, it's almost impossible for me to get out.

Almost.

Feet crossed at my ankles, a thin wire slices into my skin beneath the coarse rope binding that's also rubbed the skin raw.

Now this might be an issue.

Shit.

"Good, you're awake."

Double shit.

My entire body twitches like an addict on a good high, making my vision bounce when I raise my head to stare Rico down. It stings a little that my right eye twitches, negating the effectiveness of my death stare, but I roll with it as best I can like the badass I am.

"So we're going to do all this again," I say, my words as shaky as my body. "Last time it didn't end up so well for your minions."

Rico smooths down his short beard, a conniving smile pulling at his lips. In five slow steps, he crosses the room, moves around the coffee table, and backhands me across the face. My neck jerks to the side from the force of the blow, splitting my lip and causing my brain to slosh around in my skull.

I don't have to hold in my cry of pain, because I can't feel it. Not yet. Whatever drugs they injected me with numbed my pain sensors. Which means the ache and throbbing I feel elsewhere is so great it's pushing past the drug's effects. From the locations most of the pain is radiating from and the signs of a fever, my bet's on kidney infection or maybe even failure at this point. With the prior damage inflicted by my so-called colleagues and now dehydration, my body is slowly breaking down.

"There will be no escape like last time," Rico says, moving back to his spot along the far wall. "You will not escape these restraints, and there's no one closing in, making me rush." He turns his focus back to me, watching for any response. "They are dead."

My heart somehow races faster. A low pitiful whimper tries to creep up my throat, but I swallow it down. I don't believe a single word that lying bastard says. I can't for my sanity.

"How?" I say instead of curling into a ball and crying like I desperately want to. "Did you kill them like you did my partner?"

Rico's brows rise a fraction, something glimmering in his dark eyes. "*You* killed your partner, remember? All you had to do was give me the password, and you both would've lived."

"Right. I'm no fool. You would've killed us the moment you uploaded the files."

He lifts a single shoulder. "Maybe, maybe not. Maybe I would've let you both go, but we'll never know now. You made the decision that day that set all this in motion." His gaze sweeps around the room. "If only you would've valued his life over your sense of duty—"

"You're a murderer," I say, lunging forward but not getting far. Two hands yank me back against the couch, but I'm too angry to bother acknowledging the pain. "Your weapons kill our soldiers, kill innocent women and children. I will never stop catching bastards like you and finally getting justice for all those you aided in killing. You call it a sense of duty, but I call it housekeeping, removing one more pathetic excuse for a human from this world. I will not bend or break for you, for my partner, for any other fool."

I slouch back against the couch, breathing heavily.

Shit, courage and proclamations are exhausting.

A slow, taunting clap has me glaring across the room. "Nice speech for a woman who's currently breaking right before me." I lift a lip in a snarl. "What? You think I can't see how much pain you're in? The sweat beading along your pale skin? You'll die a very slow, agonizing death if I don't help you, and yet here you are making foolish statements about shit that doesn't matter."

"Patriotism is not shit—"

"Money, power, control, that's what matters in today's world. You follow a country that thinks it can be defended, but those who still feel devotion, a sense of unity in bonding together for a single cause are *fools*," Rico shouts. "Only those who see this world for what it is, an opportunity to make something of yourself, will land on top. I will be here long after you're dead and decaying in an unmarked grave. Preach to me about sense of country and loyalty when you're gone and I'm still here living like a king."

"Selfish prick," I mutter.

Rico's in front of me before my lagging brain can register the movement. Icy fingers wrap around my cheek, his palm gripping the base of my jaw. My teeth clench with the restraint to not lurch

Chapter 21

forward and bite off his nose. His grip tightens to the point that it should hurt, but all I feel is the pressure.

"Selfish I might be, but I'm the one in control here tonight, not you." His cold, dark eyes flick between mine. "I told him it was a lost cause, to let me kill you that night, but no. The fool doesn't see past your cunt and will die a fool. Just as you will." Leaning in close, he presses his lips against the shell of my ear. "You will die tonight, Officer Smith. How brutally and how long it takes is up to you."

With a shove, he tosses me hard against the couch. This time I can't hold back a pain-filled grunt.

It hits me then that he didn't answer my question about how he killed my SEAL and McLovin. If Rico isn't gloating about it, then that means it didn't happen. No way would he spare me the horrible details if he and his men did capture and kill the two men.

Which means....

My laugh starts in my belly, slowly rising into my chest. It comes out as just a puff of air, but it builds and builds until I'm laughing like the lunatic my file claims I am. Rico stands straight, his figure blurry through my tears. They leak down my cheeks, dripping to the top of my thighs, where they immediately disappear into the black fabric.

"Oh, you're so fucked," I say between laughs. I'm hysterical, delirious from the fever and drugs, but I don't care. "They're not dead, but you will be."

That smirk of his falls, and the toothpick that's been working from one side of his mouth to the other stills.

"You want to know how they died, to prove to you that there's no one out there coming to save you. There is no hope for you living till the next sunrise, you crazy *punta*. We surrounded—"

"Tell me all the lies you want, call me crazy, but I know something you don't." My words are powerful even though I can sense my body shutting down from the inside out.

"Funny, I was about to say the same thing. You go first."

I sit up taller and look him dead in the eye. "Nothing, not even death, will keep him from coming for me. And when he does, we both have some unfinished business with you."

Something like worry crosses his face but vanishes quickly. "Well, in that case, we should move this night along. Are you ready for my surprise?"

"More electrocution and torture isn't really a surprise."

"Something even better."

"Oh goody."

My ears perk up at the sound of footsteps behind me. Rico shifts his gaze to just over my shoulder. "Perfect timing, *mi amigo*." Rico's smile is vicious when he turns his attention back to me. "This will be fun to watch."

The footsteps grow closer, and a familiar scent floats in the wind, making my mind spin. I crane my neck to the left, the muscles and tendons stretching to help me get a glimpse of who's at my back.

I blink, thinking it's an illusion and the man frowning down at me isn't real.

Squeezing my lids shut, I peel them open, expecting the face to morph into one I don't know, proving to just be a mirage.

But it doesn't.

Nothing could've prepared me for this. Anger, resentment, and guilt explode, warring inside me for dominance.

"Kurt?"

22

TONY

Kurt?

My muscles spasm with the need to shift, allowing me to glance inside for a glimpse of Elliot and the man who she assumed was dead. Hell, we all assumed he was dead based on her firsthand account even though they never found the body in the rubble.

Or maybe the agency lied, and they knew this entire time that Kurt was the mole, meaning they led Elliot into a trap of their own, hoping she'd be able to kill a rogue officer and capture Rico all in one operation.

Bastards.

Fucking conniving, manipulating bastards. Wonder how she'll feel when we get home and I demand she quit? Maybe suggest less of an asshole of an agency. Hell, if any woman could pass the SEAL assessment, it would be her, but then she'd be surrounded by my asshole friends.

Fuck no to that. Hard pass. Plus there's that minor issue of hers with large bodies of water.

I shove a curled fist to my sternum to quell the building ache at hearing Elliot's weak voice. Learning the basics of what she's already been through in this hellhole and knowing she's in pain are a hot poker to my overprotective side, demanding I rush in there guns blazing to save her.

But going in alone and without a plan will only leave us both exposed.

No, I have to wait for the other SEAL team to offer backup, even if it literally pains me.

Though a different angle might give me a view inside. I consider the edge of the window opposite where I crouch. There's less concealment from the patrolling guards, but it's not completely out in the open. It'll be worth it to see exactly what's going on in that room. If things get dangerous inside, I can step in, damning the consequences.

That is a last resort.

I take a lunging step to the side. Keeping my weight low, I move to the other side, staying below the glow of the lights inside.

"What... I don't.... You died. I saw you. You died. He shot you." Elliot's rising panic flows through her high-pitched voice as she speaks.

Inching upward, I get my first peek into the other side of the room. Elliot sits, bound, on an old-fashioned couch with a man standing over her.

A little shorter than me, he looks to be about six feet tall, lean, but his stance conveys he knows how to fight. The suit he's wearing is expensive, the fabric nearly glinting in the light. With shiny shoes and a glittering Rolex, this Kurt fucker seems to have sold his soul to the devil all for money.

"You of all people know not to believe anything unless you see it with your own eyes." The douchebag rocks back on his heels and gives Elliot a slow once-over. My fingers dig into my straining thigh muscles to keep from reaching for my gun and popping a few rounds into his head.

Elliot just blinks up at him. I narrow my eyes. Is she twitching? Fuck, whatever they gave her is running strong through her veins.

Stay strong, Half Pint. I'm coming for you.

Chapter 22

"Why?" The word comes out strangled, like it's said through tears.

Doubt creeps in, not about Elliot's loyalty to the CIA or if she had any clue he had turned into a traitor but about us. She mentioned the guilt she felt for the man knowing—well, thinking—she killed him, but she never mentioned how close they were.

Were they close like she and I have become?

Did she share pieces of her soul, open up about her past with him too?

Not that it matters, because she's still mine, and I won't let that fucker hurt her anymore. We're a team, she and I. No one, not even the fucker who should've stayed dead, will come between us.

"Why?" He scoffs as he shoves his hands into his gray slacks. "You of all people should know why, Elliot." My upper lip lifts in a snarl just hearing her name on his lips. I cannot wait to kill him for good this time. "They break us, then use us to advance whatever damn political agenda is on the table that week. We're pawns in a never-ending game, and I was tired of it." He slips a hand from his pocket and reaches out to stroke a lone finger down her face, tracing the outline of her jaw.

I see it before he does. Maybe that signals our relationship is stronger than theirs ever was.

Even though her eyes are glazed, it's the twitch of her jaw, the stillness that washes over her at his touch. The idiot's bellow of surprise and pain thankfully covers my chuckle. Kurt yanks his hand back, stumbling into the coffee table to wrench his finger free from between Elliot's teeth. How she snapped at just the right moment and caught his finger is amazing, and a little worrisome.

Note to self: don't ask for a blowjob when she's pissed off.

"You fucking bitch." After inspecting the finger to ensure it's still attached, which unfortunately it seems to be, Kurt raises the injured hand in the air. The smack echoes around the room, and Elliot's head snaps to the side. The last time this happened, I couldn't see, just heard Rico's hit. This, watching, is so much fucking worse.

Blood streams down her lower lip and drips off her chin, giving her responding smile a malicious appearance. Pride swells as I watch her stare down the fucker while twitching against the bindings.

"You crazy-ass cunt," he yells, tossing his hands out wide. "I did all this. Not you, not them, me," he says with an incredulous laugh. "And I thought—"

"You thought I'd give you a nice slow fucking clap and be impressed. I almost died that night. I thought I killed you."

"That," he grits out with a pointed glare over his shoulder to Rico, who's watching the drama unfold from the other side of the room, "wasn't supposed to happen." He turns back around and points at Elliot. "You didn't tell me there were two codes to get inside the flash drive."

"Clearly I was right in not divulging that part of the night's mission."

"You chose the agency over me. You let him kill me," he shouts, spit flying. "You were supposed to choose me," he says, chest heaving. "We were both going to die in that damn house for a cover with those SEAL fuckers. But you, you fucked it all up with your sense of duty. You could've had all this. You could've had me."

"And why would I have wanted that?"

This time, his hand's curled in a tight fist when it connects with her face. Elliot topples over the side, giving me the first glimpse at the bindings behind her back. Unable to catch herself, she falls to the floor, landing at his feet. I don't look away when he kicks her in the stomach.

"I loved you," he says, curling his foot back to kick her again.

"Loved me," she rasps, barely loud enough for the words to be audible at the window. "You loved yourself, you narcissistic asshole. It was sex. Terrible sex at that."

This time his foot connects with her upper thighs, sending her rolling to the side.

"I built this for us," he growls, his voice low and menacing. "Built this for you, for our future—"

"Future?" Elliot's voice is high-pitched, warning everyone in the vicinity that she's reaching the last bits of her sanity. "You want to know what your plan that night did for your future? When I fucked up your grand plans to pull us both into working with Rico Fucking Suarez? You killed the only connection you and I will ever have that night. I was pregnant with your baby."

My eyes mist over, blurring my vision.

Pregnant.

Oh, Half Pint.

My heart breaks for her while my blood boils with rage. Now I'm trembling and jerking as badly as Elliot was. But I'm not on anything, only ruled by the insistent need to make them all pay for what they did to her. Did to her because she wouldn't lower her principles, was willing to die to keep that password a secret so Rico couldn't hurt anyone with our technology.

Fucking hell, I don't deserve her. Someone so strong and loyal and selfless.

"You're lying." Kurt's voice comes out crackling, proving he does in fact believe Elliot's words.

"I wish I was." Her voice trembles. I can't see her from where she's positioned, but it's clear she's crying. "Oh hell, I wish I was. Because now... now... oh fuck," she screams. "I'm so damn glad it happened. So fucking glad I lost that baby so it never had to know its father was a weak excuse for a man. A traitor."

Something else is said, but I don't hear the words.

All I can focus on is the cool metal pressed against the back of my head, its rounded edges digging into my scalp.

"Up." The clipped word comes from directly behind me.

Closing my eyes, I say a quick prayer to anyone who's listening that I at least live long enough to save Elliot and avenge my men.

With those accomplished, I can die knowing I at least did two things right in my life.

My knees pop as I slowly stand, staying out of view from those inside the house. The barrel of the gun pushes harder in a silent demand for me to move. Every cell on high alert, I dutifully follow the guard's orders, turning to head for the patio area and the opened double doors. If I allow him to take me into the house like this, I won't come out alive. He'll take me to that dipshit Kurt and Rico, who will have their fun, then kill me in front of Elliot to add a new emotional side to her torture.

The tips of my fingers twitch in the air as I plot a plan of attack.

Seven feet separate me from the patio. If I want to take the guard—hell, maybe guards—out behind me, I have to do it now before the light can maximize my exposure to being caught again or killed.

Now.

I have to do this now.

My body flows through the motions, my muscles acting on memory from years of training. Ducking and twisting, I reach up, grabbing the end of the barrel and pushing it the opposite direction. The guard's eyes widen, and his finger moves, ready to fire off a few warning shots to signal others. With a silent grunt, I yank on the barrel as hard as I can, ripping it from his hands. With my free hand, I slip the knife from my belt and send it soaring through the air.

It hits its mark right in the center of the man's throat, preventing him from calling for help. He falls to his knees before slumping to the ground.

One down.

Two thumps have me whirling the guard's gun around and positioning it against my shoulder.

The silhouettes of two additional bodies lie in the grass. Creeping closer, I zero in on the single holes in each of their foreheads.

McLovin.

Not wasting any time, I give a thumbs-up toward the jungle and turn back to the patio.

I can't wait any longer, backup SEAL platoon or not. My position is exposed. Others know I'm here. Might as well make my presence known with a bang.

Excitement roars through me as I reach into my pocket and pull out the hand grenade I grabbed at the last second as a reminder of Elliot, who I was fighting for. Pulling the pin, I keep a firm hold on the lever and wrench my arm back before launching it forward. It sails through the air, over the stone patio, and between the double doors before dropping to the ground.

I hear the faint clink of it rolling.

Moving behind a wall, I tense my body, waiting for the boom.

Time for me to save my girl.

And then never let her go.

23

ELLIOT

I'm dying, gasping for breath that won't come.

Every emotion and memory I've bottled up since I woke in that hospital bed has cracked open inside me, and I can't stop it from its leaching poison. The few tears that actually leaked out have dried, yet I still lie sobbing, trembling uncontrollably on the floor.

Kurt is alive, a damn traitor. He fooled me into believing that body was his, thinking it was the perfect cover for later when the building exploded and the agency assumed we were inside along with the SEALs. I've never been more thankful that a fucked-up mission played out like it did as I am right now. If I hadn't kept the additional password to open the contents on the flash drive a secret from him, if the night had gone according to his plan, I'd have been his captive—pregnant captive, at that—under the guise of him loving me and wanting me as part of his deranged plan for wealth and power, all provided through human trafficking.

For eight months I've mourned a money-hungry monster and our unborn child. I should be furious at his deception, but all that consumes me now is unending sorrow and grief. Like my entire chest is a gaping hole, a bottomless pit of despair.

My grief is so heavy, I can't voice the many unanswered questions.

How did Kurt even barter an agreement with Rico? At what point in our eighteen-month stint did he turn? What does Kurt bring to the table that Rico would've wanted? If he faked his death, all connections with the agency would've died with him, so what did Kurt...?

Holy unending questions, Riddler.

It all fits together.

His human trafficking connections from that previous operation in Central America. That's what Kurt offered Rico. Kurt is why Rico has ventured into human trafficking.

Bile burns up my throat, and I turn my head just as what little is in my stomach spills out of my mouth.

My lips part, ready to beg Kurt to kill me now, to put me out of my misery, when the entire house trembles from a nearby explosion. The boom vibrates the air, the ground beneath me quakes, and particles of plaster rain down from above. My ears ring, keeping me from hearing what all follows.

Dense white smoke fills the room, forming a stagnant cloud. Frantically I search for Kurt through the chaos, hoping to gain a clue about what the fuck just happened. I find him inches from where I lie, on his knees, body canted toward Rico. Face flushed, his lips move quickly as if he's shouting at Rico, who looks just as angry and, if I'm not mistaken, worried.

I watch the two men until it clicks into place. If they didn't set the explosion, that means they're here.

He's here.

My seaman.

A whimper catches in my throat as a fresh wave of hope surges. I just have to hold on a little longer.

Each movement slices the bindings around my wrists, arms, and ankles deeper into my already torn flesh, but still I shift along the floor inch by inch toward the couch. Using the edge as leverage, I work my exhausted body up the side until I'm able to sit up, using the couch as support.

Rico and Kurt continue fighting, both now brandishing pistols.

Their shouts are muffled, but with each second that passes, my hearing slowly returns.

Quick flashes outside the open window snag my attention.

Gunfire.

Lots of gunfire.

Optimism soars in my chest, only to drop like a lead weight into my empty stomach when the lights flicker and blink before failing completely, dousing the house in sudden darkness. The crack of two guns firing rattles my eardrums, the flash searing into my eyes.

Pulse racing, breathing erratic, I stare wide-eyed into the dark, begging my eyes to adjust quickly. More gunfire pops, but the sound is more distant than this room.

A sticky, wet hand wraps around my bicep and pulls. With a scream, I fall to the floor, my knees cracking on the tile. Then I'm moving. The hand wedged beneath my armpit tightens to keep from slipping as I'm dragged roughly behind. My shoulder nails a piece of furniture, and the bindings at my feet snag, jerking whoever is hauling me away but only slowing their pace, not stopping it entirely.

Some of the bright moon's rays leak through the windows, casting streaks of silvery gray across the room, just enough light to make out the shape of furniture and movement. Movement we're leaving in our wake.

Panic rises with the utter feeling of helplessness.

But unlike when I suffered at the hand of my uncle, I might be helpless, but I'm not alone.

Something in me breaks, giving up a sliver of my pride, but I'd rather need help than to die with my pride intact.

"Tony," I scream at the top of my lungs. There's an edge to my shriek. I part my lips, ready to scream for him again, only to have something hard slam against the side of my head.

I hear the crack against my skull. It vibrates down my spine and explodes with pain. My eyes droop, black bleeding into my diminished vision. Completely limp, my head lolls back and forth as I dance on that line of unconsciousness.

My lips move, saying his name over and over and over again,

hoping my pitiful pleas will somehow make him appear. That he'll feel my desperate need for his strength, for his protection, and come for me.

"It's over, Rico."

My heart leaps, skipping a literal fucking beat at the gravelly voice that can make me feel protected and powerful in the same breath.

"I can make you rich, give you everything you want."

"All I want is you dead."

"I'll give you the bitch—"

"You won't give me anything."

Rico hauls me up and wraps an arm around my waist. "You kill me, you kill her—"

The pop is muffled, a different sound from the guns Rico's men used. It's a puff, nearly silent with the ringing in my ears and throbbing head. I wouldn't even know Tony fired his weapon if it weren't for the spark of the gunpowder firing.

Then I'm falling, Rico's hold on my waist pulling my rag-doll body as he slumps behind me.

A new grip wraps around my shoulders, catching me before I hit the hard floor. These arms feel safe, comforting, protective. In an instant, my body knows whose hard chest I'm now cradled against and drains of all resistance.

The pain in my head and the heat building beneath my skin come back full force. A sad whimper escapes my tight jaw.

"Shh. It's okay, Half Pint."

I release an exhausted sob.

A male voice rumbles through the now quieted house, followed by another.

"Come on." Tony's lips feel cold against my sizzling forehead. "Let's get you home."

"Kurt," I rasp. "He's—"

"I know, Elliot, I know. Just relax for me, okay? Let me get you out of here and to a doctor." His stubbled cheek brushes against my forehead. "You're on fucking fire."

Each of his jogging steps causes me to bounce, head lolling from side to side, but I don't care. I'm safe and going home.

At some point, another figure looms over me. Tony says something, and the bindings around my arms release, followed by my wrists and feet.

"She's bad off, T." Tony's chest rumbles with a response. "Wrap her head wound." I barely hear Tony say something about drugs. "Fuck, we don't know what they gave her."

"Half Pint." The worry and pain in that voice make me want to open my eyes, but I can't. It's too much effort. "Elliot, I need you to stay with us a little longer, okay?"

"Flakes, what the hell—oh shit. What happened to her? Calling for the chopper."

"Hold on, Elliot." Tony's whispers brush against the shell of my ear, his lips moving against my cheek. "Please fucking hold on. I can't lose you. You're it for me. You're all I need. Please don't give up."

I don't want to. I want to stay with him, to live an actual life by his side. But I can't feel my legs anymore, the numbness slowly spreading to the rest of my body. Each breath is harder to take than the last. The world vanishes for a second, the darkness blanketing me in its icy stillness.

"No." The panicked yell yanks me back awake. "Don't you fucking leave me, Elliot." His voice rings in my ears. "Elliot, please, please fight for me."

But I've fought for so long.

I know I've lived a good life. Found a love that was made for me and no one else. I'm not leaving this world forgotten. He will remember me—always. And for the first time in my life, I do the unthinkable. Not because I want to, but because I have absolutely nothing left.

I give up.

Muffled voices, the rattle of metal, the whirl of a chopper blade, and excruciating pain.

So much soul-sucking pain.

"She's back." I swear it's yelled inside my skull. "Where's the fucking IV bag?"

I wince. I think I do. Internally I wince, at least. My lids are sealed shut, preventing me from opening my eyes to witness the chaos I can sense going on around me.

I barely register the prick in my arm, but it triggers a bolt of fear-coated panic.

My muscles are weak, barely responding, but I'd give all I have to move away from whatever the hell they're trying to pump into my body.

"Fuck," someone curses near my face. "Hold her fucking still. Flakes, calm her ass down. She doesn't know what the hell is going on."

"She'll crash again—"

"Half Pint." Immediately I still, my tensed muscles going lax. "Good girl. Calm your tiny ass down for us. We're doing what we can for the pain until we get you to the base." A cool, calloused hand cups my cheek, turning my face. Soft lips brush against my ear. "Don't you dare leave me again, you hear me? You're mine. *Mine.* I will follow you in death just to drag you back. I'm not letting you go, Elliot. Not now, not ever. You hear me? Never."

I hear him. I want to tell him I agree with him, that I want the same thing. That I don't want to give up again, that I don't want to leave him, not when something good finally entered my life. But I'm tired. I'm so tired.

"I love you, Elliot."

Those words are like a shot of Red Bull in my veins. I feel it, feel my heart thump a little harder, my consciousness clearing.

"Seaman," I rasp. It hurts. Everything hurts. Not under my control, my muscles spasm, making me flop against the hard surface I'm lying on.

Chapter 23

"We're losing her again." The words make sense but feel far away.
"Elliot," Tony yells, his grip on my face tightening.
I want to comfort him, tell him it will be okay.
But I can't before I slip back into the darkness.

24

TONY

I failed her.

The heat from the afternoon sun warms the window, making my forehead burn as I press it against the thick glass. My eyes close on their own, sheer exhaustion from not sleeping for seventy-two hours making me sway on my feet.

"Anthony."

"What?" I grumble, not bothering to turn and greet Lucia. Thin fingers slip between my own and squeeze. "When will she wake up?" The question is meant for the universe, a plea to know when my suffering will end rather than actually expecting an answer.

"Come here." I follow her gentle tug and allow her to guide me to the small couch tucked in the corner of Elliot's hospital room, avoiding looking at the hospital bed and the woman still fighting for her life lying on top. I haven't been able to look at her since they wheeled her in from surgery. I did this to her. I didn't get to her in time to avoid their torture that weakened her already-battered body. "She's a fighter. She'll pull through. The doctors are optimistic."

I flex and extend my free fingers. It's not enough. I want her awake, not their empty promises.

She's been out of surgery for six hours. The surgery where they removed the ruptured spleen and kidney. The kidney infection mixed with severe dehydration set her other organs into failure, and the prolonged high fever fucked with her heart. How someone with her strength can be here, helpless on the hospital bed connected to so many machines and tubes, is infuriating and terrifying.

Twice Elliot died in my arms.

Twice I died right there with her.

If she dies a third....

I shake my head, not able to go down that dark path.

Elliot will wake up. She has to.

"Tell me what happened," Lucia says softly beside me.

I shoot her a hate-filled glare. "You want to fucking debrief me while—"

"Watch it, Flakes." I snarl at my best friend standing guard at the door. "She's trying to distract you, you idiot."

"Sorry," I grumble, meaning the single word. Lucia doesn't deserve my grief-fueled anger. "Where do you want me to start?"

Lucia frowns. "Well, I'd like to skip to the end and learn how the asset you needed to apprehend and bring in for agency questioning ended up with a single bullet between his brows...."

A corner of my lip twitches. "It was an accident. Finger slipped."

"Right." Lucia sighs. Leaning back, she rests two hands on top of her belly. "Fine, start with the officer we assumed was dead."

"I wanted to be the one to kill that fucker," I snap. Taking a deep breath in, I close my eyes and think back to just a few days ago, which feels like years. "From what I could piece together, he went dirty during the previous operation with Elliot. Used his knowledge of human trafficking as an in with Rico. Planned his own death down to putting a dead body at the scene in case it wasn't destroyed in the explosion. He planned on taking Elliot with him that night, but she threw a wrench in his plan."

I swallow hard and turn to look at Lucia. "Did you know she was pregnant?" I flinch at her tense nod. "Shit," I hiss. "She's had so much to deal with. What if... what if she doesn't want to come back to it all?"

What if I'm not enough to come back to? is what I really want to ask.

"You're breaking my heart, Tony," Lucia says with a sniffle. I force my stare to stay locked on the laminate floor. "I've never seen you like this."

"Broken, you mean."

"No, Tony, I've seen you broken. That was you these last eight months before she blew into your life. Right now, you're giving up."

My muscles tense as I slowly turn to face Lucia. "What?"

G pushes off the door, moving to step between us, clearly hearing the warning in my one word.

"She's right there. She's alive, and you're acting like you've already lost her. Her coming back to you twice means she's fighting. What are you doing?"

"What do you want from me?" I grit out. "If there was something I could do, I would. If giving her my heart would bring her crazy ass back to me, I'd rip it out of my chest and hand it to her on a silver fucking platter. Give me a target, I'll kill it. Give me a mission, and I'll complete it. But this... I'm useless to her."

"No you're not," Lucia says with more patience in her voice than I deserve. "She needs you to be strong when she can't."

"Do you know why she's here, why she's missing two organs?"

"Because Rico—"

"Because I didn't see the trap to grab her. Because I didn't get to her before those two fuckers did who the fuck knows what—"

"You know that's not true, Anthony."

I huff and press the heels of both hands into my eyes. "I know nothing anymore."

"You know her." Those three words sink in deep. "If she were awake right now, do you think she'd be blaming you?" My shoulders slump. "Elliot knew the dangers of going into this operation, as she does every time she's sent out, and she still went. What happened to her isn't your guilt to wear, Tony. Just look at her. *Really* look at her."

It takes all my strength to drop my hands. The room is blurry at first, slowly becoming clearer as I lock my gaze on the hospital bed I've done my best to avoid. Elliot's slight frame lies tucked under a thin white blanket. Tubes and wires sprout from several areas of her body. The heart monitor near her head pulses up and down with each beat. A thin tube tucks beneath her nose, her dry lips parted.

Before I even realize I've moved, I'm halfway to the bed, and then I'm there, my shaking hand reaching out for hers. Her thin fingers are limp as I interlace my own with hers and squeeze. Her normally light bronze skin is paler; long dark locks splay across the right side of the pillow, the other side stark white.

I swallow down the lump forming in my throat as I inspect the stitches along the left side of her scalp, visible from where they shaved her thick hair to suture the gash.

Another injury she wouldn't have if only I would've moved faster.

My whole heart hurts, throbbing from the sharp stab of failure as I take in her battered body. A road map of all the ways I let her down when she needed me most.

A wave of emotion hits me so hard my knees give out, sending me crashing to the floor beside her bed. I stay there, holding her hand while kneeling at her bedside. Leaning forward, I press a hard kiss to the back of her hand. In the distance, the faint click of the hospital door closing tells me Lucia and G left, giving me some privacy.

Pressing my forehead to the mattress edge, I squeeze both eyes shut, hoping to stop the sudden dampness building beneath the lids.

"I'm so sorry, Half Pint," I rasp, my throat raw. "I let you down, and now... now you're here. I don't deserve to ask this of you, not when you've been through so much, but I'm a selfish asshole who doesn't want you to go. You broke me in the best way possible, or maybe you fused the already shattered pieces of who I was into someone better. All I know, the only thing I'm certain of anymore, is it hurts to even think about any of this without you. Please, Elliot, please come back to me."

Over and over I repeat those last few words, hoping the more I say them, it will somehow make her hear my desperation and wake up.

The steady beep of a machine, the rhythmic tick of the old-school round clock on the wall, and the murmured voices beyond the closed door are all I hear in return. Even still, I stay kneeling beside her bed, holding her hand.

The pain in my knees morphs into numbness, my thighs tremble from holding the same position, and the sun pouring through the window at my back set long ago, all proof of how long I've knelt here, but still I wait.

At some point, I fall asleep, leaning against the bed with my arm along the top of the mattress and my face stuck to my forearm.

Then something changes.

I go from asleep to alert as if someone fired a gunshot beside my head. Mind still foggy, I visually scour Elliot, searching for whatever snapped me awake.

My heart literally stops for a beat before kicking into hyperdrive when I find those amber eyes locked on me. I'm frozen in place, my throat working but no words coming out.

The tip of her tongue pops out and swipes across her lower lip.

"Seaman," she barely whispers. The hand I'm crushing with my own tentatively squeezes.

"Half Pint." Keeping my movements slow, I push off the bed to stand, wincing when my legs almost give out under my weight from being in the same position for too long. "You're back in San Diego, in a hospital." My mind is bombarded with everything I need to tell her, becoming jumbled and confusing. "I'll go get the doctor—"

Her grip on my hand tightens, reminding me how strong my little fighter is despite everything she's gone through.

"Don't ever leave me," she says, eyes fluttering closed like she's about to slip back asleep. "Never leave me."

When her eyes don't flicker back open, I just stare at her relaxed face.

Elliot woke up, saw me, and didn't push me away.

She doesn't want me to leave.

Ever.

Keeping our fingers interlaced, I stretch as far as I can toward the chair against the window. Using the toe of my boot, I drag it inch by inch closer until I can wrap my hand around the metal armrest and pull it the rest of the way, situating it next to her hospital bed.

The thin cushion sinks beneath my weight. Leaning forward, I rest my head on my outstretched arm, face turned toward hers, and allow my heavy lids to flutter closed.

No matter what happens from this point, I know everything will be okay because she doesn't want me to leave.

Ever.

I don't dare look at the nurse who's wrapping a new bandage around my bicep after inspecting the stitches the medic hastily sewed while they stabilized Elliot. My lips twitch, fighting the wide grin that wants to take over my face as I watch the woman glaring from her hospital bed.

"Just keep it clean," the nurse says, oblivious to the hellcat behind her, clearly plotting her death for daring to touch me.

I fucking love it.

With my childhood and history, you'd think I would balk at Elliot's clear possessiveness, but there's something different when it's coming from her than what I witnessed with my mother.

After securing the edge, the nurse rolls down the sleeve of my T-shirt. The feel of her gaze is heavy, begging me to turn and pay attention to her for even half a second, but I don't. It's not even a hardship to ignore the woman. My full focus and heart are taken.

Elliot's calculating glare follows the nurse until she's through the door and we're once again alone. Immediately, she relaxes against the mound of pillows at her back and closes her eyes.

"I hate this," she says, not for the first time.

"I know."

Her eyes flick open, finding me. "When do I get to leave again? I'm over everyone hovering over me like I'm a damn invalid."

"That's not—"

"It's been three days. Plenty of time for me to get used to all this."

She waves a hand toward her head before sweeping it down her body. "It was one kidney. I have another."

"And a spleen."

"It's not a vital organ."

"And the heart murmur?"

Her lips press together. "I just want to get out of here. Get back to being me."

"A crazy pain in the ass?" I offer, no longer fighting my smile. With a groan, I push off the couch and move to stand at her bedside.

"Strong," she whispers.

"You're still strong, Half Pint, just recovering. Give yourself time to adjust—"

"I don't want time to adjust," she snaps. "I want to go blow something up that I shouldn't. Start a fight I know I can finish. Run until my lungs bleed and my muscles fail."

"Is that what I have to look forward to?"

Her brows furrow, clearly unsure how to answer that. Between the doctors, nurses, visitors, and her sleeping, we haven't talked about anything. When she first woke up, all she wanted to know was what the hell happened that night; we've been ignoring the elephant in the room—us—since.

A look of determination clouds her face. "Tony, you don't have to do this." Her voice trembles. The blanket shifts as she fists the material.

My heart thunders, and my skin flushes with a sudden heat.

Is this it? When she pushes me away because of what I did to her? What I failed to keep from happening, which put her in this damn hospital bed?

"I've been thinking about it," she continues, "and—"

"I know I don't deserve a second chance, but I'm going to ask for one anyway," I blurt, cutting her off. Her amber eyes widen. "I know I let you down—"

"What the hell are you talking about?" she says, mouth gaping. "What did you do?"

A deep line forms between my brows. "I didn't get to you in time. You're here because of—"

"Because of Rico and Kurt," she finishes, shaking her head. "Tony, that's not what you really think, is it?" This time it's me sealing my lips shut. "Do you know what I am?"

"Um...." *Is this a trick question?*

"I'm a tool for the agency. I've known that since I joined, and I'm okay with it because it's who I am, and I like it. I enjoy what I do and who I am, even when it almost gets me killed. It's a challenge. It keeps me somewhat sane and gives me an outlet to be me. What happened that night would've ended with me either as Kurt's prisoner or dead after being tortured at Rico's hand. You're thinking what happened was your fault, but you saved me. Again."

"But—"

"And pretty sure my opinion is the one that matters."

"Is that right?" I sit on the edge of the bed, facing the windows.

"But I don't want to tie you down." Her hand slides across the bed and covers my own. "I don't know how long it will take me to get back to normal. It might be two or three weeks"—that makes me huff and shoot her a side-eye glare—"of me struggling to find my footing again. It won't be easy. I'll be difficult and bitchy. I don't know how to do this"—she motions between us—"on a good day. Add in my pathetic state, and it just won't work. It won't be what.... I'll just drag you down, and you don't deserve that."

My chest fills with my deep breath, giving myself a second to form the right words.

"Every time you died, I died with you," I admit softly. Her audible gasp fills the hospital room. "The only way you're getting rid of me, Half Pint, is if you tell me to leave." Turning, I lean across her thighs, resting my elbow along the mattress. With a single finger, I trace along her face that's finally losing some of the swelling. "I love you, Elliot Smith. Like this, like you were, and who you'll be tomorrow. Give me a chance to show you who I can be, to show myself the better side of life. I know it won't be easy, either in the short term while you heal or long term when we disagree, but for the first time, I don't want it to be. I want the challenge you bring me. I want to be the man, the SEAL, you push me to be, making me see who I can be with the right person by my side. That's you, Half Pint. It's you now and forever, if you'll have me."

A knock on the door and the whoosh of it opening breaks the mood.

"Miss—"

"Out," Elliot commands, never looking away from me. "Give us a second."

"I'm Dr.—"

I go from heartrending emotions threatening to strangle the air from my lungs from the pressure to all the blood rushing to my cock. In a blink, Elliot's hands went from clutching the blanket to one holding a nine-millimeter, the gun pointed toward the door.

Where the fuck did she get that?

Guess it could be worse. Could've been a hand grenade.

That crazy smile of hers that makes me want to fuck the sass right out of hers spreads across her face. "If you don't leave, I will—"

A slam echoes through the room.

She turns a happier smile my way. "Sorry, what were you saying?"

"Fuck, I love you," I breathe. "I love you crazy and explosive. I love you sane and confiding. No matter how I can get you, I'll take you and forever be grateful."

"I'm damaged," she says, settling the gun on her lap but keeping a tight grip on it. "Kurt... he fooled me. I didn't know. I didn't see—"

"Elliot, I know."

"No, you don't. I slept—"

"Elliot, I know. I know it all. You and him...." I swallow hard and shoot a cautious glance to the gun, hoping she doesn't turn it on me when I bring up what else I heard that night. "The baby."

A stifled sob makes her shoulders tremble. When I go to pull her close, she jerks away, holding a hand between us.

"I didn't love him. I never even felt.... Hell, that sounds terrible, doesn't it?"

I offer her a sad smile. "You're preaching to the wrong person on that front. There are things we did when we were lost and alone that don't define us now."

"I was so alone. I didn't realize it until now. It's why I was so excited about the idea of a baby. Of having one good thing in my life. Then it was gone, and now... now I know it was for the best. Because I have something else to look forward to. You give me that, Tony. You give me a future to be excited about. A real one."

Shoving her hand away, I lean forward and bury my face against her neck.

"I love you, Tony." My chest cracks open, pouring out all the pent-up worry and fear, leaving only happiness and joy in its place. "I don't know how this will work, but I know I want it too. I lost my heart to you that night you saw me raw and beaten and somehow still made me feel strong. I didn't fight my way back to keep doing this alone. If there's a life without you in it, I don't want it."

I press my lips to hers in a searing, promising kiss. Pulling back, I wait for her eyes to open and find me.

"Never again. Never again will either of us have to do this alone. We're in this together now, and I can't fucking wait to see what's in store for us."

And I mean it.

Every damn word.

Because she's mine, and I'm hers.

Partners. Equals. Lovers. Friends.

Forever.

25

ELLIOT

"Slow the hell down, Half Pint."

I flip him the bird over my shoulder as I continue to speed-walk through the first floor toward the stairs. Am I in incredible pain because of my need to prove otherwise? Hell yes. I'm working to keep the tears at bay, but no way will I let him see how every step leaves my body feeling like it's a twelve-mile sprint instead.

I'm pathetic.

Sure, it's only been a week since my discharge, but I'm a damn CIA officer. Losing two organs shouldn't affect me like everyone else.

The emotional shit is throwing me for a loop too. It's not just a physical recovery that's proving to be more of a challenge than I expect but the mind fuck I was given that last night in Cartagena. Kurt is—no, *was* our mole. Sold his soul for money and expected me to just jump on board to sell women, all for a fancy house and him.

My lip curls at the memory.

How did I ever let that fucker touch me? Every time I think about it, I hate myself a little more. And now I carry the burden of being thankful I didn't bring his child into the world. For months I mourned Kurt and the baby, and now I'm... hell, I don't know what I am.

Confused. That's what I've been since waking up here in San Diego.

But not alone.

"You're a pain in my ass, you know that?" Tony says, now at my shoulder as I slowly ascend the stairs. "I'd pick you up and carry you—"

"But I'm too fragile," I hiss through my panting breaths.

"You're not fragile." I release an incredulous huff. Right, that's why he hasn't touched me since leaving the hospital. A woman has needs, and he's too scared of popping an incision to start anything fun. "Healing, Elliot. You're healing from—"

"Yeah, I know what I'm recovering from, but I keep telling you I'm golden, Seaman. See?" I say and turn to face him, smiling through the pain and exhaustion.

"You're such a damn liar." He chuckles. "When you end up back in that hospital, I'm taking away all your guns and knives so you can't hold the medical staff hostage... again."

"They didn't think I was ready for release. *I* did." I shrug, even though it hurts to do so. "We came to a mutually beneficial agreement. They didn't receive a bullet wound, and they discharged me."

There's only so much cross-stitching fun phrases with cuss words that one woman could take before she snaps and demands release.

"I love your crazy ass."

"Ditto, Seaman. Though...." Pausing outside the CO's door, I turn to him, needing to get this off my chest in case shit goes down inside. "I haven't heard from my handler or the agency since returning. I don't know what they'll want from me for a debrief, or..." I swallow hard. "I'm damaged goods, Tony. They might take me and never bring me back. We need to be prepared for that."

His earlier worried expression morphs into something that would scare most people, except me. It turns me on.

"I've discussed the situation with the CO and Lucia. We're prepared for any course of action we'll need to take to keep you with us."

Stepping forward, I press my forehead to his chest to hide the tears lining my lower lids.

His calloused hands rub up and down my biceps. "Come on. Let's get this done and get you back in bed."

Shifting to press my chin to his breastbone, I smile. "With you on top of me?"

His responding laugh vibrates my face. "Soon, baby." Raising a fist, he pounds on the heavy wooden door, shaking it on its hinges.

A deep voice calls out from the other side for us to enter.

Inhaling deep, I pull away from Tony and put my crazy, easygoing mask on. A blast of ice-cold air smacks me in the face, chilling my clammy skin the moment the door swings open. A steady, warm hand presses to my lower back when I stop two steps into the office.

A fresh wave of icy chill—this from fear, not the temperature—races through my veins. Two men in black suits have stood from where they occupied the two chairs in front of the CO's desk. Lucia and Gabe stand tense along the wall with the bookshelf.

Her eyes find mine. Is that fear or fire pouring off her?

"Officer Smith," CO Williams says, pushing off his desk to stand. Crossing both thick arms, he narrows his brows at the two men in suits, but they don't notice, their attention solely on me. "These men are—"

"Here to take me to a black site where I'll never be seen again?" I finish for him. I'm no idiot. I know what's going on here. I'm about to be relieved of my duties—permanently.

"It's just a debrief," one says, his face a blank slate. But I hear the lie.

And so does Tony, apparently.

His fingers flex along my back, forming into a fist.

"You'll come with us, Officer Smith—"

I feel it the moment Tony snaps. In a single move, he's in front of me, blocking the two officers' view of my smaller frame.

"You'll have to get through me first."

My heart races and swells at the same time.

Damnit, Seaman. I love him so fucking much. I haven't had someone stand up for me like this, put their own life and career on the line, ever before. And now here he is, standing up to the most feared agency because they're shady as hell, all for me.

Before I can tell him it's fine, a feminine voice fills the office.

"And me."

There's no stopping the tears from leaking out.

"And me."

I cover my mouth to stifle the sob at Gabe's declaration.

"That makes four of us." My mouth gapes open. Stepping around Tony, I stare through my watery vision at the CO. "We will have a new assignment proposal for Officer Smith by the end of the day. But she will not be returning with you two today, or any day after. After the recent mission, the Navy sees the value in Officer Smith that your agency was okay with tossing away. Let your superiors know they will hear from me and Officer Wilcox by 1700. Dismissed, Officers."

Hot damn, Robin.

"Do you know who you're talking to?" one of them snarls.

I suck in a breath that hurts like a motherfucker when, between blinks, the CO somehow brandishes a military-issued Glock, along with the two SEALs, all guns pointed at the officers.

"I suggest you leave," Lucia says with a smirk. "They get trigger-happy when you disrespect their superior."

If hate and loathing were a palpable thing, I would've been pushed over by the sheer force as the two suits stalk out of the office. Their glares burn into me, but I offer a smile and four-finger wave as they pass.

The moment the door shuts, the tension in the room deflates like a popped balloon.

"Well, that was exciting," I say, my voice breaking. Clearing my throat, I move toward the CO's desk. "Thank you, sir." Instead of sitting like my body demands, I stay standing in an at-ease stance.

CO Williams motions toward the chair and replaces his gun in the concealed holster at his back.

"Sit. You look like shit." I offer him a weak smile in response and gladly take the offered seat. "Officer Wilcox."

"Sir," Lucia says, stepping forward and stopping at my side. I have a sudden flashback to a few weeks ago when my life changed forever. "I have the assignment change proposal ready to go. I just need Officer Smith's okay to move forward."

I glance up, finding her pleading gaze already on me.

"You guys just saved me from a certain, probably painful death. Anything you suggest is a step above that." I flick a glance at CO Williams. "Unless your proposal is to feed me to the sharks. Then I'm out."

He chuckles, and Lucia grins.

"Explain to Officer Smith so she doesn't go out and order a harpoon."

"Oh, I wonder if Amazon has one."

"No harpoon needed," Lucia says, placing a hand on my shoulder. "I'd like for you to be permanently stationed here in San Diego on my team."

"Your team?"

"I'm the CIA intelligence liaison between the agency and SEALs. I have a few analysts working under me, but no active field officers."

I deflate. "You want an active field officer missing two organs?"

Her hand tightens around my shoulder. "It won't be any long stints like you're used to. More flying in and assessing the situation on the ground to report back to me. I think it'll be extremely beneficial for me to have someone with your experience and skill assessing the situations when I can't."

I chew on my lip for a second. "Do I still get to blow stuff up?"

Her laugh as well as the others' roll through the room. "Not without prior approval."

"Deal," I say and hold out my hand, wincing when the muscles strain and tremble. Her lips dip into a frown, but she takes my hand and squeezes.

"Now that business is conducted and we're officially keeping Officer Smith"—I grin at CO Williams, absolutely loving the sound of that—"I need your debrief on the Cartagena mission." He holds up a palm to the approaching figure at my back. "I want to hear her version first, Hackenbreg. Your chance is coming."

With a deep breath, I do just that, telling him every detail from the moment we landed to when I woke up in San Diego. Well, minus the head I gave Tony in the jungle that turned into one hell of a quickie for me. Once finished, I slump back, hissing when the stiff cushion presses against my incision.

"Understood. Hack—"

"Did they know?" I ask. CO Williams's black brows furrow. "Did the agency know Kurt was the mole and still alive? Did they send me in there knowing I probably wouldn't return?"

"We don't know," Lucia answers. "I find it suspicious though. I think they didn't have conclusive facts but probably suspected."

"Bastards. Motherfucking bastards."

"Agreed," the other four in the room say in unison.

"Hackenbreg," CO Williams commands. "I've read over your report. Though the CIA is not happy with Rico Suarez not being brought in for their interrogation, I've sanctioned the termination because of the circumstances. With Officer Smith's declining condition and—"

"Permission to speak, sir," Tony cuts in.

"You already are, Hackenbreg. Don't absorb her bad habits. You're not nearly as scary as she is."

I preen in the chair, making CO Williams laugh.

"I didn't kill Suarez because of Officer Smith." Turning in the chair, I blink up at his stiff posture. "I knew she could handle herself, even with the drugs in her system and the head wound. I took the shot because he was about to escape, again. That man deserved to die by our hand after killing so many of our brothers and sisters in arms due to the weapons he sold to our enemies. I pulled that trigger knowing the world would be a better place without that motherfucker taking another breath. I'll take the reprimand or mark, but I could not allow that man to continue living."

There's something messed up in my head. It should offend me that he didn't kill Rico to save me, but I'm grateful. He could've made me out to be the weak link—the main objective of the mission failed because of my injured ass—but he didn't. I'm not one who wants to be saved, not that damsel in distress who's waiting for her white knight. I'm a badass officer who needs an alpha-hole who will get the job done that I couldn't.

He's so getting laid later... if he'll let me.

My mood sours at the thought.

"Noted." But the CO's hands don't make a move toward a pen. I smirk. "Now, something came across my desk earlier this week that I wanted to ask you two about. Lovall stated he knew nothing about the incident at the Cartagena base."

I roll my eyes. "It was one tent!"

"Excuse me?"

My eyes widen. "Nothing. Erm, what are you referring to? Because clearly we are not on the same page."

CO Williams holds his hard stare for several seconds before turning his attention back to the paper in his hand.

"I received a notice that the commanding officer at the Cartagena base was dishonorably discharged after admitting to several counts of sexual harassment and assault. It also states he had to have help off the base because of two broken hands."

His chocolate-brown eyes peek up through his black lashes to the man at my side. "Any comment on that, Hackenbreg?"

"Should I, sir?"

"I suggest not."

"Yes, sir. All I know is while they worked on stabilizing Officer Smith and stitching up my arm, there was some kind of commotion. No other details. Sir."

"The logs say you and the other platoon were at the base for two hours while they worked on Officer Smith. Your stitches took the whole two hours, did they?"

I smirked at the leading question.

"Yes, sir. The medic was very thorough on cleaning the wound."

"Noted." This time he writes Tony's statement. "Wilcox, Wilcox, and Hackenbreg, you're dismissed. I need a moment with Officer Smith."

I feel Tony's hesitation. Smiling up at him, I tilt my head toward the door.

"This man just held two officers at gunpoint so they wouldn't take me. I think I'm good in here alone."

With a reluctant grumble, he follows the two Wilcoxes out the door.

When I turn back to the CO, the stern mask he's worn since we opened the door is gone. A soft, concerned expression now mars his handsome features.

"You're pushing yourself too hard." I open my mouth to deny it, but he shakes his head. "I see it in my men all the time. I know what it looks like, so don't deny it. I understand your readiness to get back to normal, but give yourself time. You deserve that, Elliot."

"I've never stopped," I say with a sigh. "I'm bored, hate this weakness I can't seem to shake, and I just want to be me again."

"It will come with time. Now, regarding your personal relationship with my SEAL." I swallow hard. Sure, he just saved my life, but if he tries to keep me and Tony apart, I'm not sure what I'll do. "As long as it doesn't interfere with your work with Wilcox and the other platoons, I approve."

I sag against the chair. "Good. Because I wouldn't take no for an answer."

His lips twitch as if holding back a smile. "I know. Oh, and thank you." He leans down, followed by the sound of a drawer opening. Standing back up, he holds up the cross-stitched fabric swatch I sent him while in the hospital. "I've always wanted something that says 'I can kill you' somewhere in my office."

My cheeks burn, the earlier exhaustion gone. "You're welcome. It was between that or 'Fuck this shit.' I figured that one would fit better in a CO's office."

"Rightly so. I look forward to working with you, Elliot. I have a feeling my life will never be boring again."

Pushing off the chair's armrests, I stand. "I aim to please, sir. And thank you, for everything."

"You deserve it. You're a damn excellent officer and woman. I'm proud to have you as an addition to our CIA liaison team."

Well, fuck. Why did he have to say that?

Sniffling, I turn quickly so he can't see my tears.

"Thank you, sir. Dismissed?"

He laughs. "Yes, dismissed. Take care of yourself, Elliot."

"I will."

I find Tony leaning against the metal filing cabinet, flipping his knife in the air, catching it as his eyes flick my way. He slips the blade into the sheath connected to his belt.

"What was that about?" he asks, running a calculating scan over my body as if checking me for injuries.

"He thanked me for the gift I sent and a few other things." I grin. "So, now that I'm sticking around San Diego, I'll need to find a place."

He wraps an arm around my shoulder, and we walk down the hall side by side.

"Funny, I was just thinking it's time for me to get out of my shithole apartment and find something new. Want to go apartment hunting together?"

I lean a little more into him at the hope in his tone. "Sure, Seaman. Though I've heard this place is hell of expensive. We could always go in on an apartment together. Us being home at the same time—"

"Sold. Now, will you let me help you down the stairs, or will it be by force?"

"I'll allow it." He immediately reaches for me, but I shuffle out of his hold. "But first. Handsy Hank?"

"I told you I'm making a list," he says with a twinkle in his brown eyes. "He deserved worse."

"Between the two of us, I think he got what he deserved."

He eyes me cautiously. "Now can I take you home?"

Home.

What he doesn't know is home isn't a place. It's him.

Have you read Book 1, Covert Affair? Grab your copy to read how Gabe and Lucia found their happily ever after!

EPILOGUE
ELLIOT

Sweat slips down my temples, dripping to the floor. My every breath is ragged, muscles twitching and straining as I haul myself off the floor.

Thirty.

Thirty measly push-ups.

Having had enough, my arms give out halfway, sending me falling face-first to the new carpet. Everything hurts. Probably a sign I pushed it too hard today, but when have I not? Rolling over, I splay my arms and legs out to get the full effect of the overhead fan's breeze against my bare skin.

I'm sure I'm a sight to behold. A tiny see-through black bra, matching boy shorts, and a white lab coat.

The lab coat is a recent addition to my normal black wardrobe. The doctor who signed my discharge papers said it would take me at least six weeks to resume regular activity after surgery. Okay, fine, he said I needed to wait six weeks to resume regular activity, but even so, I heard a challenge. So I told him I would run five miles by week three. He said no way in hell.

The fun lab coat was my reward for winning yesterday, and I thoroughly enjoyed taking it from his clenched hand. Everyone has underestimated me and my will to get back to normal. Even Tony, who's the worst with his overprotective, cautious self. I know he cares. It's clear in the way he's treating me like a fragile doll. I should enjoy it, love the way he's doting on me and waiting on me hand and foot.

But I don't.

The complete opposite, in fact.

And it's not just because we haven't had sex in what feels like ages.

Biting my lip, I press my sweaty thighs together just reminiscing about the last time he had me tied to the bed and that night in the jungle. Every time we're together, his dick or tongue pushes me so high I see stars. Chest heaving, pressing my peaked nipples against the see-through mesh bra, I feel my heart rate spike, having nothing to do with the exertion from the workout.

It's all him. The memory of him. And fuck, I want to feel that high again.

The faint jingle of keys, the scrape of the metal slipping into the deadbolt, has me turning my head to face the door. *Speaking of the devil....* Bright afternoon light pours through the widening crack as Tony pushes open the door of our new apartment. The smell of the nearby ocean wafts in along with his musky scent, driving my desire even higher.

I squint to keep from being momentarily blinded.

"Elliot?" I tense at the worry in his tone that hasn't eased since I woke up in the hospital. Either bossy or worried, those are his two tones. Though I'm okay with the bossy one, if only it was ordering me to take his cock deeper down my throat. "What the hell are you doing on the floor? Are you okay?" His duffel smacks the stone entryway and he strides closer, kneeling by my head. "Let me help you back in bed. Are you hungry—"

"I'm bored," I say on a groan. He stills, clearly not knowing what to say about that. "Fine." Pushing off the floor, I don't get far before he scoops me in his arms and carries me toward the bedroom. "No, shower first. I'm all sticky."

"You shouldn't be pushing yourself so hard," he grumbles beside my ear.

Moving my lips silently, I mock his words while rolling my eyes. Am I being a brat, sure, but fucking hell, I'm over this babying shit. I need him. I want him.

My toes press to the cool tile, Tony's hands holding me steady until he knows I'm good standing on my own.

"Join me?" I ask, my voice breathy.

His jaw clenches, the muscles twitching as he stares me down, not letting his eyes drift lower than my face.

"You know I can't. The doctor said nothing for—"

Without thinking, I press both hands to his chest and shove. His eyes widen as he stumbles back a step. I advance, ready to shove him again and again and again until all this pent-up energy and frustration dissipate.

Before I can push him again, his hand encircles my wrists and twists. With a controlled yank, my arms cross over my chest, and my back seals against his chest.

Well, fuck, that's hot.

Not caring about anything other than the feel of his body against mine, I press my ass back, grinding against his cock that's desperately pushing against his fatigues to come out and play. A warm burst of air brushes past my ear, his following groan making my knees weak.

"Elliot, we can't—"

With a twist and push, I wrench myself out of his grip and turn the tables by grabbing his hands. Guiding both to my stomach, I play puppeteer, making his fingers brush along my sizzling skin the way I've wanted since the day they released me from the hospital. Tony's chest rises and falls at my back, clearly putting effort into restraining himself, but he doesn't stop me.

"This is what I need, Seaman," I say with a moan when I make his hands cup my heavy breasts. "I need us to feel whole again. Can't you see that? I'm dying for you."

I nearly whimper in relief when his hands and fingers move on their own. Dipping a finger into each thin cup, he tugs the flimsy material down, exposing both pebbled nipples to the cool air. My back arches, shoving my breasts harder into his hands when he squeezes both, pinching my aching nipples at the same time.

"Yes," I cry. "More. I need more."

"Oh I know what you need, baby." He grinds himself against my ass and thrusts. My knees grow weak, threatening to give out with the overwhelming rush of pleasure coursing through my system. "Are you sure you're ready?"

Annoyance flares. Turning in his arms, I wrap my own around his neck and jump, tightening my legs around his trim waist.

Gripping what I can of his short hair, I give it a hard tug. He hisses, jaw muscle twitching with tension.

"Give me everything you've got, Seaman."

His eyes sparkle, and a slow grin takes over his face. Walking me over to the sink, he keeps one hand beneath my ass, holding all my weight so I don't have to—fuck, I love him—and reaches inside the medicine cabinet with the other. The bright bathroom lights glint off the metal scissors.

It would terrify most people about what was to come, but I trust him, and I'm a little messed-up in the way it turns me on even more. The cold metal glides along the soft skin of my hip before slipping beneath the cotton fabric of my boy shorts.

We don't break our stare-off as he cuts along one hip before moving to the other. A loud clatter echoes when he tosses the scissors to the granite counter. Instead of asking or commanding, Tony skims a hand over my ass, dipping his fingers into my slick center, and uses that hold to pull me back an inch, allowing the ruined underwear to fall to the floor.

"Your turn," he says, pumping those two fingers in and out in shallow strokes. "If you want me, you'll need to help. I have my hands full of you." With that, he curls his fingers, scraping along my inner walls.

Head tossed back, I press my weight harder into his hand. Keeping one arm around his neck, I use the free hand to work his belt loose and then his pants. A sharp bite along my shoulder has my eyes fluttering closed. Boxer briefs tugged just below his hard cock, pants hanging around his hips, Tony twists, the wall gently pressing to my back, the coolness seeping through the lab coat.

"We need to play doctor with that coat," Tony says, staring greedily between us where his cock is now wedged between my slick lips. "I'll be the doctor, and you're my naughty patient."

"Who needs her temperature checked with your cock," I finish with a smirk.

Leaning back, I rest my head against the wall and close both lids. With him doing all the work, he lifts my hips higher, positioning me right over his dick. We moan in unison as I slowly sink lower, wiggling at the base to take all of him. The wall vibrates when his fist connects with the drywall, leaving a small indention.

"I can't hold back," he says, voice strained. "Tell me this is okay, baby. Tell me you'll let me know—"

Not letting him finish, I press a hand to the back of his skull and force his lips to mine.

He releases a relieved breath. Using the wall as leverage, he presses me harder to keep me upright and holds both hips in a bruising grip.

"Yes, Seaman," I encourage. "Take it. Take me. Take it all."

His biceps flex, straining against the cuffs of his fatigues as he lifts my slight weight until just the tip teases my entrance. Then he yanks me down again, thrusting his hips at the same time.

I watch him move, firm ass bunching beneath his partially removed boxer briefs in the mirror behind him. Skimming both hands lower, I grab handfuls of it and squeeze as hard as I can, no doubt leaving tiny Elliot prints.

He grunts into my ear, thrusting harder. Each time he bottoms out, a burst of pleasure sparkles through my veins, coiling the tension in my lower belly tighter and tighter.

"Fuck, I love you, Half Pint," he says into my ear. "I want to be buried deep inside you every damn second of every day. The way you squeeze the cum right out of my dick makes me see fucking stars. Can't wait to find out what that ass of yours does." A pitiful whimper squeaks up my throat. "We might need to take leave once I finally get to sink myself in your ass while I fingerfuck your sweet, needy pussy."

Holy dirty talk, Batman.

It's too much. The pent-up need from weeks of watching his naked ass walking around the apartment erupts. Pitching forward, I seal my forehead to his shoulder, squeezing the life out of his cock as I work myself up and down, chasing my looming release.

"That's right, baby. Take it."

And I do.

With a praising curse, I fall over the edge, the tension bursting and flooding my veins with euphoria. Holding me close, Tony grinds me against his pelvis, rubbing my swollen clit and sending me over the edge a second time, this time falling with me.

Breathing hard, body aching, I smile at my reflection like a sated fool in love.

Because that's exactly what I am.

And with Tony, I have many, many more moments like this to look forward to.

Together.

For better or worse, through war and peace.

We have each other, finally. After everything we've been through on our own, we have the other's strength to lean into when needed.

And me...

I've found a family in him.

Maybe one day we'll grow from two to more.

But for now, for a while, I'll soak up every moment of our time together.

Because finally... I'm not alone.

Thank you for reading! Check out book 1 in my Protection Series, Mine to Protect!

ALSO BY KENNEDY L. MITCHELL

Standalone:

Finding Fate

Memories of Us

Protection Series: Interconnected Standalone

Mine to Protect

Mine to Save

Mine to Guard

Mine to Keep (Coming December 2021)

SEALs and CIA Series: Interconnected Standalone

Covert Affar

Covert Vengeance

More Than a Threat Series: A Bodyguard Romantic Suspense Connected Series

More Than a Threat

More Than a Risk

More Than a Hope

Power Play Series: A Protector Romantic Suspense Connected Series

Power Games

Power Twist

Power Switch

Power Surge

Power Term

ACKNOWLEDGMENTS

Another book done!

Wow. This one has been a long time coming. I've wanted to write Tony's story for a while but coming up with a character that would compliment him too a WHILE. I loved writing their story so much. Elliot spoke to me on an odd level. She's crazy and owns it in her own badass way. Honestly I wish I could be more like her.

So first I have to mention the amazing women who help me form the story from a one line though to a full book. Em, Chris and Kristin - Thank you so much for all that you do. Supporting me at all hours of the night, putting up with my relentless questions and chapters sent. You guys make this more than job, it's so much fun writing for you three.

I never thought I'd do this full time, but now here I am and it's surreal. Thank you to all the readers who buy my books, download via KU or listen via audio. I couldn't do this without each and every one of you. Thank you for making this a dream job!

The last few months I changed some things up with my ARC team and it's made a huge difference for me. I feel all your support and enthusiasm for my writing with our super fun chat group! Thank you all for everything you do to support me during the writing process, cover selections, and of course reading and reviewing my books. You guys rock and I wouldn't want to do this without you.

Printed in Great Britain
by Amazon